The Heartland
EXPERIMENT

Darold Crist

iUniverse, Inc.
Bloomington

The Heartland Experiment

iUniverse books may be ordered through booksellers or by contacting:

iUniverse
1663 Liberty Drive
Bloomington, IN 47403
www.iuniverse.com
1-800-Authors (1-800-288-4677)

ISBN: 978-1-4620-8371-8 (sc)
ISBN: 978-1-4620-8373-2 (hc)
ISBN: 978-1-4620-8372-5 (e)

Printed in the United States of America

iUniverse rev. date: 12/27/2011

Acknowledgments

To my wife, Linda:

I'm the luckiest man on Earth and thank God for sending you to be my life partner. You are a patient, caring, gentle, kind, considerate and loving soul. I look forward to sharing our love for eternity. With each passing day, you amaze me more and more!

To my mom, Nancy Malaponte Crist:

Everyday that goes by I miss talking to you. Your smile is etched in my mind and I can still hear your voice in my ears. Thank you for setting such a loving example for me. You and Nana were so right. Life is about family, love, God, and doing good deeds for others. I take comfort in knowing that you are at peace in the brilliance of the Lord!

To all of the associates at iUniverse:

Thank you for helping me to accomplish a lifelong dream!

CHAPTER ONE

*"Minds that are ill at ease are agitated
by both hope and fear."*

Ovid

His left cheek swollen with chewing tobacco, Staff Sergeant Will Blanks spat a dark brown spot onto the pristine white snow. At twenty-five, Blanks was one of the youngest members of the Union Army regimen. He chewed tobacco because it seemed to have a numbing effect on his nerves. However, it had quite the opposite effect on his teeth, staining them a harsh yellow.

Blanks gently rocked back and forth in the saddle. His horse crested the hill. Looking to the southeast, he recognized the back of a farmhouse and a little red shack nearby. The dull echo of a smacking sound filtered through his ears. He smelled the aroma of burning wood and saw smoke ascending from the chimney. The McKenna farmstead was within sight.

The six soldiers in dark blue uniforms continued to ride through the field in single file. They left the fort at ten that morning. Leading the procession was Major Aaron Wilkerson. He was forty-one years old and a twenty-year veteran of the army. His hair was reddish-brown in color. He was a very fit man, approximately six feet tall. The Major was born and raised in Kansas. However, he'd seen his share of fighting during this bloody Civil War. At Gettysburg, he witnessed human flesh and bone being shredded into countless, gruesome pieces. The images replayed constantly in his mind. The war certainly had changed him.

A brown rabbit scampered past in the shallow snow. The legs of the horses seemed to rise and fall in unison. Vapors from their nostrils snorted little mists into the cold, dry air.

Along with Major Wilkerson were five of his most trusted men. Second in command was Corporal Jeremiah Livingston. He was a short man about thirty years old. He'd fought side by side at Gettysburg with Major Wilkerson. Corporal Livingston was from Connecticut. He wasn't married. After the battle at Gettysburg, he followed the Major to Kansas. The two men were best friends.

"We're getting close", Major Wilkerson relayed back to the Corporal. With this, he'd broken about an hour's worth of verbal silence.

Major Wilkerson raised his right arm and pointed to the southwest. The riders were about one hundred yards away from the house. There was little noise other than the occasional neighing from one of the horses.

The horses made a wide turn around the southwest corner of the house. The Major noticed a young man chopping wood. He slung a long handled axe. Two young black men stood near a woodpile and eyed the Major.

The Major commanded his horse to halt. It came to an abrupt stop, as did the other horses in the single file line.

Benjamin McKenna slammed the axe head into the tree stump. Looking over his left shoulder, he saw the Union soldiers climbing down from their mounts.

"Afternoon men", he said, in a greeting fashion.

"Afternoon", the Major replied.

"Mother and father are just finishing supper. If you men are hungry, there should be plenty of food for all of you. We'll be glad to water your horses while you warm yourselves by the fire."

The Major looked directly into Benjamin's eyes. He sternly said, "We're not here for a social visit son."

"Is there a problem?", Benjamin asked.

"That's what we're here to find out", the Major replied. I need for you and those other two to join us inside the house. We have a few questions to ask you and your family." This last statement came more as an order, as though the Major was instructing one of his own men.

"Sure", Benjamin replied. "Samuel, Marcus, follow me into the house."

"Yes sir", they both said, nodding their heads in the affirmative.

Benjamin led the way into the house. He handed the door off to the Major.

"Mother, father, we have visitors", Benjamin called out toward the kitchen.

The sound of chairs scooting against the wooden floor echoed from the kitchen. Alexander and Molly McKenna walked down the short hallway to the living room.

"Would you men care for some supper, Molly asked?"

"No ma'am", the Major replied. "But thank you kindly for the offer."

"How can we help you?", Alexander McKenna asked.

"Sir, my name is Major Aaron Wilkerson and this is Corporal Jeremiah Livingston. We're here to investigate allegations that have been raised against you and your family."

"Allegations against me and my family?", he asked in disbelief.

"Yes".

"What kind of allegations are you talking about?"

"Numerous sources have accused you and your family of harboring slaves."

A young woman gently walked into the living room from the kitchen. She stood quietly next to Alexander McKenna. Sarah was the McKenna's daughter, and at nearly seventeen, their youngest child.

"Slaves, that's outlandish!", Alexander McKenna spouted loudly. "Marcus and Samuel work the fields and perform household chores. They're not slaves. They're like family."

"But do you pay them?", the Major asked.

"Listen here Major, you can't come into our home like this and make these kinds of wild accusations." Alexander paused, collecting his thoughts. Even though it wasn't hot in the room, he began to perspire.

"But are they paid?", the Major once again asked.

"Sir, I just told you they are treated well. I pay them in kind. They receive food, clothing and a roof over their heads. Your charges are groundless and insulting to my family and me. We're not on trial here!"

"Well sir, that's exactly what we're going to have us here, a little trial!"

"You have no authority to do so", the elder McKenna said. His face flushed with anger, he prepared to do battle with the Major.

"Mr. McKenna, we have the full authority of the government of the

United States of America to investigate this matter. I strongly suggest that you and the members of your family fully cooperate."

An evil grin crossed the face of Staff Sergeant Blanks. Standing near the fireplace, he walked in front of it. He spat a chunk of the brown, leafy material through his teeth and into the fire. This caused the flames to briefly dance higher. Feeling a trickle of juice running down the left side of his mouth, he took his right shirtsleeve and wiped it away. The grin on his face disappeared. He returned to his original position.

"Surely there's some mistake?", Molly asked.

"No ma'am, I'm afraid there's no mistake." The Major paced a couple of steps closer to the center of the room.

"I'm going to ask you all to have a seat while we conduct our investigation."

"Why you can't be serious!" Alexander McKenna now pointed his right index finger in the Major's direction.

Molly grabbed her husband's arm firmly in an effort to calm him. Both men stared directly at one another for several seconds, neither seemed to blink.

"I'm asking all of you to please have a seat!", Major Wilkerson repeated.

Sarah was the first to comply, taking a seat on a red chair located in the northeast corner of the living room. Molly and Alexander walked over to a divan along the west wall. The divan was gold in color. She was still holding on to Alexander's arm as they sat down. Benjamin took a seat on the floor in front of his parents. The two young black men stood silently near the front door. The Major paced back and forth like a nervous animal. The other five soldiers were scattered about the edges of the room.

Cathy stood breathlessly as she watched the proceedings taking place in the living room. She was spying through the slight crack in the bedroom door that had become her hiding spot.

Her mind shifted focus to the two men still hiding in the little red shack. For some reason, Josh was able to scramble back to the bedroom. He now stood quietly, hiding in the bedroom closet with Brea.

Cathy knew their best chance was to try to recreate the energy force that brought them here in the first place. However, Terrance and Professor

Brammer were still outside. There was no good way to communicate with them, especially Dr. Brammer. He'd become more than their Psychology Professor. He was now their best chance at survival.

The bedroom was dark and cold. Although she was standing just a few feet from where the group started their experiment, she was at the same time a world away. The group just traveled one hundred and fifty years into the past and now her primary focus centered on finding them a return ticket home.

"Take a look in those rooms", the Major barked to one of the privates.

"Yes sir", the private responded quickly. Rifle slung over his right shoulder, he walked down the short hallway to the kitchen. He didn't see anything. Halfway back, he noticed a white, wooden door. It faced north. He grabbed the knob and turned it. Staring into the darkness, he saw the outline of two steps leading down. The basement smelled of musk. He closed the door.

Cathy held her breath, as the footsteps were now on the other side of the door. She closed her eyes.

The private opened the door and swung it back, concealing Cathy. He walked into the bedroom and looked around. He looked behind the bed, but saw nothing. He turned and left the room, closing the door to a crack behind him. Cathy felt like crying, but knew it wouldn't accomplish anything.

"All clear Major", the private reported.

"Good, now let's get down to the business at hand." The Major took on the posture of a trial lawyer. As he lifted his head, his eyes locked onto Sarah's hazel eyes. Alexander McKenna said nothing, but he didn't like the way the Major eyed his daughter.

"Several members of the community have made the claim that these two black men are slaves." He turned briefly and pointed at Samuel and Marcus who were standing like statues near the front door. "These are serious allegations and we aim to get to the bottom of this." He then scanned the others in the room as if they were a jury.

The Major walked in front of the mahogany secretaire that was just north of the fireplace. As he did so, one of the privates inched closer to Sarah. The Major now controlled the pace and direction of the proceedings.

"Sergeant, bring those two forward." He pointed in the direction of Samuel and Marcus.

Sergeant Blanks walked over to where both men were standing and ushered them to the center of the room.

"That's fine right there Sergeant. Now, please turn them so they're facing south."

Blanks did as instructed.

The McKenna family watched intently.

"I want both of you to unbutton your shirts and remove them", the Major said.

"But they'll catch a chill", Molly said.

"Ma'am this won't take but a minute."

The two men began the process of unbuttoning their shirts. After loosening all of the buttons, they took their shirts off.

"There you have it!" The Major exclaimed, while pointing to the backs of the two black men. "Slaves, look at those whip marks. Those aren't the signs of well cared for workers!"

CHAPTER TWO

"All the art of living lies in a fine mingling
of letting go and holding on."

Henry Ellis

Sarah gasped at seeing the backs of Samuel and Marcus. She hadn't seen them without their shirts. She instinctively raised her right hand and covered her mouth.

Alexander McKenna was well aware of the Underground Railroad that aided slaves from the south on their journey north to freedom. He knew it was a well-organized operation. Mostly during the cover of night, those known as "conductors" would lead small groups of slaves from one obscure location to another, called "depots". Alexander was determined not to let this happen to Samuel and Marcus. At night, his son Benjamin shackled the two to a post in the small shack where they slept. Alexander felt that intimidation was the best method of prevention.

The elder McKenna's mind now began to speculate. Which of his neighbors turned him in? Did they do it for a reward? How were they able to manage their crops without the aid of slaves?

"Now just a minute!", Alexander rose from the couch, contesting what the Major just said. "These are runaway slaves. They came here escaping the brutal conditions of the south. We took them in when they had nowhere else to go. We've fed them and given them shelter. We've clothed them as well. How dare you make these false and unproven allegations?"

"Well sir, let me take it one step further." The Major turned his body to face the secretaire. He fixed his attention on two, slender drawers. Each drawer contained a knob and a keyhole. He pulled on the left drawer and opened it. It held a jar of ink and a quill pen. He closed it.

"Now just a minute, you've gone too far sir. I'm going to have to ask you and your men to leave at once!" Alexander was red in the face and angrily screaming at the Major. Sarah was quite familiar with this side of her father.

The Major ignored his warning and pulled on the second knob. He found the drawer locked.

"Where's the key to this lock?", he asked, glaring back at Alexander McKenna.

"The key has been missing for years", Alexander snapped in disgust.

"I'm going to ask you one more time for the key. Where is it?"

"Lost!", he replied.

The Major looked at the two privates standing at either end of the divan. "Make sure they're restrained", he said. Facing toward the McKennas, the two soldiers moved a few paces in front of the divan.

Major Wilkerson took his knife from the sheath of his belt. He wedged the three-inch blade between the drawer and the desk. Next, he pulled mightily, causing the drawer to fly open and out onto the top of the secretaire. Looking down at the papers in the drawer, he picked them up. As he brought the papers closer, he clearly made out the words, *Indentured Servant Contract*, at the top of each page. Holding one paper in each hand, he turned around and faced the room.

"As I said, slaves, and here are the documents to prove it!"

Molly was stunned. Sarah was somewhat surprised, but suspected this might be the case. Alexander McKenna lowered his head in a defeated manner. He didn't have a reply for the Major at this time.

The tension in the living room was growing extremely high. Major Wilkerson waved the two *Indentured Servant Contracts* in front of everyone in the room as if he were waiving his claim to the Mother Load Silver Mine.

Alexander McKenna slouched onto the divan in a defeated posture. Molly tried to comfort him.

"Just a minute", Benjamin said to the Major, rising from his sitting position on the floor.

"Yes son?"

"How do we know those are real documents? You could've planted them there after breaking open the locked drawer."

The Major carried the two papers over to Benjamin so that he could get a closer look at them.

"See, son, signed by Alexander McKenna. He pointed at one of the papers while moving it closer to Benjamin. Is this not your father's handwriting? Also, there's the seal from the State of Alabama stamped onto the documents."

Benjamin looked them both over closely. The signature did indeed appear to be that of his father. He could barely comprehend what he was looking at. Finally, he turned around facing his father and shouted, "Why father, why?"

Alexander McKenna didn't look at Benjamin, but instead stared blankly down at the floor. "We needed help with the crops and there weren't enough available hands around these parts. I did what I felt I had to do. I haven't mistreated these two. Quite the contrary, I've given them food, shelter and clothing."

Major Wilkerson quickly broke in, "but in doing so you've violated the very principle many of my fellow Union soldiers have laid down their lives to stamp out. The President of the United States of America has made it clear that slavery will not be tolerated. Those sacrificed lives will not be in vain!"

He said this so loud that Brea and Josh could easily make out every word from the bedroom closet. Cathy stood still behind the bedroom door. It was a good thing that breathing came automatic, she thought. She saw the burning fire in Major Wilkerson's eyes. It was scary. The Major looked like a demon possessed. This was the most frightened she could remember being at any time in her life.

Major Wilkerson continued. "I want to see Corporal Livingston and Staff Sergeant Blanks in the kitchen at once. You other three men stand guard over these people."

The Major set the two pieces of paper down on the secretaire and walked through the hallway into the kitchen. The Corporal and Staff Sergeant followed directly behind him. The three stepped back into the kitchen and out of eyesight. They huddled.

"We have to punish these people", the Major whispered to the other two. "They've gone too far and have betrayed their own country. We need to execute Alexander McKenna."

Upon hearing this, Staff Sergeant Blanks shifted his giant wad of chewing tobacco from one cheek to the other. "We gonna' hang him or shoot him?", he asked inquisitively.

There was momentary silence. The three men looked at one another and then shifted their gazes about the room.

"Not enough", Major Wilkerson said.

"Not enough?", the Corporal questioned. "You want us to torture him first?"

"No, not torture", said the Major. "I'm talking about the family and the two black men. We can't just kill the old man and leave the rest of the family to go about their business as usual. They are witnesses. They can identify us. We could be tried on murder charges."

"But we have the evidence", Sergeant Blanks suggested.

"We would need to bring this man to trial on slavery charges. The court would likely find him guilty, but how severely would they punish him? They may decide to hang him. They may give him life in prison. On the other hand, they may give him a lighter sentence. The three of us have all seen our friends and brothers butchered by the enemy. They died for our cause. Heck, it could've been any one of us out there instead of them. We'd want them to do the right thing if it was our blood and bones lying around on those battlefields."

"So, are you saying that we need to kill all of these people for what one man did?" Corporal Livingston asked this with a bit of disconnect in his voice.

"That's exactly what I'm saying Corporal."

"How do you want this handled?" Sergeant Blanks asked the Major, showing little facial expression.

"Wait a minute", the Corporal tried to interject. "These others may not have known the two were slaves?"

"Maybe, maybe not", the Major replied. "But they can't be left alive to testify against us."

"Let's just arrest them all and put them in front of a judge. Let the judge decide." The Corporal didn't like the idea of killing all of these people, especially since two of them were women.

Wilkerson and Livingston fought side by side at Gettysburg. They were mostly inseparable, but now found themselves on opposite ends of a life and death argument.

Major Wilkerson said, "The discussion is over. We'll execute all six of them. Have the men dig four shallow graves in the basement. I think I noticed a couple of shovels leaning against that little red shack when we first rode in. Blanks, have your men fetch them."

"The two black men will be hung side by side from that large oak tree out back. Once the four family members are buried have the men look for something heavy to place over the graves. This is an order, do you understand Corporal?"

Corporal Livingston paused and begrudgingly said, "Yes sir".

"What about you Staff Sergeant, do you understand?"

"Yes sir", he replied to his commander.

Major Wilkerson led the procession of the three men from the kitchen back into the living room.

"You two run out to that red shack and fetch those shovels", Blanks ordered, as he pointed at two of the privates.

"Yes sir Staff Sergeant", one of them verbally replied.

The men made their way out the front door and through the thin layer of snow. They quickly returned, each carrying a shovel at his side.

"Staff Sergeant, lead these men to where they are needed", Major Wilkerson ordered with authority.

"Yes sir", Staff Sergeant Blanks replied. "You three men follow me". Blanks began to walk from his spot near the front door toward the kitchen.

"Where're they going with those shovels?", Alexander McKenna asked.

"Never you mind sir", the Major said. He signaled for Staff Sergeant Blanks to come closer. "Blanks", he whispered, "I think I saw an oil lamp in the kitchen. Take it with you downstairs so that the men can see where they're digging. Also, dig your holes about three feet deep. Have your tallest man lie down on the ground and use him as an outline for your length and width, okay?"

"Yes sir", The Sergeant said.

"Let me know when you've finished."

"Yes sir, Major".

Blanks continued his slow march toward the kitchen. The three soldiers followed closely behind him. He picked up the oil lamp that was sitting in the middle of the kitchen table. Turning, he parted the three soldiers like Moses parting the Red Sea. His right hand took hold of the doorknob and twisted it open. There was just enough natural light for him to descend the stairs without having to fire up the oil lamp.

Once in the basement, he lit the lamp and looked around the room. There was a large, wooden, wine press located on the east wall. It was five or six feet tall. A wide, flat board slanted down from top to bottom. This acted as a slide for the grapes. After dropping about two feet, the grapes met a metal mashing wheel operated by a hand crank. Buckets lined up on the floor would catch the streaming juices.

"Set your rifles down over by that wine press", Blanks directed. The men lifted their rifle straps over their heads and laid down their rifles. The three men made their way back to where Blanks was standing.

The Sergeant sized the three men up. "Jenkins, I need you to lay on the ground in this direction." He used his right arm to indicate that he wanted him with his head near the west wall, his feet pointing east.

"Sergeant, do what?", the private replied, with a puzzled look on his face. Kenny Jenkins had been in the regiment for nearly a year now. He was twenty-three years old. Tallest of the three, he stood six-feet, two inches tall.

"You heard me!", Blanks said, with a bit of frustration in his voice.

Jenkins quickly made his way to the spot where Blanks was pointing. He lowered his lanky frame to the ground. Turning onto his back, he stretched out looking east toward the wine press. Motionless, he wondered what the Sergeant had in mind.

"Bring those shovels over here", Blanks barked out at the remaining two. They each picked up a shovel and stood in place as instructed.

"I need you two to dig an outline around Jenkins. Then I need the three of you to repeat the process three more times to his left, do you understand?" Blank's was accustomed to the Major asking him this same question, do you understand? He rarely missed the opportunity to use it himself. This imitation was indeed a sincere form of flattery.

"Each hole needs to be about three feet deep", Blanks followed.

The assignment became quite apparent to the men. They were digging graves.

CHAPTER THREE

"Doing what you love is the cornerstone
of having abundance in your life."

WAYNE DYER

Donald Brammer looked up at the white clock hanging on the back wall of the classroom. It was three twenty-five. He sensed the restlessness in the body language of his students. His Monday Psychology and the Paranormal class officially ended at three-thirty. He nervously coughed into his right hand in an effort to clear his throat.

"Are there any questions?"

"Yes Brea", he punched the words out and shifted his gaze in her direction.

"Dr. Brammer, will we meet here at school on Thursday or do you want us all to meet at the site?" Her voice was high pitched. It sounded more like Minnie Mouse than a graduate student.

"Brea, that's a good question". He nodded in affirmation.

"We'll meet here at twelve-thirty on Thursday afternoon, two hours before our normally scheduled class period. I'll have all of the equipment we need to conduct the experiment packed into my van. All four in your group can ride with me to the site. I've budgeted two hours for the entire experiment, including set up. We should be finished, packed up, and back here at school around three-thirty."

He saw a wry, little smile curling up on Brea's lips. He heard the squeaky voice offer, "Sounds good, Dr. Brammer". Donald still couldn't get used to the idea of someone addressing him as doctor. He hadn't performed any surgeries nor had he delivered any babies. It appeared early on in life that

Donald would have blue-collared shirts hanging in his closet. Somehow, he didn't get the message.

Growing up, most people simply knew him as Donnie. He started out at a young age flipping burgers in order to scratch out enough money to keep the fuel gauge of his Chevy Impala from dipping below empty. His father and his father before him were both high school dropouts. Donnie's father carved out a living driving an eighteen-wheeled, seventy-thousand pound monster around the city delivering groceries to local super markets. His grandfather's working life encompassed numerous occupations, most notable of which were chasing women and drinking himself into oblivion at any watering hole that could fill a tall glass full of Hamm's beer.

Somewhere along the line, Donald managed to take a zig in the road instead of a zag. Not only did he finish high school, but he also did the unthinkable, he went on to college. He ended up going to college so long that they gave him three letters of the alphabet to tag along to the backend of his last name, Ph.D. He earned a Doctorate Degree in Psychology. No big rig, no womanizing, no tall glass of suds for him, he had what people often referred to as a respectable profession.

"Are there any other questions?"

Reaching down with both hands, Donald gathered the stack of completed quizzes from the table and laid them neatly into his briefcase. He heard the shuffling and squeaking of shoes making their way to the door. There was the usual small talk and banter as well. Donald liked to take his time putting away his textbooks and other papers in case one of his students had a question. After clicking shut the metal clasps of his briefcase, he looked up and found himself standing alone.

Carrying the briefcase in his right hand, he felt the winter chill penetrate through the Levi jeans he was wearing all the way to the core of his bones. Both of his knees stiffened. It felt to him as though he had two tree trunks for legs. All those years playing sports were finally catching up with him. He opened the door of the white, Chevy van and slid into the driver's seat. He buckled his seat belt and started the engine. Yes Dorothy, you are in Kansas, he thought.

Donald Brammer steered the van up the driveway. As he did so, his wife Patty saw the reflection from the headlights stream through the living room window. She decided to slide the thermostat north a few clicks from seventy-two to seventy-four degrees. Being born and raised in Florida, she wasn't yet acclimated to the cold Midwestern winters. Midway through December in Florida wouldn't require one to wear a coat or turn on a heater.

He pressed the remote opener button to the garage door that hung above him on the visor. It was a two car, detached garage. It would be nice to have an attached garage he thought, but in this type of winter weather, he was just happy to have shelter for the vehicles. He turned off the engine, unbuckled his seat belt and opened the driver's side door. After taking a couple of steps outside of the garage, he clicked the remote. The garage door began to close automatically.

Walking back into the kitchen, Patty stirred the pot of boiling water that was on the stove. She knew how much her husband liked spaghetti, so she tried to cook it for dinner at least once a week. Stepping over to the pantry, she grabbed a bottle of pre-made spaghetti sauce from the shelf. She opened the lid and poured the contents into a pot. Her looks were still quite stunning for a woman in her early fifties. Soft blonde locks gently lay down upon her shoulders. However, her ocean blue eyes were what first attracted Donald's attention. That was nearly twenty-eight years ago. Although they had no children of their own, they both took a keen interest in their eight nephews and two nieces. Patty gave up her career as a court reporter when Donald took his most recent assignment at a nearby college in Topeka. The college was a fifteen-minute drive south from their rural home.

They were both proud of their home. It was predominately a brick ranch. The brick was a good insulator. The house was about twenty-five years old, but in very good shape. It sat on a one-acre lot. Both Donald and Patty liked the space and breathing room. There was a small shed in the backyard where Donald kept his riding lawn mower and other tools. Patty liked to garden. She cleared out an area roughly six feet wide by twelve feet long. Tomato and pepper plants were the mainstay of the garden. Of course, at this time of year, the garden was nothing more than a two-inch thick blanket of white, powdery snow.

"Lucy, I'm home", Donald said, using his best Cuban accent while entering the living room.

"I'm in the kitchen Ricky", Patty replied in jest, using her Lucy Ricardo imitation.

"It smells good in here", he said. He wanted her to know he recognized the aroma of the pasta sauce.

"Wash up and grab a seat at the table honey. Dinner will be ready in about five minutes", Patty said, in a voice filled with approval.

He and Patty began to twirl their forks into the piles of spaghetti on their plates. The normal dinner table chat soon followed.

"Did anything exciting happen at school today?", Patty asked. She said this in a begging tone, hoping to flesh out some new details in what otherwise had been a typical day for her.

"Now that you mention it, I'm kind of excited about my final group of graduate students and their semester project." He said this with a twinge of exhilaration in his voice.

"I think this group of students has chosen a great topic and have spent a pretty decent amount of time researching it too." After finishing this sentence, he took the napkin from his lap and raised it up. He wiped away a line of sauce that had soaked its way onto his brown mustache. Donald was a very neat and orderly person. He was self-conscious about his outward appearance. He placed the napkin back onto his lap.

"Really", Patty replied. Those swimming pool blue eyes locked onto his face like two laser beams. She shot him her sweetest smile, the one that she often used to elicit either his money or attention. With little pause she inquired, "And what topic might that be?"

Donald realized he'd fallen for the bait - hook, line and sinker. He knew he'd be required to spill the beans to her regarding the project.

"Well honey", he said, swallowing hard to clear his throat. "Their project, or more precisely their experiment, involves the use of telepathy and paranormal techniques in an attempt to solve a mystery."

"What mystery?" She was now goading him on with the enthusiasm of a Girl Scout sitting around a campfire.

"He took a sip of the Merlot from his wine goblet and continued, "Have you heard about the old McKenna farmstead that sits just off of highway ninety-three?"

"I have", she responded. "Isn't that the place local residents claim is haunted, something to do with the Civil War?"

"Exactly", he nodded his head in agreement. "Story has it that in the winter of eighteen sixty-four, the McKenna family was paid an unannounced visit by five or six members of the Union Army. The soldiers were in receipt of allegations from several local sources that the McKennas owned slaves. Slavery would not be tolerated this far north. If proven true, it would have serious repercussions for the McKennas and the purported slaves. Union troops at the time executed swift judgment and justice. Reprisals could include torture or even death. He paused here as he caught a fleeting glimpse of shock beginning to materialize on her face.

"Well, what happened?"

"That's just it", he said. "Nobody really knows for sure. By the time the war ended in eighteen sixty-five, the farmstead was abandoned. The McKennas and their alleged slaves weren't seen or heard from again. In addition, there's no written record detailing the fate of the Union soldiers, ergo, the mystery."

Patty shook slightly as a ripple of goose bumps made their way up her spine. "How many members of the McKenna family were there?"

Donald fidgeted with his wedding ring as he often did when he was a bit anxious. Patty picked out a very beautiful ring for him. The band was fourteen karat gold. On the top of the ring was an indentation implanted with five, one-tenth karat diamonds. He gazed at the diamonds as if he were gazing into a crystal ball.

He took in a medium breath, let it out, and continued. "There were four family members. The head of the household was Alexander McKenna. He was born and raised on the farm. He took control of the property after his mother died. He was a very strict man who focused the majority of his time and attention on making money. On occasion, he'd strike the backs of the two black workers. Rumor had it that he'd purchased the indentured servant contracts of the two. Further, it was believed that Alexander kept the contracts hidden in a small, locked drawer in his mahogany secretaire located in the living room.

Donald took another sip of Merlot. "Alexander was married to Molly. She was a simple but stunning woman who devoted most of her time to the care and welfare of her children. As with most women of the time, Molly was predominately submissive to the needs of her husband."

"And the remaining two family members were their children?"

"Yes, two children lived with them. A male child named Benjamin and a daughter named Sarah. Benjamin had a very astute mind and gift for numbers, which endeared him to his father. However, he also had an independent streak. Benjamin was a very good-looking young man of twenty years. Unlike his father, Benjamin would just as soon see the two black workers paid for doing household chores and tending the fields.

Finally, there was Sarah. She was the spitting image of her mother. Beautiful brown hair with a fair complexion, she possessed a charming smile and inviting hazel eyes. Sarah was nearly seventeen years of age. While doing research for the project at the local library, one of the students in the group came across a daguerreotype photograph of Sarah. We hope this might help in identifying her should her spirit appear at the session."

"What session?", Patty asked.

"The session taking place this Thursday", Donald's voice quivered a bit, as he knew this part of the mystery yarn could create some concern for his wife. "I and four of my students are going to meet at the old McKenna farmhouse in an effort to conjure up spirits and entities. We're hoping to get some answers regarding the fate of the McKennas, the black workers and the Union soldiers."

"You know how I feel about these conjugations!" Patty's voice began rising to the next highest octave. "Besides, she offered, I don't think the McKenna farmhouse is structurally safe."

"I understand your concern", he said, in a reassuring tone. "We had an engineer look at the place and he told us that the first floor living room was safe. We also obtained written permission from the current owners. There's no need to worry. Besides, there will be five of us. I'm bringing the digital video camera, the infrared thermal scanner, the EMF detector and a digital tape recorder to the event. We should be wrapped up by about three-thirty."

He saw the trepidation painted on her face. She abruptly pushed out her chair and began collecting the dirty plates from the table. She carried them toward the kitchen sink. Patty was stepping into the kitchen when Donald said, "Patty, we both know this is what I do and what I love to do".

"I know, but those ghost hunting stories on television always give me the creeps!"

He rose from his chair and joined her at the kitchen sink. He gave her a reassuring hug from behind. She turned toward him and half whispered, "Don, I'm kind of nervous". She addressed him as Don. She didn't use the usual honey, babe, sweetie or Donald, but Don. He knew this meant she had serious reservations about the experiment.

He gave her a gentle stroke, passing the fingers of his right hand through her velvety soft blonde hair. He followed that by giving her a passionate kiss on the lips. After, he backed up a step and in a calm voice said, "Baby, nothing bad has ever happened in the past and nothing bad will happen at this experiment either".

In a slightly surrendering voice she responded, "Okay, but I'll be glad when it's over. You know that I love you more than anything darling." She hugged him tightly.

"I know you love me babe and I love you more than anything in the world. It's the tail end of the semester. After this it's our favorite time of year, the Christmas Season."

"I can't wait", she said, with a bit more pep in her voice.

"I can't wait either", he said. He beamed a smile toward her and added the softest look that his teddy bear brown eyes could muster up. "I can't wait either!"

CHAPTER FOUR

"Through others we become ourselves."

Lev S. Vygotsky

A brisk breeze began to pick up outside of Bruno's Bar. Bruno's was a popular hangout in this college town. Located on the corner of Third & Main streets in downtown Topeka, it was within walking distance of most college dorms. On weekends, it was usually standing room only and so noisy that one could barely hear the voice of the nearest person. However, this was Monday night, and at 7:00PM, it was half-full at best.

Brea Taylor took her tanned left hand and lifted the half-full mug of beer to her mouth. She took a healthy swig of the malt and barley combination. Feeling some of the foam sitting on the outside of her lips, she took her sweater sleeve and wiped it away. Brea felt good, not just from the buzz the beer provided, but because she was really enjoying the Psychology and Paranormal class this semester. Dr. Brammer was easy going and an expert in the subject. Studying topics like telepathy and paranormal activity were right up her alley.

She looked across the table eyeing the young, blonde haired man. He looked too young to be drinking. She also doubted if he'd shaven for the first time. "Josh", she queried, "do you think we'll contact any spirits on Thursday?"

"Maybe, Josh replied?" His voice sounded as though it had recently graduated from puberty.

Although he'd just answered, maybe, Josh Crenshaw was very skeptical about this whole experiment. He considered himself well grounded in reality. He was from Missouri, *The Show Me State*. He was looking for credible proof to win him over into the believer category. Of the four-member group, he'd need the most convincing.

"Come on Josh", both Terrance and Cathy blurted out in unison. This caused everyone at the table to laugh aloud, except Josh, who maintained a somewhat stoic face. Terrance Bell and Cathy Reynolds rounded out the group.

"Great minds think alike", Cathy offered.

"You know it", Terrance countered, raising his mug toward Cathy's in a toasting jester.

While Josh was born and raised in Kansas City, Terrance and Cathy were both transplants.

Cathy grew up in corn country, Iowa. Her parents owned a two-hundred acre farm on which they raised corn and soybeans. Cathy learned the ropes of farming at the heels of her father. She had no siblings, so Cathy took on the personification of a tomboy by default. She knew how to drive the big combines and John Deere tractors. In addition, she could perform most maintenance functions on them as well. She studied weather patterns and followed the corn and soybean prices in the business section of the local newspaper.

She mostly wore blue jeans and cotton flannel shirts in the winter. Her appearance was plain. She had a light complexion and wore her auburn colored hair short. She often felt intimidated by Brea's seductive smile and knockout body. Cathy's eyes were a common shade of blue. Brea had hypnotic, hazel colored eyes. Nevertheless, for Cathy that was just fine. She wasn't interested in earning the crown of Miss America. Her focus was on obtaining a Master's Degree in Business Administration. She was taking this class for two reasons, and two reasons only. One, she needed a three hour elective course, and two, the course sounded interesting to her.

"Well people, I hate to be a party pooper, but it's time for me to head home", Terrance said, half apologetically. "It's Monday and that means Monday Night Football. The Patriots are playing the Packers tonight and it's going to be a good one", Terrance said, with a great deal of anticipation in his voice.

Brea looked up at Terrance and asked, "Do you mean to tell me you'd rather watch football than drink beer with your friends?"

Terrance beamed a charming smile back at her and said, "No comment".

The remaining three at the table lightly laughed and giggled.

"Just get some rest", Josh said to Terrance. "We want your legs fully rested when it comes time to chase down those ghosts."

Terrance countered, "I'll catch my share of ghosts, just make sure you catch yours".

"Don't you worry", the normally quiet Cathy interceded. She lifted her right arm over her head and began imitating a cowboy twirling a rope. "I'm going to rope me some doggies!"

All of them were now in full laughter.

Of the four, Terrance was by far the most mature. He, too, was taking this class as an elective toward his graduate degree. However, Terrance favored Finance over Business Administration. As a young boy, college didn't seem like much of an option for him. Growing up in a very seedy and dangerous part of Detroit, many young black males like Terrance didn't live long enough to see their twenty-fifth birthday. By the age of twelve, he'd pretty much seen and heard it all; the gangs, the drugs, the prostitutes, the gunshots, the police sirens and the mortuary station wagons.

Terrance's mother had seen it all too, and it worried her about his safety. She was also trying to kick a bad heroin addiction. He didn't know it at the time, but she called her parents in St. Louis asking if they could help Terrance escape a city that seemed to hold no future for him. His grandparents were more than willing to help. They loved Terrance and knew he was a bright boy with good manners. They also liked the way he treated others with respect. From the age of twelve until graduating from high school, he and his grandparents formed a bond filled with tremendous love and respect. He called them from his apartment at least once a week to see how they were doing.

With his buffed physique and athletic frame, most students probably assumed Terrance was on an athletic scholarship. If they did, they were wrong. He'd earned a scholarship all right, but it was an academic one. He finished high school with a three point eight grade point average and graduated with honors. He wasn't exactly sure where the finance degree would lead him. He had aspirations of being either a stock trader or a chief financial officer. With his drive, persistence and intellect, he could easily fit into either of those roles.

"See you all on Thursday", Terrance said.

The three chimed back in an awkward harmony, "See you Thursday Terrance."

He walked to the front of the bar and pushed open the glass door. Terrance headed out into the cold night.

Josh scooted back his chair. Half-standing, he looked toward Brea and Cathy. "How about I buy us one more round before we call it quits?"

"Sure thing", Brea replied.

"I'm in", Cathy followed.

Josh slowly made his way to the bar. About half way there, his eyes zeroed in on the bartender. She had it going on. She was wearing a tight, low cut black t-shirt with the word, *Bruno's*, stenciled in white just above her breasts. As he reached the bar, he leaned over onto it and noticed a glass jar full of green one and five dollar bills. It didn't take much inductive or deductive reasoning on Josh's part to figure out why the jar was full.

"What're you having?", she asked.

"I need three, Boulevard Light's from the tap".

"You've got it sweetie", she said. "Just give me a minute."

Josh reached into his pocket and pulled out a five and a ten-dollar bill. He figured the ten would cover the beers. The five, he thought, would find comfort joining its counterparts in that big glass jar.

Back at the table, Brea pulled her chair a little closer to Cathy. "Cathy", she asked, in a low and whispering voice, "can I count on you to keep a secret?"

"You know you can. Mum's the word."

"This Thursday, there's just going to be the five of us at the old McKenna place."

"Right", Cathy nodded.

"Well, there just might be six of us instead". Brea said this with the look of a child who'd just snuck a cookie from the cookie jar.

"What?", Cathy asked, in a slightly confused voice.

"You know my boyfriend Brian who is a writer at the newspaper?"

"Yes".

"Well he's been working there for about three years now. He's a great writer but his boss doesn't give him a chance to write about interesting things. He always gives him the lousy assignments. You know, like covering the town picnic or the annual fireworks show."

By now, Cathy locked onto what Brea was telling her and was sure where she was going with it. Cathy shook her head and said, "Brea, tell me you didn't invite Brian out to the farmhouse for the experiment?"

"Well Cathy, he won't actually be involved. He'll just be an observer."

"More of a reporter, you mean", Cathy scoffed.

"I guess so", Brea sheepishly answered. "But he could use a lift right now. He's really in the dumps. I thought if we did have contact with spirits, he could write an article describing it. It might be just the break he needs."

"Oh my God", Cathy stammered. "I can't believe you did this. Dr. Brammer was okay with it?"

"Well, I haven't quite gotten that far up the chain of command yet."

Cathy heard the sound of drinking glasses clanking behind her. She took a quick peek over her right shoulder and saw Josh nearing the table carrying three beers in his hands.

As he set them down onto the table, Josh smiled and queried, "Did I miss anything ladies?"

Cathy gave Brea a quick sneer and looking up at Josh said, "No, you didn't miss a thing!"

CHAPTER FIVE

B rian Foster pushed down on the silver handle, but no soap came out. He moved to the next sink and tried again. He got the same result. There was one sink remaining. He pushed down several times on the pump but obtained the same result, nothing.

"Damn!" Brian vented aloud in the otherwise empty restroom.

He was beginning to think life was conspiring against him. He was in a rut. His job as a beat writer at the Reporter was going nowhere fast. His boss didn't seem to have much faith in him. He was hoping that attending his fiancée Brea's paranormal project tomorrow would give him a lift. He was looking forward to it. It sounded bizarre, but interesting. They were going to conduct an experiment out at the old, rundown, McKenna farmhouse in an attempt to solve a mystery. She thought it might be a good story for him to cover, one that could help turn things around. Who knows, he thought to himself, she just might be right.

As he finished washing his soapless hands, Brian picked up a small stack of paper towels sitting on the sink counter. He wiped his hands dry but didn't throw the paper towels into the trash bin. He quickly checked his overall appearance in the mirror and made his way to the door. Brian used the paper towels to grab onto the door handle. He'd watched plenty of men in the past use the restroom without washing their hands before leaving. Brian wanted nothing to do with touching the door handle with his bare hand.

Heading back to his cubicle, he passed a couple of his colleagues and exchanged the customary nods and smiles. He discarded the paper towels into the trash can next to his desk. Pulling back on his chair, he looked at his computer screen and saw it, the dreaded yellow sticky note with the words, "come see me", scribbled in red ink. It was attached at the upper middle part of the screen so that he couldn't miss it. It was signed at the bottom, "Hank Edwards". Hank was the Reporter's editor and Brian's boss. Brian crumpled the little square of paper into a small ball. He shot the little paper ball into his trash can as if it were a basketball.

As he approached the open doorway to Hank's office, he could see the silver haired man waiving him in like a traffic cop directing the next car to proceed.

"Have a seat Brian", he said, in a thick, course voice that was the product of many years of smoking cigarettes.

Brian eyed the nineteen-seventy style-padded chair. It was a dandy. It had two wooden armrests that were supported by metal brackets. The true beauty though was its interior, matching lime green plastic seat and back cushion. As Brian lowered his body into the chair, he waited for the big payoff, "Wooooosh!" There was no avoiding the loud bellow the cushion seat gave off when squeezed of oxygen. Better yet, Brian played a little mind game with himself each time he sat in the chair. He liked to see just how loud he could make the old relic belch.

"You wanted to see me?"

"Yes, I have an assignment for you", Hank answered. "It should be rather interesting. Tomorrow, from ten until two o'clock in the afternoon, they're holding *The Little Mini-Miss Midwest Pageant* downtown at the old Divine Theatre. Like Miss America, only the contestants are six and seven year olds."

Brian sat stunned for several seconds. He looked over the old man's facial features for any hint of a joke. There was none. Life just keeps getting better all the time, he thought. This wasn't a rut he was in, it was a full-blown sinkhole.

"You want me to cover a beauty pageant tomorrow?" Brian said this out loud to make sure he wasn't stuck in some kind of twisted nightmare.

"Yes", Hank continued. "The beauty contest contains three main parts. First, there's the parade of girls in their little evening gowns. That's followed by a talent contest. Finally, the host reads each contestant a question, like, how would you change the world, or something to that effect. They're each given one minute for their replies. After this, the judges tally their scorecards and the new *Little Mini-Miss Midwest Champion* is crowned."

Crowned, Brian thought. He'd rather get a crown or even a root canal than tackle this assignment. These spoiled little brats were coached to be three-foot tall adults. Never mind the mothers, living vicariously through their precious little darlings.

"Okay", Brian responded with the enthusiasm of a Christian being led down a hallway toward a Coliseum full of hungry lions.

"One last thing". Hank leaned back in his office chair scratching the gray hair on top of his head while at the same time combing it down. "I won't be here the rest of the week, so you'll need to submit your article to Janet for editing and review."

Finally, a silver lining in the dark clouds, Brian thought. Janet Krigle was younger than Hank. She was much more progressive, not so old school. She actually had a personality. Better yet, she wouldn't know he was supposed to be covering the beauty contest. This would give him the needed cover to attend the paranormal experiment at the farmhouse with Brea and the others. Most importantly, if he submitted an article regarding the experiment to Janet, she would be none the wiser. Sure, he may be out of a job come Monday, but it seemed well worth the risk.

"Okay Mr. Edwards", Brian smiled and exhaled deeply. "I hope you enjoy your days off."

This was all too much for Brian to digest at once. He needed to get away from the office to try to relax. Maybe a cold beer and a pizza would do the trick, he thought.

Brian gathered his coat from his desk chair and walked down the narrow hallway leading to a bank of three elevators. He heard a ding, as the shiny, silver, metal door opened on the middle elevator. To his pleasant surprise, he saw that it was empty.

A light snow continued to fall as Brian pulled his red Mustang into its usual parking spot at his apartment complex. He grabbed the cardboard box containing the pizza from the passenger's seat. After exiting the car, he briskly made his way to his apartment.

Inserting the key into the door, he snapped the deadbolt open with a sharp turn of his wrist. He closed the door and locked it behind him. Making his way to the kitchen, he removed his coat and hung it neatly over the back of a chair. He set the pizza down on the table. Reaching out with his right hand, he grabbed onto the refrigerator door handle and pulled it open. As he picked it up, Brian felt the cold glass bottle against his right hand. He closed the refrigerator door.

He twisted the metal cap off the top of the beer bottle. He raised the bottle and tilted it back toward his mouth. Relief, he thought, as the cold, yellow liquid made its way down his parched throat.

He picked up the box of pizza from the table and headed directly to the couch. Grabbing the television remote, he tapped the power button. Instantly, the sound of voices blared from the box. Now, he thought, for a slice of hot pizza.

Brian felt a buzz in his front, left jeans pocket. He also heard the ring tone of his cell phone, *I'm on the Highway to Hell*. He reached into his pocket and removed the phone. After, he picked up the television remote and pushed the mute button.

"Hello", he answered.

"Hi baby," the high-pitched voice on the other end said excitedly.

"Hey sweetie, how goes it?"

"Excellent", she replied. "I'm getting ready to send Dr. Brammer an email informing him that you'll be attending tomorrow's experiment as an observer."

"Awesome, do you think he'll mind?"

"I'm sure he won't mind."

"Great, what time do I need to be there?"

"Be there around twelve forty-five or so."

"I'll be there early. I really appreciate you setting this up for me."

"No problem", she said. "You're my fiancé and my future husband."

"This is true Mrs. Foster." He said in an endearing fashion.

Brea giggled and replied, "Brea Foster does have a nice ring to it."

"That it does", he followed.

"By the way, since I'm just going to be an observer tomorrow, I thought

I would jot down the names of all the participants. Can you give those to me?"

"Sure", she replied. "There's Dr. Donald Brammer, Josh Crenshaw, Terrance Bell, Cathy Reynolds, and most importantly, yours truly!"

"Cool, thanks. Do you know what type of equipment will be used?"

"Yes", she answered. "Dr. Brammer will be bringing all of the equipment. First, there will be a video camera mounted on a battery-operated tripod. The camera will swing back and forth covering a one hundred and eighty degree area. He's also bringing an infrared thermal scanner. This device registers hot and cold spots that might indicate the presence of an entity. There will also be an EMF detector. It detects changes in electronic fields and frequencies. I'm sure that he'll bring a digital recorder to capture any EVP's, or electronic voice phenomenon."

Brea yawned into her cell phone and said, "I'm getting kind of tired babe. I want to get some rest for tomorrow."

"Sounds good", he said. "I probably won't be up much longer either."

"I love you Brian", the sweet and squeaky voice said.

"I love you too, Brea", he answered.

"Goodnight baby".

"Goodnight".

They clicked the end call buttons on their cell phones and set them down. Neither knew it at the time, but tomorrow would be a day they both would never forget.

CHAPTER SIX

"That best portion of a man's life, his little, nameless,
unremembered acts of kindness and love."

William Wordsworth

Donald Brammer drove up the spiral-parking garage, stopping on the second level. He pulled his wife's Accord into an empty spot between a green Jaguar and a black Hummer. While driving to Kansas City, he'd spent the last sixty minutes in deep thought. His wife Patty loved shopping on the Country Club Plaza at least once during the Christmas Season. It had become an annual pilgrimage for them. The quaint buildings were decorated with Christmas lights across their roofs.

The area did have a way of putting people into the Christmas spirit. Even Donald, who would rather have a prostate exam than go shopping, seemed a bit energized.

"Look honey, there's that cool kitchenware shop", Patty bubbled, as she pointed across the street.

"I see", he said, trying to feign excitement.

They stood on the corner and waited for the streetlight to change from red to green. A light snow continued to fall. The psychologist in Donald took over. He started to size up other shoppers. There were two women walking side by side. They were wearing what appeared to be genuine fur coats. Were these the wives of Doctors? Lawyers? Successful Businessmen? One thing he felt quite sure of, they weren't the wives of college Professors.

Donald held the door for his wife as they entered the store. Once his wife was busy shopping in her favorite boutique, Donald headed for the bookshop next door. He quickly found a myriad of titles about the Civil War. One in particular caught his eye. It was a large, hardback book titled, *Up and Down the Mason-Dixon Line, a Pictorial History of the Civil War.* He skimmed through the pages and knew this was the right book. He took the book back to a black padded chair and comfortably nestled into it.

He was interested in finding photographs taken of the Missouri-Kansas area during the Civil War. He was doing some informal, last minute research for tomorrow's experiment. His thinking was that getting a better feel for the people of the period and their dress might be helpful in identifying apparitions should they appear. Thumbing through further, a particular black and white photograph caught his attention. It appeared to be a family of farmers. They were standing beside a horse and plow. Their eyes looked hardened and hollow. These people knew the harsh reality of surviving. There were no powerful machines to streamline the planting and harvesting. The backbreaking work was clearly reflected in their faces.

The woman in the photograph wore her hair up in a bun. She was wearing what appeared to be a long-sleeved, cotton blouse. It was light in color, probably white or tan. She had a full dark skirt on that fell to her shoe tops. Her waistline was very thin which made Donald think she might be wearing a corset. She looked about forty years old or so to him. The two men in the picture were most likely father and son. Their facial features bore a strong resemblance. Neither smiled and both posed awkwardly.

Donald felt the vibration of the cell phone in his right, front pants pocket. He pulled out the phone and flipped it open to see he had an incoming email message. The message was from Brea Taylor. He touched the yellow box with his finger to open the message and read it.

"Dear Dr. Brammer, I feel very bad about emailing you at this late hour, but I did something regarding tomorrow that may upset you. My fiancé Brian is going through a very difficult time at work. He's a writer for the Reporter newspaper. He's mostly been covering superficial stories. I thought it might give him a boost of confidence if he could cover our experiment tomorrow. He would strictly be an observer and not participate in anyway. The other members of our group didn't have any objections (because, except for Cathy, they didn't know). However, I will completely understand if you do. As I said, I feel horrible for letting you know so late. I won't give Brian the green light unless I receive an email from you Okaying it first. I'll check my email messages

late tonight and early in the morning. As I said, I hope that you won't be too upset. Sincerely -Brea Taylor."

It wouldn't take long for Brea to receive a reply. Donald didn't like last minute surprises. He gave himself a moment to digest what he'd just read. His first reaction was to fire off a stinging rebuttal to her explaining why this was a bad idea. Nevertheless, the more he thought about it, the more his easygoing temperament got the better of him. He typed the following reply into the keyboard of his cell phone:

"Dear Brea, I wish you'd come to me sooner regarding this matter. This has the potential to jeopardize the entire project. Not only could it affect your grade, but that of the other group members as well. However, if they've agreed to Brian being an observer, then I have no objection. I haven't met him, so I trust your judgment. Please have him meet us at the old McKenna place around twelve forty-five. I want to make sure that he completely understands the ground rules. Respectfully-Donald Brammer."

He closed the cell phone and tucked it back into his jeans pocket. He was not too thrilled. Shaking his head, he rose from the over-sized chair and returned the book to its place on the shelf. Too bad the coffee bar wasn't a full service bar, he thought. He sure could use a drink about now.

Meanwhile, next door, the cashier asked, "Will that be all?"

"Yes", Patty Brammer replied.

"The total is ninety-four dollars and sixty-nine cents. Will that be cash, check or credit?"

Patty Brammer pulled the blue billfold from her purse and removed a red and white credit card. She slid the card through the card reader and pressed the "yes" button. Almost instantly, the cash register spit out a twelve-inch long receipt. The cashier handed both the receipt and shopping bag to Patty.

"Thank you and have a very Merry Christmas".

"You do the same", Patty said. She turned and headed toward the front of the store. She quickly made her way to the bookstore. Once in the bookstore, Patty spotted her husband sitting in a square reading area bordered on all four sides by black, thin couches.

Patty sprightly walked up to him and said, "Honey, I found a couple of things."

Donald looked up and smiled.

"Good", he said, in a reaffirming voice.

"What're you reading?"

He stood up and showed her the cover of the book, titled, *Poems of Edgar Allen Poe*.

"Do you want me to buy it for you for Christmas?"

"No thanks honey, I think I have these poems pretty much memorized." Donald loved the macabre writing style of Poe, not so much the short stories as the poems. He particularly liked Annabel Lee and The Raven. Poe seemed to have a close connection to death and the spirit world. This intrigued Donald. He wondered if Poe was able to communicate with these spirits. If so, this would've been in an era before modern technology. Could he communicate using telepathy? Was he clairvoyant? There were so many questions, yet so few answers. He laid the book down on the table in front of him.

"Would you like a cappuccino?", he asked his wife.

"No thanks sweetie. Don't you want to know what's in the bag?"

"Sure".

"I found a couple of knickknacks for your mom and sister. I think they're really going to like them."

"I'm sure they'll like them." He smiled. "Did you want to do some more shopping?"

"No, I'm kind of tired now. I think I'm ready to head back home. I'll finish my shopping at less expensive stores". She smiled and offered out her left hand for him to hold. He took his right hand and locked fingers with the fingers of her left hand. They made their way out the door and through the snow to the parking garage. In an hour, they'd be back in the warm confines of their home.

The following morning, the alarm clock sounded with a loud, intermittent beep. The green LCD digits on the front were flashing nine o'clock. Donald set the alarm later than usual. He wanted to get an extra hour or so of sleep in this morning. This semester's final group experiment in his *Psychology and Paranormal* class was today. Reaching out with his right hand, he tapped the button with his index finger. This brought much needed silence. He also noticed that his wife was no longer in bed.

"Honey, are you okay?" He asked this loudly, almost half shouting.

"Yes dear, I'm in the kitchen", Patty yelled back.

"Okay, I'm going to shave and take a shower."

"Sounds good", she replied.

Donald hoisted himself up from bed. He walked over to the window and raised the shade. It was lightly snowing with an overcast sky. The weatherman on television the previous night predicted a total snow accumulation of up to three inches. Along with the snow, he forecasted a high temperature of thirty-one degrees, with a wind chill of twenty-three. The snow was pretty, but Donald knew there'd be no heat or electricity at the McKenna place.

Walking to the closet, he grabbed a large green sweatshirt from its hanger. He made his way across the room to a mahogany dresser. Pulling on the plain silver handle, Donald slid out the top left drawer. He extracted a pair of underwear and a handkerchief. Proceeding to the next drawer down, he picked up a pair of thick, white cotton socks and a white t-shirt. Finally, he pulled out the bottom right drawer and chose a pair of Levi jeans.

Donald heard Patty's voice from the kitchen, "Breakfast will be ready in about ten minutes".

"Thanks babe", he offered back, in an appreciative tone.

Carrying his clothes into the bathroom, he set them down on top of a shelf. Donald reached up with his left hand and grabbed a large fuzzy towel. He set it next to the sink. He dabbed a line of toothpaste onto his toothbrush. Looking into the mirror, he began to scrub the bristles of the brush around his teeth. First, left to right and then up and down. He carefully worked around his gum lines. Turning on the cold water, he fashioned the palm of his right hand into the shape of a cup. He let it fill with water, brought it to his mouth and rinsed. He repeated this process three times. Finally, he picked up the nearby towel and dried the outside of his mouth.

His mind started to drift. He couldn't help thinking about the McKenna family, their two black household workers and the Union soldiers. What could've happened to these people? How could they have disappeared into thin air?

Picking up a can of shaving cream, Donald pushed the button on top, filling his left palm with foam. He spread it liberally over both of his cheeks, his chin and neck, avoiding his upper lip. His mind frantically raced as he pictured the McKenna family. He saw them as a tight-knit family. He could imagine the backbreaking labor they had to perform with all of the early hours and late nights. No engines, no electricity, and at that time no indoor plumbing to make life easier. The soldiers, he figured, probably came from a nearby fort. They were at war with their own compatriots and no doubt had witnessed some horrific atrocities. The men must've been both mentally and physically exhausted.

He finished shaving, showered and got dressed. Picking up the red handled hairbrush on the sink counter, he combed back his dark, brown hair. Yes, his hair was thinning, but for a man in his mid fifties Donald felt good. He had just a touch of grey around the temples. A lot of his friends and associates were either completely grey, or completely bald.

Walking into the kitchen, he saw that his wife had his breakfast nicely laid out. A white porcelain plate covered with several strips of bacon, scrambled eggs and toast. There was a glass of milk and a jar of grape jelly next to the plate.

"Wow Patty, I wasn't expecting breakfast this morning."

"It's not much", she said. "Besides, you have a long day planned in the field."

As he pulled his chair out to sit down, he noticed his wife standing at the countertop making sandwiches. He saw a blue plastic cooler next to her.

"Baby, what're you doing?", he asked, in an incredulous tone.

"You and your students might get hungry for lunch. It's not much, just a few ham sandwiches and bottles of water. We have plenty of ice in the freezer."

"You do way too much", he said adoringly.

"I like doing it", she said. "It's just a small way for me to help out. I feel like nesting today. I want to clean a little and do some laundry. I might put up the Christmas tree this afternoon. I've decided to postpone the rest of my shopping until this weekend."

"One thing's for sure, God gave me the best partner in the world!" He said this with a choke of emotion in his voice.

"Ah honey, what a nice thing to say. You know I feel the same way about you."

"I know", Donald said, as he sat down and began to eat his breakfast.

Patty finished preparing the final sandwich and set the cooler down on the kitchen table.

"It's all ready to go", she said. "Please don't forget it."

"I won't", Donald answered, while finishing a bite of bacon. "I still need to get all of my equipment together and check it out. I'll probably do that here at the table so I don't forget the cooler."

"Okay", Patty said. "If you don't mind, I'm going back to bed and snooze for a little bit."

"Sounds good", Donald replied. "Thanks again for all your help."

"You're welcome." She walked through the kitchen doorway and toward their bedroom.

CHAPTER SEVEN

"If you don't learn to laugh at troubles, you won't
have anything to laugh at when you grow old."

Ed Howe

The bright, red Mustang pulled through the parking lot and up to the drive-thru speaker. Immediately after pushing the driver's side window button, Brian felt the cold air hit his face.

"Order when you're ready", the female voice directed from the other end of the speaker.

"Yes, I 'd like a cheeseburger meal and a large coffee to drink."

The same female voice said, "Does everything on the screen look correct?"

"Yes it does", Brian answered.

"Okay, that'll be five dollars and twenty-seven cents at the first window."

"Thank you", Brian blurted back, as he hurriedly raised the driver's side window. He checked the heater control on the dashboard. It read thirty degrees for the outside temperature and seventy-two inside. Small snowflakes continued to trickle onto the windshield as he waited for the car ahead of him to pull to the next window.

Brian lowered his car window when he saw the woman slide open the little glass window.

"That'll be five dollars and twenty-seven cents", she smilingly said.

"Okay", Brian replied. He reached into his brown leather billfold and pulled out a one dollar and five dollar bill. He handed both bills to the woman.

She punched a couple of buttons on her computer keyboard and reached into the opened drawer. She pulled out two quarters, two dimes and three pennies, handing them to Brian. She then finished, "thank you".

"Thank you." Brian took the coins she just laid in his left palm and dropped them into the red box hanging below the window. The box collected money for charity. He always dropped coins returned to him into the box. Although he couldn't actually see the coins physically being invested in a hospital or medical treatment, Brian believed wholeheartedly they'd make a difference.

He picked up his order at the second window and drove to the side of the parking lot. He checked inside the bag to ensure the order was correct. It was. In addition, it contained several paper napkins and a packet of sugar.

Brian unfolded the piece of wax paper covering the sandwich. He held the bottom of the burger, still wrapped in the wax paper. He took a bite. It was ten minutes until noon and he hadn't eaten a thing all day.

Pulling out of the parking lot, Brian made a left turn and pulled up to the red stop light. After the traffic light turned green, he took another left on Main Street and drove for a quarter of a mile. He steered the Mustang into the left lane and stopped again at a red light. A green highway sign stood about ten feet tall and fifteen feet to his left. It had the outline of the state in white and the number "93" stenciled in black.

The light turned green and Brian stepped on the gas. He felt the power of the car as it zipped up the entrance ramp. He liked the muscle feel of the car. The car accelerated straight and true despite the pavement being wet from snow. He turned on the left blinker signal and merged from the right lane into the next lane to his left. He peeked out of his rear view mirror, then turned his head around. He didn't completely trust the view in the mirror.

Immediately after hearing the sound of the siren, Brian looked back in his rear view mirror and saw the spinning red and blue lights on top of the car. Putting down the napkin, he steered the Mustang over onto the right shoulder. He set the remaining half of the burger on the napkin. Wonderful, he thought. I haven't even eaten my first French fry yet.

Brian brought the car to a complete stop and pushed the gearshift into the park position. He pulled out his billfold and removed the laminated driver's license. Next, he reached across the passenger's seat toward the glove box. After opening it, he reached in and pulled out a black folder containing the registration papers for the Mustang.

Brian recoiled to an upright position. He heard a tapping noise on his driver's side window. He saw a man in a brown uniform with matching brown hat looking in at him.

He hit the button to slide down the window.

"Hey officer, is something wrong?"

"I need to see your driver's license and owner's registration papers, please." The officer said this in a no nonsense way. He had little expression of his face.

"Here you are", Brian said, as he handed the laminated plastic card and black folder with the registration papers to the officer.

"Sit tight, and I'll be right back", the officer said. He walked back to his patrol car.

Brian looked down at his watch and saw it was noon. He still had a twenty-minute drive ahead of him in order to get to the McKenna place. Reaching into the white sack, he felt the stiff, cold French fries. He took the lid from his coffee cup and took a sip. He didn't bother to pour in the sugar.

Sheriff Mark Preston climbed into the driver's seat of his patrol car. He was about six feet, two inches tall, with a medium build and clean-shaven face. His hair was short and black. His eyes were dark brown. Law enforcement in this small county was his life, first as a patrol officer for eighteen years and then as sheriff for the past ten.

He quickly punched in the nine-digit driver's license number from the small, laminated card into the dashboard computer. Almost instantly, the name Brian Foster popped up on the screen. There were no outstanding wants or warrants. Next, he did a search of the car's license plate number. Ownership came back to Brian Foster.

Mark Preston picked up the traffic ticket pad sitting on the front passenger's seat and began writing up a speeding ticket. In the space marked fine, he wrote in, one hundred and ten dollars. After, he signed the ticket above the line marked, "officer's signature".

Brian took another sip of coffee when he heard the tapping on his window once again. He slid the window down.

"Did I do something wrong officer......he looked at the badge on the brown shirt and then finished, Preston."

"Mr. Foster, you were driving ten miles over the legal limit."

"I was?"

"Yes sir, you were doing seventy-five in a sixty-five zone."

"It sure didn't feel like I was going that fast."

"Well sir, you were. The roads today aren't in optimal condition. I'm going to have to issue you a speeding ticket. I need you to sign the bottom of the ticket. Your signature is not an admission of guilt. It simply states that you received a copy of the ticket. You can pay the fine by mail, or if you wish, you can go to court on the appointed date and appear in front of a judge. Do you understand?"

"Yes", Brian said grudgingly, as he took the ticket pad and pen from the officer. He signed his name on the bottom line and handed them back. Sheriff Preston ripped the pink copy from the pad and handed it to Brian.

"Be careful in this weather", the officer said. Sheriff Preston then walked back to his car.

Brian raised his driver's side window. It was about two-thirds of the way up when he disgustingly blurted out, "asshole".

He put the Mustang into gear and once again resumed his trek to the old McKenna Place. Brian ranted and raved to himself the entire twenty-minute drive to the old farmhouse. If it isn't one thing, it's a half-dozen of another, he thought to himself.

Brian made out the silhouette of the run down, weather beaten structure to his right. It sure didn't look too safe to him.

Veering to the right off the exit, he proceeded down County Road. He came upon an old, mostly missing barbed wire fence. The two fence posts were badly aged and leaning. Carefully, he pulled his Mustang through the opening and toward the haunted looking house.

As he climbed up the stairs of the front porch, he noticed one of the steps was missing. He turned the doorknob and opened the creaky front door. Leaning up against the west wall of the living room, he looked out the window. He heard music coming from his right, front pants pocket. Taking the phone out of his pocket, it blared the *Highway to Hell* ring tone.

Brian pushed the green talk button.

"Hello."

"Brian this is Janet Krigle down at the Reporter."

"Hey Janet, how are you?"

"I'm doing well, thanks. I just wanted to remind you of the deadline for submissions to make tomorrow's newspaper. I'll need to have your article emailed to me with any attachments no later than ten tonight. If possible, I'd like to receive any emails by nine, which would give me a little bit of time to review them?"

"Sounds fine", Brian said. "I'm hoping to have an article to you no later than eight o'clock."

"That's great", Janet replied. "Just remember to call me if you have any questions."

"I'll do so", Brian replied. "Thank you for calling Janet and look for an email from me by eight."

"Sounds good, take care Brian."

"You take care as well Janet. Bye for now."

"Bye".

Brian hit the red end call button on his cell phone. Janet hung up the black handset of her desk telephone.

CHAPTER EIGHT

*"The thing always happens that you really believe
in; and the belief in a thing makes it happen."*

Frank Lloyd Wright

Brea pulled the hood of her coat up and braced herself. She opened the front door of her apartment. In rushed a stinging, cold wind. Her breath condensed into a little cloud as she pulled the door shut and locked it.

Normally, she enjoyed the two-block walk to campus. However, this wasn't normal weather. It got cool in her hometown of Atlanta, but never this cold. At least she was walking with the wind. She was still thinking about the email message she'd received from Dr. Brammer the night before. She hoped she made the right decision inviting Brian.

Brea grabbed the metal handrail with her right hand and climbed the ten or so cement steps. Reaching the top, she looked toward the building straight in front of her. Damn, its cold, she thought to herself. The sign above the two glass doors on the front of the building read, *Regal Hall*. Brea pried the right door open to escape the cold. She stomped the snow from her boots onto the blue strip of carpet just inside the door. Taking a right, she made her way to room number one forty-five.

Entering the room, she began unzipping her coat.

"You made it", the young, male voice sitting in the front said. It was Josh. Cathy was there as well, standing near the front of the room where Dr. Brammer normally gave his lectures.

"I made it but I'm an ice cube", she replied, as she tried to shake off the cold.

Josh stood and said, "I'm going to the vending machine to get a coffee. Would either of you like one?"

"That would be awesome, thanks," Brea said.

"No thanks, I'm good," Cathy said, while taking a seat.

Josh quickly made his way to the door and out into the hall. The vending machine was on the other side of a large stairwell that split the building in two.

"How's it going Cathy", Brea asked, as she took her coat off.

"I'm doing good thanks." Cathy gave Brea enough time to sit down in the desk across the aisle from her.

"Did you get in contact with Dr. Brammer?", Cathy asked.

"Sure did", Brea said with confidence. "He didn't have a problem with Brian attending today."

"Wow", Cathy exclaimed. "Aren't you the little snake charmer?

Brea put her right elbow up on the desktop. She curled her wrist in a downward position imitating a cobra. She wiggled it up and down in a motion simulating the undulations of a snake.

Both women laughed aloud.

"Boy, what did I miss?", Terrance asked the two, as he entered the room.

Brea quickly dropped her arm and both women took on a more serious posture.

"You didn't miss anything Terrance", Cathy said, while trying to hide the last remnants of laughter.

"I don't know about you two!", Terrance remarked, producing one of his signature smiles. He walked into the room but didn't take a seat right away.

"Hey, hey, the gangs all here", Josh half sung, as he carried the two coffees to where Brea was sitting.

Josh handed Brea one of the coffees.

"Thanks", she said.

"You're welcome", he replied.

"I need to tell you guys something before Dr. Brammer gets here." Brea said this in a somewhat hesitant tone. Cathy mockingly made the cobra gesture right after she said it.

Terrance gathered closer to the other three as Brea began to explain.

"I told Dr. Brammer that you were all okay with my fiancé Brian attending the experiment today. I'm sorry that I didn't run it by all of you first."

"Would've been nice", Josh commented.

"Yeah, would've, been nice", Terrance seconded.

"I kind of sort of already knew", Cathy, responded, which caused Josh and Terrance to slightly shake their heads in confusion.

"Anyway, I sent Dr. Brammer an email last night and he said it was okay. Brian will just be an observer. I wanted to give you guys a heads up so that you wouldn't look surprised if Dr. Brammer mentioned it, or if you saw Brian when we got to the McKenna place."

"Thanks for all the notice", Terrance said jokingly.

"Come on you guys", Brea replied, half pleadingly. Brian is having a difficult time at work. They keep giving him the loser stories to cover. I just thought this might give him a lift. He really needs a boost right now."

"Calm down, its cool", Terrance retorted. "I was just giving you a hard time."

"It's cool with me too", Josh said.

"Not a problem with me", Cathy said, in an agreeing fashion.

"Thanks you guys. It means a lot to me and I know Brian appreciates it."

Donald Brammer pulled his white Chevy van into its assigned faculty parking space. After turning off the engine, he grabbed the black duffle bag sitting on the front passenger's seat. He'd cleaned and straightened the van before leaving home. Donald wanted to give it a quick look over to make sure everything was in order. He half amusingly shook his head when he spotted the blue plastic cooler sitting on the very backbench seat.

Brushing the little snowflakes from his coat, he entered through the doorway of the classroom.

"Good afternoon everyone", Donald said, with a jovial tone in his voice.

"Afternoon Dr. Brammer", the four responded.

He made his way to the small table next to the lectern near the front of the room. After setting the black duffle bag down onto the table, he removed his coat.

"I'm very excited about performing this experiment with you," he said. "However, before we go out to the McKenna place I thought it would be best if we went over a few things."

All four students were now sitting and each nodded in agreement.

"First", Dr. Brammer began, "Each of you is aware that Brea's fiancé

Brian will be attending today. Brian's role will strictly be that of an observer. He will not take part in the experiment in anyway. From our standpoint, we'll treat him as if he's invisible. Are there any questions?""

Terrance and Cathy verbally said no while Josh and Brea nodded their heads from side to side in a no fashion.

"Good", Donald Brammer affirmed. "Now, I'd like to go over with all of you the equipment that we'll be using today. He reached over and unzipped the black duffle bag. Reaching into the bag, he pulled out an oblong black instrument. He walked around the podium and in front of the table. He wanted to get closer to them in order to give them a better view.

"This is an EMF detector", he said, holding it up facing the students. "This instrument is designed to pick up electronic fields over different frequencies. Disruptions in electronic fields may indicate the presence of a spirit. The sliding scale of numbers and colors signifies the strength of the signal. The numbers one through three are in red and indicate a slight disruption in the electronic field. Number's four, five and six are yellow in color and signify a medium disruption. Seven, eight and nine are green in color and represent the highest disruption in electronic frequency. This indicates a high probability that there's a spirit present. I'll pass this around so that each of you can look at it. I'd appreciate it if the last one viewing it would place it on the table."

Donald Brammer handed the instrument to Josh who was sitting closest to where he was standing.

He took another item out of the bag with all of the care of a magician performing a trick. "This is a normal video camera. I have a tripod that's out in the van. The top of the tripod mount swivels so that the camera can get a panoramic view. We'll set it for a one hundred and eighty degree sweep." He laid the camera down on the table.

"Next, is a digital recorder. Its primary purpose is to pick up any electronic voice phenomenon that may occur. Sometimes these voices aren't clearly heard or interpreted the first time around. This instrument allows us the chance to go back and listen for spoken words or phrases that we may have missed." Like the camera, he set the recorder on the table.

"Finally, we have an infrared thermal scanner." He held the grey instrument up so that they could see it better. "It kind of looks like a handheld bar code scanner that you might see at a Wal-Mart or Kmart. The purpose of the scanner is to detect cold spots. These areas may indicate the presence of a spirit." He again handed this instrument to Josh.

Terrance was the last to look at the EMF detector and laid it back on the table. He returned to his seat.

"Excuse me, Dr. Brammer?"

"Yes Terrance."

"Who's going to monitor these instruments?"

"I'm glad you brought that up. The digital camera will run unattended. I'll monitor the digital voice recorder. If it's okay with the two of you guys, I thought Cathy would manage the EMF detector and Brea the infrared thermal scanner. That's, if it's okay with the both of you?"

"Sure thing", Terrance said.

"Fine with me", Josh added.

Donald Brammer picked up the digital recorder and placed it back into the black bag. Taking the digital camera in hand, he did the same thing with it. He also reached over and grabbed the EMF detector that Terrance just set on the table. He placed it into the bag. Folding his arms across his chest, the professor patiently waited as Cathy passed the infrared thermal scanner to Terrance. Terrance looked at both sides of the scanner, then from front to back. When he was finished, he handed it back to Dr. Brammer who placed it into the black bag.

After zipping the black bag shut, Donald Brammer asked, "Do you have any questions?"

None of them had a question.

Excitedly, Terrance half shouted, "I'm ready to do this thing!"

"Yeah, me too", the others chimed in.

"It sounds like we're set to go. Everyone please follow me out to the van." Donald Brammer put his coat on. He picked up the black duffle bag with his right hand and started toward the door. The four students quickly put their winter gear on and followed closely behind him. Brea threw her empty coffee cup into the trashcan next to the door. Josh was the last one to leave. He threw his coffee cup away and turned off the lights.

CHAPTER NINE

*"I did not direct my life. I didn't design it. I
never made decisions. Things always came up
and made them for me. That's what life is."*

B.F. SKINNER

M adge Stewart walked over to the cash register. She was wearing her
iconic light green, cotton dress draped in the front with a white apron.
Her hair was mostly blonde, although if one looked close enough, one could
see some light grey hairs peppered in above her forehead. Over the years,
Madge had managed to keep herself in good shape. It was hard physical work
running the diner, but it provided her with steady exercise. In addition, she
wore just the right amount of makeup that helped her appear five to ten years
younger. The sixty-year-old woman threw out her heartwarming smile and
asked, "Hey Luke how was it?"

"Good as always Madge. You won't hear any complaints from me", he
said, in a complimentary manner.

Luke first started coming to the diner when Madge and her husband
operated it together. Jim Stewart passed away five years earlier. He was a
fighter, but the battle with lung cancer finally overwhelmed his body. His
death put a real strain on Madge. It wasn't quite the same diner without
him. However, she knew the business well and always took care of her
customers.

"That'll be six dollars and sixteen cents", she said, flicking a couple of
buttons on the register. This caused the money drawer to pop out near her
waist.

Luke reached into the back pocket of his dark green slacks and pulled
out a black leather billfold. He was wearing a matching dark green, button

down shirt with a white patch that read, "Floyd County Electric" in green thread. Below that on the patch was,"Luke", also sewn in green thread. He set his white safety helmet down on the counter. Taking his right hand, he reached into his billfold and pulled out a five-dollar bill along with three one-dollar bills.

"Here ya' go sugar", he said, handing her the bills. "The rest is yours."

"Why you're such a dear", she said, accepting the four bills from his hand. Madge slid the five-dollar bill and a one-dollar bill into their respective drawers in the cash register. After, she folded the remaining pair of one-dollar bills and tucked them into the front pocket of her apron.

"I wish we had better weather for you to work in Luke", Madge said, at the same time closing the cash register drawer.

Luke looked down for a second and hesitated. He replied, "I wish it were seventy degrees and sunny everyday, but that's just wishful thinking. I guess you could look at it as job security."

"I'm sure there are enough power outages to keep you busy."

"This weather really puts a strain on the lines and equipment."

"Speaking of which, do you mind taking a glance at the transformer and the line next to the building on your way out?"

"Will do Madge", Luke said, as he flipped the white hard hat onto the top of his head.

"I sure hope we don't lose power", she said, with a hint of concern in her voice.

"If you do, you're my priority one!", Luke said, with all the warmth and confidence of a son reassuring his mother.

"You be careful out there".

"See ya' tomorrow Madge", Luke said, as he did everyday before leaving. He strode across the tile floor toward the front door, his heavy electrician boots making a clopping sound. Five seconds later, he was out of sight, disappearing into the light flow of snowflakes.

As he placed the two hot dishes of food onto the stainless steel shelf, Marty rang the silver desktop bell to his right and barked out, "order up!"

"Coming", Cindy answered. She made a beat toward the rectangular opening in the wall that separated the kitchen from the front of the diner.

Cindy was a very attractive woman. She didn't quite have the measurements of a beauty queen, but they weren't far off either. Her hair was long and black which she pinned up while working at the diner. She wore blue jeans and a red sweatshirt. The front of the sweatshirt contained a decorative iron on patch. It showed a cute male and female moose in a canoe. Beneath, the caption read, "We're in the same boat together!"

She picked up the two plates, turned, and carried them out to a booth near the front of the diner where an elderly couple sat. Marty stayed at the window and stared intently at her as she did so. He always liked to watch her walk away from him.

"Here ya' go darlin's'", Cindy cheerfully said, as she laid the plates down in front of them. "Is there anything else I can get you right now?"

The two looked up at her and both shook their heads in a negative gesture without audibly speaking a word.

"Enjoy", she said. Cindy returned to her station behind the front counter. The front counter ran nearly the width of the diner. It was made of Formica and accommodated fifteen bar stools. The stools were the metal kind, with red, cushioned tops.

Suddenly, a strong blast of cold air blew into the diner. Two men in matching uniforms entered. They were regulars as well. Each wore tan slacks with a dark brown stripe up the side. Their tan, buttoned-down, collared shirts matched their slacks. A gold badge adorned each tan shirt. One badge contained the name Mark Preston in black letters along the bottom. Written in black lettering across the top was Sheriff. The other badge was similar. The name Merle Vickers stretched across the bottom with Deputy Sheriff at the top.

"Hey, look what the wind just blew in", Madge said, with a chuckle in her voice.

"Afternoon Madge", Sheriff Preston responded.

Deputy Vickers, in keeping with his quiet disposition muttered, "Day all".

The two men proceeded to their regular stools located in the very middle of the long, dining countertop. Madge was already pouring each a hot cup of coffee as they sat.

"Some weather, huh?", she blurted out, almost by rote.

The Sheriff replied, "You aren't just a kiddin'."

Both the Sheriff and the Deputy were loyal family men. Mark Preston and his wife had three children. The youngest of the three, a girl, was a senior at the local college. Deputy Vickers was about fifteen years younger than the Sheriff. He was also married and had two boys, ages six and eight. The Deputy carried around a few more pounds than his counterpart did. He was stout in build. He was six feet tall and weighed two hundred pounds. Sheriff Preston had a two-inch taller frame than the Deputy did. He weighed roughly one hundred and seventy-five pounds.

"I'll have the usual", Deputy Vickers said, in the general direction of where Madge was standing.

"What about you Sheriff?", Madge asked in a charming way. She fully expected him to say he was having the usual as well.

"I think I'm going to try something different today", Sheriff Preston replied.

"You feelin' okay darlin'?", Madge quipped.

"I'm doing fine. I'm just in the mood for something different."

After completing this statement, he took a glance toward Cindy. She couldn't help but smile and blush with the officer having just said the words, "...in the mood for something different". They both glanced away from the other, not wanting to embarrass or be embarrassed.

"Just let me know when you're ready to order Sheriff", Madge said, turning her back toward the rectangular, metal ordering area.

"I need a bacon burger and fries", she shouted through the opening.

"Got it", Marty confirmed.

Mark Preston did something he hadn't done in recent memory. He drew the plastic covered menu from its metal holding stand. The first thing that caught his eye were the words, **No Finer Diner** printed in bold letters across the front of the menu. Mark could remember the days before Madge and her husband took over the diner. Back then, it was called "Mooreland's".

He looked over the menu for a minute and blurted out, "Madge, I think I'm ready to order now".

"Okay Sheriff, what'll it be"?

"I'm going to have the spaghetti topped with chili."

"Wow, are you sure? I don't want you to go out on a limb here or anything. This is a real departure from your regular order, a bowl of chili." She said this in a teasing manner, which he quickly recognized.

"I'm pretty sure", he answered, in a halfhearted fashion. Sheriff Preston smiled and grinned.

"All right then", Madge confirmed. Turning back toward the ordering window, she bellowed out, "I need an order of spaghetti red".

Again, Marty answered from the other side of the window opening, "got it"!

Cindy walked over to the booth to check on the elderly couple. "How's everything?", she inquired caringly.

"Delicious", the grey haired gentleman responded. His wife smiled up at Cindy, but didn't utter a word.

"Great", Cindy answered. "There's no hurry, but I'm going to leave the check with you for when you're ready".

Both nodded in an acknowledging way. Cindy went to the next booth and gathered some dirty plates and glasses. She carried them through the swinging kitchen door located just to the left of the ordering window.

"Anything exciting happening out there today?", Madge asked. "You know, besides all the rear end accidents."

Sheriff Preston looked toward Madge and replied, "I'm still trying to figure this current generation out. I stopped a young man today that was going seventy-five in a sixty-five zone. Mind you, it's snowing out and he was eating his lunch at the same time."

"Mercy!", Madge exclaimed. "Whatever happened to the day when a person just drove his or her car down the road?"

"That's what I'd like to know", the Sheriff replied.

"Order up!", Marty boomed from the kitchen area.

It was the Deputy's bacon burger and fries. Madge shuffled to the window. She picked up the plate with her left hand and laid it gently down on the counter in front of the Deputy.

"What else do you need honey?", she smilingly asked.

"That'll do it", the Deputy replied. When he was hungry, he was not one for small talk.

"So, did you give the kid a ticket?", Madge asked, referring to the Sheriff and their previous conversation."

"You bet I did".

"Good for you", she responded.

"Order up!", Marty once again hollered from the kitchen.

Marty was a good kid. He was about five feet, six inches tall and slender. He had long brown hair that layered down the back of his neck. While some of his friends were in college, he had no desire to study. It wasn't Marty's bag. He was twenty-one years old and worked at the diner for the past three years. Marty was dependable and a hard worker. He preferred work to studying. Marty was happiest when he made enough money to support his three major expenses; gas for his car, rent and drinking money.

"Madge, I think I'm going to go out and shovel the front walk again, if that's okay with you?"

"Sounds good Marty", Madge replied, in an agreeing voice. "Can you throw down some more of that rock salt?"

"Will do", Marty obligingly said.

Marty took off the hairnet he was wearing and placed it into a plastic bag. Next, he donned his blue coat and green stocking hat. He picked up the snow shovel with his left hand and the bag of rock salt with his right. Marty made his way through the swinging door, past the counter and to the front door. He pushed open the front door and stepped out onto the sidewalk.

Madge felt the cold wind against her skin as the door finished closing. She walked to the order shelf and with her left hand grabbed up the plate of spaghetti smothered with chili. She turned and walked toward the counter. Reaching down into the refrigerator, she produced a glass jar half filled with parmesan cheese.

"What else can I get you Sheriff?", she asked, while laying down the plate and glass jar of cheese.

Looking down at the plate of long noodles and chili, he grinned and said, "That'll do it."

The sound of Marty's shovel scraping against the cement sidewalk sent a chilling echo throughout the diner.

CHAPTER TEN

*"Whenever you're in conflict with someone, there is one
factor that can make the difference between damaging your
relationship and deepening it. That factor is attitude."*

William James

Dr. Donald Brammer and his four graduate students began to make their way across the parking lot to his white van. He unlocked the front door. "Brea, you can sit up here in the front passenger's seat."

"Thanks Dr. Brammer", Brea said, in her high-pitched, giddy voice.

Cathy rolled her eyes in a condescending fashion. Everything is Brea, Brea, and Brea, she thought to herself. Brea was the group leader. Brea was allowed to bring her boyfriend to the experiment. It seemed as though Cathy was having a private pity party. Dr. Brammer did, however, choose her to run the EMF detector. Of course, Brea was chosen to operate the infrared thermal scanner!

The professor held the front passenger's door for Brea as she climbed up into the seat. She wore a pair of tight fitting blue jeans. A tan Ugg boot covered each foot. The blue sweatshirt she wore had the University logo on the front. She slid back the hood of her coat and buckled the seat belt.

Dr. Brammer closed the front passenger's door and walked around the van to the driver's side door. He unlocked it and climbed into the seat. He hit a button on the dash that caused the large sliding passenger's door to open automatically. Josh seemed mesmerized by the door opening on its own.

Cathy, Terrance and Josh all piled into the black leather captain's chairs located behind the front seats. Cathy took the chair behind the driver's seat. Terrance scooted further back and sat in the chair behind Cathy. Josh was the last to board and took a seat across from Cathy.

"Josh, I'll close the door electronically from up here."

"Awesome", Josh replied with a large grin.

Terrance turned around in his captain's chair and sized up the interior of the van. The blue cooler sitting on the backbench seat caught his eye.

"Hey professor, are you packing some beer in that cooler?" Terrance rather chuckled as he said it.

Dr. Brammer laughed. "No Terrace, not beer. My wife decided to make us some sandwiches in case we got hungry. There's also some bottled water."

Dr. Brammer, your wife is awesome!" Cathy said, in an excited tone.

"For sure she's the better half", he replied.

"If it's okay with all of you, I thought that anyone who was hungry could eat a sandwich before we set up the equipment."

"Sounds good", Brea said.

"Yeah, sounds good to me too", Terrance followed. The other two members of the group also agreed.

Terrance was wearing a dark blue pair of sweatpants. He had on a dark blue sweatshirt. A white pair of Air Jordan's adorned his feet. He wore a large, black, snow-skiing type coat. It was obvious that he was in great physical shape.

Cathy and Josh were attired as one would expect a Midwesterner to be in December. They both had on a pair of blue jeans. Josh was wearing a large pair of black boots that came up to his calves. He also wore a shirt, a sweatshirt and a large brown coat. A blue stocking hat covered his blonde hair. Cathy was wearing snow boots that came up to the top her calves. She had on a red and blue flannel shirt. She was wearing a green coat. A red scarf draped loosely around her neck. All five were dressed for the cold.

Donald Brammer swung the van around the parking lot and toward the exit. He turned the van left and headed west on Campus Street. The van was warm inside, but he wanted to make sure everyone was comfortable.

"Is it too hot in here or is it okay for everyone?"

"It's okay back here", Cathy confirmed.

"Fine", Terrance agreed.

"I think we're okay", Brea said, as she smiled over at the professor.

Dr. Brammer veered into the left turn lane. This was the lane he needed in order to catch the entrance ramp going north onto highway ninety-three.

The twenty-minute drive seemed to fly past.

"Well, it looks like we're here", Dr Brammer said, with a hint of excitement in his voice.

"Cool", Cathy clamored loudly.

"This place looks pretty spooky", Terrance said.

Donald Brammer took a right turn off highway ninety-three onto County Road. He drove about fifty yards east and turned left in between two old wooden fence posts. There was little fencing connected to the outside of either post. Pulling the van through the posts, he followed the fresh tire tracks in the snow. There was a red Ford Mustang parked on the south side of the badly weathered structure. He parked the van next to it.

"I'll grab the cooler", Terrance offered.

"Sounds good", Dr. Brammer replied. "Josh, can you grab the light blue bag containing the tripod?"

"Will do", Josh answered in a shrill voice.

"That's Brian's car", Brea said, looking over at the Mustang.

"Nice car", Cathy commented.

Dr. Brammer reached back and grabbed the black duffle bag full of equipment sitting behind the driver's seat. He clicked the button that opened the side door of the van. They each exited the van. Brea and Cathy were the first of the bunch to start toward the front porch. Right behind the two were Dr. Brammer, Terrance and Josh, each carrying an item in his right hand.

As she climbed the wooden front porch steps, Brea noticed that the third step was missing.

"Careful everybody, there's a step missing", she warned.

All five climbed up the stairs and onto the porch. Brea swung open the front door and saw Brian leaning up against the west wall.

"Hi Brian", she squeaked.

"Hey sweetie", he replied.

"Everyone, I'd like for you to meet my fiancé Brian Foster."

First, turning to the professor she said, "Brian, this is Dr. Brammer." Brian reached out and shook his hand.

She continued, "This is Cathy, this is Terrance and this is Josh". She pointed to each one as she called out their names.

"Nice to meet all of you", Brian said gracefully.

"Nice to meet you too", they chimed back.

The group of five that just entered the house took a panoramic assessment of the living room. The walls and ceiling were badly cracked. It appeared that many holes were intentionally knocked out of the walls with crowbars or sledgehammers. Plaster and lathe could be found lying around the bottom of the walls. Empty beer bottles were strewn about the room. It was apparent that this once elegant farmhouse now served as a party hangout for local teenagers.

"This place smells like urine!", Terrance said in a defiant snicker while holding his nose.

"All right everyone let's get started", Dr. Brammer said. He set the black duffle bag on the floor next to the east wall of the living room....or what was left of the east wall.

"This place is even more run down than I expected. We need to take a few minutes to clean the area and get organized before we start." Donald spanned the entire room with his eyes. It was a mess. It smelled of musk and urine.

"Terrance, I need you and Josh to do me a favor. I need for the two of you to go out to my van and grab a few things. You can open the pair of back doors, they're unlocked. Under the seat is a shop broom. You should also find a black plastic trash bag and four high beam lantern style flashlights. The first thing we need to do is sweep some of the plaster and wood from the middle of the room. Do you guys mind grabbing that stuff for me?"

"No, not at all", Josh responded.

"I'm with ya' Josh", Terrance followed.

The two young men turned toward the south and walked out the front door.

Looking at Brea, the professor continued. "Brea, I'd like for you and Cathy to help pick up empty beer bottles and any other sharp objects and put them into the trash bag."

"Sure thing Dr. Brammer", Brea confirmed.

"No problem", Cathy added.

"Brian, I'd like to take a minute and briefly go over where you'll be sitting today." Dr. Brammer said this maintaining solid eye contact with Brian.

"Sure", Brian answered.

Donald Brammer walked over to the north wall of the living room. "I think this is the area that I'd like for you to sit." He motioned with his right hand to an area up against the middle of the wall. "I'm going to set the video camera up so that it's pointing south. It'll pan back and forth from roughly the middle of the east wall to the middle of the west wall."

"Sounds fine professor, I'll sit against the wall back here and take notes. I won't say anything or participate in anyway."

"Excellent", Dr. Brammer said, with a congratulatory hint in his voice.

Terrance was the first through the door with Josh right behind him. Terrance carried the shop broom in one hand and the trash bag in the other. Josh carried two flashlights in each hand by their handles. It reminded Cathy of the way he carried the beer mugs at Bruno's Bar.

"I ate a big breakfast this morning, so I'm not hungry. Now would be a good time for those of you that are hungry to eat a sandwich. That includes you too Brian, as there are five sandwiches in the cooler. There should be five or six bottles of water as well. While all of you are eating, I'll begin setting up the video camera. Once you've finished eating, please sweep the room and pick up trash."

"Sure thing", Brea said. The others nodded their heads in agreement.

"Just throw the sandwich bags in the big black trash bag when you're finished. The same goes for the plastic water bottles too."

Terrance set down the broom and trash bag while Josh laid down the four lantern type flashlights.

"Come on Brian", Brea encouraged, as she smiled and motioned for him to join the group.

The five gathered against the east wall. Brea opened the cooler and began passing a sandwich to each person. She handed each a bottle of water as well.

CHAPTER ELEVEN

*"If you care enough for a result, you
will most certainly attain it."*

CARL GUSTAV JUNG

Donald Brammer picked up the black duffle bag and carried it to the middle of the room. He unzipped the bag and pulled out a video camera. He laid it down on top of the bag. Next, he walked over to a light blue plastic bag containing a tripod for the camera and snatched it up. Carrying it back to the camera, he removed the three-legged metal tripod. Two snaps later, the legs of the tripod locked into place. Delicately, the professor connected the camera to the flat metal plate located on top of the tripod. His right index finger pushed a button on the back of the tripod stand causing the camera to rotate from left to right.

"Awesome", Cathy said. "I'm a little shy about being filmed though."

"Don't be", Dr. Brammer warmly responded. "We all have butterflies at first, but they soon go away. There's nothing to be nervous or shy about."

After finishing a huge bite from the sandwich he was eating, Terrance asked, "What if we need to go to the bathroom?"

"Anyone who needs to empty their bladder will have to do so through that doorway and in the next room." Dr. Brammer pointed in a northeasterly direction. For our purposes today, it will be a makeshift bathroom. If you need to relieve yourself please do so expeditiously and in a quiet manner."

Josh and Cathy looked at each other, trying to fight back grins. Terrance didn't miss a beat, taking the last bite out of his sandwich. Afterward, he placed the small, clear plastic bag into the larger black trash bag.

"I'm going to start sweeping if that's okay professor?", Terrance offered.

"Sounds good, Terrance. Can you start by getting the area behind me where Brian will be sitting? Do your best to sweep away any glass or other sharp objects."

"You got it!", Terrance said, in a pleasing way. He picked up the shop broom, walked behind the professor and started sweeping.

"Thanks for the sandwich Dr. Brammer", Brea said, as she took her last bite.

"Don't thank me Brea. You'll need to thank my wife", Dr. Brammer replied modestly.

"It was awfully nice of her to think of us."

"It sure was", Josh said, agreeing with Brea's comment.

By now, all had finished eating. Cathy took a gulp from her water bottle and set it on the floor behind her. Brea and Brian set their water bottles down in the southwest corner of the room. There wasn't a drop left in either water bottle of Terrance or Josh. Josh grabbed both bottles and flipped them into the black trash bag. Cathy and Brea began collecting empty beer bottles and other pieces of trash from around the room. Josh followed behind them with the black trash bag.

"Just as soon as the area is clean, we'll go over the ground rules. Some types of questions are more conducive to receiving feedback than others." After saying this, Dr. Brammer drew in a deep breath and exhaled.

He walked over to the cooler and looked inside. There was one bottle of water left. He picked it out of the ice, opened it, and took a medium swig. His hand tingled from the chill of the ice. Twisting the white plastic bottle cap back on, he made his way to the middle of the room and set it down. He turned to check on the progress of the group.

"It's looking better already", he said.

"Yeah, but it still stinks like pee in here", Terrance said, while scrunching his face. "I would've brought some air freshener had I'd known." This caused two or three of the others to cackle.

Dr. Brammer looked at Terrance who was sweeping the dirt and other trash toward the outer edges of the room.

"Terrance, we aren't going to move in out here. We're just going to conduct a two hour experiment."

"Thank God," Terrance exclaimed, producing a laugh from everyone, including Dr. Brammer.

The professor walked over to the camera and tripod. He wanted to make sure the camera was working properly. Looking into the side-mounted viewfinder, he saw Terrance sweeping while the others picked up trash. Brian walked to the north end of the room, carrying his pen and legal pad with him. He seemed like a very well mannered person, Donald Brammer thought. He was glad he'd given Brea permission for Brian to attend today.

The four students were nearly finished picking up the trash and sweeping the floor.

"I think this is about as clean as we need the space for our purposes", Donald Brammer said. He pointed to the southeast corner of the room and said, "Terrance please set the broom down in the corner. Josh, you can set the trash bag next to it." He waited about twenty seconds or so to allow them to complete this task.

"At this point, we need to go over some of the ground rules, such as where each of us will be sitting, the equipment we'll be monitoring and what type of questions we'll be asking."

Donald Brammer nervously coughed into his right hand to clear his throat. He had a habit of doing this when starting a lengthy speech.

"First of all, let's go over seating assignments. I'll be sitting just in front of the camera. Josh will be sitting to my left. Brea, you'll be sitting next to Josh, and Terrance next to Brea. Cathy you'll sit in between Terrance and me. Let's try to make it as even a circle as possible. We may want to actually hold hands when we start to ask questions of the spirits."

All four shook their heads affirmatively and walked to their assigned positions. They stood as the professor continued.

"As you all know, Brian is attending as an observer only. He'll be sitting next to the north wall behind me. He's not to participate in the experiment, so please do not elicit any responses from him."

Reaching into the black duffle bag, Donald Brammer pulled out a small, digital recorder. "I'm going to position the recorder in between Josh and myself. If we think we may have captured an electronic voice phenomenon, or EVP, we'll rewind the recorder and replay it. Sometimes EVP's aren't heard clearly at regular speed. Therefore, we have the ability to go back and take a second listen."

Brian was sitting about ten feet behind the professor. He held the yellow legal tablet flat against his knees. He furiously took notes down as the professor spoke.

Dr. Brammer reached into the bag and pulled out the infrared thermal scanner. He looked at Brea and said, "Brea, you can come get the infrared thermal scanner". He held the device out in front of him. Brea walked over and took the instrument from his hand as if were meant for a mystical sorcerer. She had a large smile on her face. Brea returned to where she was originally standing.

He reached into the bag again and removed the EMF detector. He held it up and asked Cathy to take possession of it. She too, smiled and took it from him. She returned to her spot as well.

"Now, if you'll recall, these two devices are used to measure spirit presence. The EMF detector picks up disruptions in electronic fields. Remember red is low, yellow is medium and green is high. The infrared thermal scanner detects changes in temperature. Cold spots often indicate the presence of a spirit. Brea and Cathy will be monitoring these instruments and will let us know if either one gives off a strong indication."

"Are there any questions so far?"

Terrance raised his right hand.

"Yes Terrance."

"Dr. Brammer, you said something earlier about all of us holding hands when we ask questions of the spirits. How are Brea and Cathy going to hold hands and their detectors at the same time?"

"That's a fair question Terrance", Dr. Brammer replied. "They won't need to actually hold the instruments in their hands. They can set them down close by and just monitor them for activity. Does that make sense?"

"Yes", Terrance answered.

Donald Brammer took a quick glance down at his watch. It was ten minutes after one. "Let's do a quick review before continuing. We'll be sitting in a circle, holding hands while asking questions. Those with instruments will keep an eye on them for significant activity. Oh yeah, I almost forgot, the flashlights."

"We'll set three of the flashlights face up in our circle for light. Once we begin, please center them inside of the circle."

"Brian, the fourth flashlight is for you. Hopefully, it'll give you some better light for your note taking."

Brian set down his pen and tablet and approached the professor. As Dr. Brammer handed him the flashlight, he smiled and politely said, "thank you". He took the flashlight and returned to his spot. After sitting down, he picked up his pen and tablet. He flipped the switch on the flashlight to the "on" position. A powerful stream of light shot up onto the ceiling.

"The rest of you can sit down and turn your flashlights on", Dr. Brammer instructed.

Brea, Terrance and Josh picked up flashlights and flipped them to the "on" position. They set them down in the middle of the circle, which caused three powerful beams of light to bounce off the ceiling.

"Now, we need to go over the types of questions we want to ask. I'd suggest asking questions that try to identify the spirit. Once identified, we can ask follow up questions. I can tell you from past experience we've had more success when asking questions in a sensitive manner."

Donald Brammer reached down and picked up the bottle of water that was next to him, opened it, and took a swig. He closed the lid and set the bottle down.

"Go ahead and switch your instruments on."

Brea and Cathy pushed the buttons on their respective pieces of equipment until the "on" indicators lit up. Dr. Brammer pushed the red, record button on the digital recorder.

"The camera is scanning, the video recorder is running and it appears that both of the other instruments are in working order". He said this with a slight pitch of relief in his voice.

CHAPTER TWELVE

"All houses are haunted. All persons are haunted. Throngs
of spirits follow us everywhere. We are never alone."

B. SARECKY

"We can get started now", Dr.Brammer said. Don't be afraid or hesitant to ask questions. Please pay close attention to the instruments and any unusual noises that you may hear. If need be, we can stop the digital recorder in order to play it back for possible EVP's."

"In order to give you an idea of how the questioning works, I'll ask the first question. Once a question is asked, please try to be as quiet as possible for the following fifteen to thirty seconds so that we can all listen closely for a response."

"Here we go." Dr. Brammer reached out with his left and right hands. Josh and Cathy quickly grabbed one each. The others followed in kind until all were holding hands in one, uniform circle.

He asked, "Are any spirits present?"

There was dead silence in the room after the question was asked. As instructed, the group maintained quiet while waiting for a possible response. Twenty seconds transpired when a low sound came from the east wall. It sounded like someone tapping. For that matter though, it could've been a piece of old plaster sliding down the wall.

"Dr. Brammer, the number "two" button just lit up on the infrared thermal scanner". Brea said this with the excitement of a miner panning for gold.

"Good Brea", Dr. Brammer replied. "That means it's detecting a cold spot in the room that could be a spirit."

"To simplify things, let's go around the circle in a counter- clockwise fashion with our questions? Cathy, you can go next."

"Thanks Dr. Brammer", she said nervously. "I'm not really sure what to ask."

"Don't feel nervous, just pose a question."

"Okay", Cathy responded. She asked, "What's your name?"

Again, all was quiet. Roughly, fifteen seconds passed when Terrance broke the silence. "I think I heard something", he said. "It sounded like a voice, but I couldn't understand what it was saying."

Dr. Brammer picked up the wallet sized digital recorder and pushed the rewind button. He turned the volume to its highest setting in order for all to hear. They heard the voice of Cathy asking her question, "What's your name?" They quietly listened for about ten seconds then heard what sounded like a female voice saying, "Maaalayyyyy".

"Oh my God, that's so weird. She said Molly, at least that's what I heard", Brea said.

"I heard the same thing", Terrance said.

"Me too", Josh confirmed.

"I did as well", Dr. Brammer said, pressing the red, record button on the digital recorder and setting it back down.

"You're up Terrance", Dr. Brammer said, as he looked in his direction.

Terrance took a minute to gather his thoughts. You could almost see the wheels turning in his head. Finally, he asked, "Are you alone?"

They didn't have to wait long, nor did they need the digital recorder to interpret the answer. The same female voice answered in a more pronounced and easily understood manner, "no".

"Spooky", Josh said.

"Cathy, is there anything registering on the EMF detector yet?"

"Nothing yet professor", she said, in a disappointing fashion.

"That's okay, we're just getting started and that could very well change."

"Brea, it's your turn", Dr. Brammer encouraged.

Brea thought for a second or two then asked, "Can we do anything to help you?"

There was silence for about twenty-five seconds, when they all heard the same female voice. This time it was inaudible.

' "Let's play that one back", Dr. Brammer suggested. He picked up the digital recorder and pushed the rewind button. Hitting the play button, the very end of Cathy's question replayed along with the spirit's response. As the digital recorder kept rolling, Brea's high-pitched voice could be heard asking her question. There were ten or fifteen seconds of silence, followed by a muffled female voice saying something that wasn't clear.

"Let me slow it down a bit", said Dr. Brammer.

He took his finger and adjusted a setting on the recorder. After, he hit the rewind button. Clicking the "stop" button, he pushed "play". Brea asked her question. They waited, and in the slower speed made out what the female voice was saying. The female voice said, "You must all leave!"

They looked at each other sitting around the ring.

Dr. Brammer reassured them. "It's okay, we can continue. Sometimes we get negative responses from these entities."

By this time, Brian was taking notes at a frantic pace. He'd taken one full page of notes. Flipping the page over the back of the notepad, he revealed a fresh piece of yellow lined paper.

"All right Josh, go ahead with your first question", Dr. Brammer said, smiling in his direction.

They continued to hold each other's hands as Josh hesitated for a minute. Finally, he asked in a nervous manner, "Where are you?"

Once again, a short silence followed. They heard the faint tapping of what sounded like someone walking. Cathy blurted out, "the EMF detector is climbing".

A white figure lurched from the darkness of the next room. It was a white cat. The cat snarled loudly as it pranced around the circle behind Terrance. Both Cathy and Brea screamed in chilling tandem. Brea let go of the hands of Josh and Cathy. She placed her right hand over her mouth in fright. The cat let out a terrifying shriek as it shot between Terrance and Cathy, then to the other side of the circle. They all reacted quickly, taking evasive action. Terrance leaned to his right. Brea scooted back a foot or two while Cathy dodged to her left. Josh swung to his right. The cat darted to the doorway from which it came and then sprang back into the darkness.

"I think I just had a heart attack", Terrance stuttered.

"That thing scared me to death", Brea said, her voice cutting in and out.

"I think we all got a little jolt of adrenalin from that one", Dr. Brammer remarked. "Let's take a minute to get settled."

Once their breathing slowed down, Brea and Cathy rejoined their hands. Dr. Brammer took a swig of water from the bottle next to him and closed it.

The odd thing was that the cat jumped through the doorway closest to where Brian was sitting. It appeared as though Brian didn't even flinch. Nor did he react when it ran back into the dark room. Maybe his writing distracted him, or maybe he just didn't scare easy?

"Since we got such a good response from that question, why don't you ask another Josh", the professor said.

Josh thought for a minute. "Molly, can you give us another sign?"

Again, there was the usual few seconds of silence. The high beam flashlight sitting in front of Brea began to flicker wildly. How strange, Brea thought to herself. The flashlight near me is flickering but the other three are steady as a rock. It wasn't long after that when the flashlight completely went out.

"Dr. Brammer, the EMF detector went to number five, the high yellow area", Cathy said, with a twitch in her voice.

"The thermal scanner also detected something", Brea added.

"Sometimes equipment can do weird things when there's a spirit presence nearby. Equipment can even malfunction as we just saw with the flashlight."

"Brea, would you push the button on the flashlight to see if it comes back on?"

She picked up the flashlight and flicked the on-off switch several times, to no avail.

"Nothing Dr. Brammer", she said.

"That's okay Brea. We'll spread the remaining two flashlights a little closer to the edge of our circle to cover more ground."

Josh grabbed the flashlight nearest him and moved it a foot or two closer to the professor. Terrance did the same with the middle flashlight, moving it closer to where Brea was sitting. Brea took the non-working flashlight and set it to her right, just outside of the circle.

"Why don't we take a five minute stretch break here? If anyone needs to relieve themselves, now would be a good time."

Terrance indicated that he needed to relieve himself. "I'm not sure I want to tangle with that cat though."

"Terrance, that cat is more afraid of you than you are of it!"

"I'm not so sure about that Dr. Brammer", Terrance responded. He made his way to the door and into the darkness.

Donald Brammer pushed himself up from the floor. Both of his knees made a cracking sound as he stood. Cathy and Josh stretched in place while Brea got up and walked over to where Brian was sitting.

"Are you doing okay?" she asked him.

"I'm doing fine babe", he replied. "This is kind of creepy and interesting all at the same time."

"I agree", she said, with a slight jitter in her voice.

About five minutes passed when Terrance made his way back into the living room. "Cathy, can I use some of your water to rinse off my hands?", he asked.

"Sure thing", Cathy responded.

"Thanks", Terrance said. He reached down, picked up the half-full bottle of water, and untwisted the cap. He poured the water with his right hand onto his left. The water was cold. The room was cold, which made the water feel that much colder. He set the bottle down with his right hand. Taking his left hand, he brought the water to his right hand and began to rub the two together. There were no paper towels. Terrance dried his hands the best he could on his dark colored sweatpants.

"Let's return to our positions now. We still have more questions to ask", Dr. Brammer said.

All four students returned to their positions and sat back down. The professor was already sitting.

"We need to get a little more pointed and detailed in our next round of questioning", he said.

They once again joined hands in a circular formation.

Terrance thought to himself, I wonder what Dr. Brammer is going to ask this time?

CHAPTER THIRTEEN

B rian sat against the middle of the north wall, quietly finishing his notes regarding the spooky appearance of the cat. He mentioned how the cat seemed to set the instruments off. Not taking his pen from paper, he also added the strange incident with Brea's flashlight.

"I think it's my turn for a question", Dr. Brammer said.

"Molly or any other spirits present, can you tell us if something bad happened in this room?"

Terrance had the feeling the professor was going to ask just a probing question.

There was silence. The circle of hand holders sat motionless. Brian watched from behind the camera with intent.

Then it happened! The house began shaking as if an earthquake was pummeling it. They felt the floor vibrate beneath them. The members of the group began making eye contact with one other. The flashlights were shaking. There was a look of uncertainty on Josh's face. Brea and Cathy had wide-eyed looks of panic on their faces. Terrance squeezed Cathy and Brea's hands a little tighter. Donald Brammer maintained a calm and poised posture, like that of a Texas Hold'em Poker player not wanting to reveal a tell.

The room began to shake more mightily.

"Is it an earthquake?", Cathy asked, in a startled tone.

"I don't think so", Donald Brammer said, trying to reassure her. He added, "Everyone keep your hands together and let's see where this goes".

"Dr. Brammer, the infrared thermal scanner is at its coldest setting", Brea excitedly said.

"The EMF detector is in the high green range", Cathy added.

Brian was trying to jot down notes, but his hand was swaying wildly from the shaking house. He was doing his best just to steady his hand to form legible words.

He looked over the camera toward the ceiling, near the middle of the room. Brian saw it, but he didn't believe it. There was a blue-green energy field rotating above the circle. He shaded his eyes with his right hand in an effort to keep watching the bright illumination. It was almost like trying to look directly into the sun. He was about to shout out to the group until he remembered their agreement, he was only to be an observer.

"Oh my God", Brea screamed, as she noticed the blinding energy force descending from the ceiling.

"Hang on everyone", Dr. Brammer implored.

The light was just above their heads. None of the five looked directly into it. The green-blue swirling ball of energy continued its downward trajectory. Brian tried to maintain eye contact with the orb, but it was too bright for his eyes.

The floor of the living room was shaking violently. Everyone except for Dr. Brammer was screaming. Even the professor let out an audible grunt.

The orb reached the wooden planks of the floor. Brian saw the light through the side viewfinder of the camera. It was some kind of pure energy. He was no longer holding his yellow tablet, as writing was not an option. He continued gazing into the viewfinder of the camera and saw sparkles inside of the circle. They were unlike any sparkles he'd ever seen, and he'd witnessed a ton of fireworks shows.

The screams and yells coming from the group were beginning to become more and more muffled. The sparkles were everywhere, and the green-blue field was spinning like a tornado. Brian sensed the panic in their voices. The old house continued to wobble and creak. He couldn't watch the light through the viewfinder any longer, as it was too bright. There was a giant banging noise. The orb was sucking the oxygen from the room, causing labored breathing for everyone. Brian wondered if the experiment might be more than he had bargained for.

Suddenly, the spiraling energy field was gone. Brian adjusted his eyes once again to the mostly darkened room. He was stunned. Not only was the blue-green orb gone, but so were the five people that'd been holding hands.

The only things remaining of the circle were the instruments, the flashlights and a puddle of water lying where Dr. Brammer had set his water bottle. The flashlights were not working. Brian broke his silence and half yelled, "Bea, Professor, where are you?" There was no answer. He picked up the one working flashlight from where he'd been sitting and walked over to the now empty space. He reached out with his right hand, but felt nothing, no heat, no energy, nothing.

A sense of panic overtook Brian. He walked to the front door located at the south side of the house. Opening the door, he looked for any footprints in the snow leading away from the house. The only footsteps he saw in the snow were those coming into the house.

His mind was spinning a million miles per hour. What was the blue-green orb? Where did it take them? Who'd believe him?

Brian took a deep breath in and exhaled loudly. He tried to override the panicky feeling that gripped him. There was only one thing to do at this time, and that was to notify the authorities. He'd have an impossible job explaining to them what had happened, but what choice did he have?

He reached into his right front pants pocket and removed his cell phone. He steadied his right index finger and pushed the numbers nine, one, one.

"Nine, one, one emergency", the female voice on the other end said calmly.

"Yes ma'am, I need to report some missing persons."

"Some?" the operator inquired.

"Yes ma'am, five to be exact. They just disappeared into thin air. I know it sounds crazy, but that's what happened." Brian was breathing heavily into his cell phone.

"Okay sir, please calm down. Where are you?"

"I'm at the old McKenna farmhouse just off of highway ninety-three."

"The old McKenna farmhouse off of highway ninety-three", she repeated back to him.

"Yes. They were conducting an experiment when something went terribly wrong."

"Okay sir, can you give me your name?"

"My name is Brian Foster", he said, with tension in his voice.

"Brian, please stay calm and remain at the farmhouse. I'm going to send help out to you."

"Please ask them to hurry."

"I will", the female voice said, reassuringly. "Can you wait outside for them? It'd be best if they can see you when they approach."

"Will do", Brian responded. He clicked the end call button of his cell phone and put it back in his front pocket.

Moments later, Sheriff Mark Preston heard a female voice coming over the police radio in his car.

"Emergency dispatch to one-eighty two and one-eighty three", the female voice said in a manner of fact tone.

"One-eighty-three here", Sheriff Preston barked back into the microphone.

Deputy Vickers heard the same call coming over his radio as well. "One-eighty two here", Merle Vickers commanded.

The female voice continued, "We just received a call from a male who said he was at the old McKenna farmhouse off highway ninety-three. His name is Brian Foster. He sounded quite shaken, something about an experiment going terribly wrong. He said there were five people missing. I asked him to meet you on the front porch of the farmhouse."

"Ten-four, we're in route", the Sheriff answered.

Brian stood with his back against the wall of the front porch. He had gloves on and his jacket zipped up to his neck. The snow was starting to ease, but it was still very cold. He heard the faint sound of police sirens off in the distance. The sounds were getting progressively closer and louder. Several cars pulled off onto the shoulder of the highway. He saw the red flashing lights as the two cars turned the corner of highway ninety-three onto County Road.

The cars quickly made their way through the snow. They pulled up to the house and parked side-by-side, just east of the white van. Sheriff Preston was first out, quickly followed by Deputy Vickers.

"Brian Foster", the Sheriff yelled out toward the porch.

"Yes sir", Brian answered loudly.

As the officers approached the porch, they were careful to avoid stepping through the missing stair. Sheriff Preston took a hard look at Brian and said, "I think we've already met once today?"

Brian looked at the man in uniform and studied his face. The man had knocked twice on his car window a little over an hour earlier. This was the same officer who'd written him a one hundred and ten dollar ticket for speeding.

"Yes, officer, I think you're right", Brian responded impishly.

"Brian, let's go back inside where it's warmer so that you can explain to us what happened in detail."

The Sheriff opened the front door and held it for Brian and Deputy Vickers. He quickly followed them inside, closing the door behind him.

"Looks like a lot of equipment here?", the Sheriff stated in an inquisitive way.

"Yes", Brian answered. "My fiancé Brea and three of her friends along with their psychology professor were conducting an experiment. Are you familiar with the McKenna mystery, Brian asked?"

"I think everyone in the county is familiar with the McKenna mystery", said Deputy Vickers.

"My fiancé is a graduate student in psychology. Her semester project was to come out here and try to use telepathy and paranormal means in order to get some answers regarding the mystery." Brian was now talking very fast.

"Slow down, I'm with you so far", Sheriff Preston said.

"Okay", Brian said, as he took in a deep breath and exhaled.

"The five of them were sitting in the middle of the room in a circular shape. Each one of them would ask a question and then they'd all wait quietly for a response. A green-blue orb twisted like a tornado and swept them up from the floor. It was giving off bright sparks. Finally, the orb disappeared, as did the five of them. I know it sounds crazy, but that's what happened, honest."

Deputy Vickers turned toward the Sheriff and asked, "Sheriff, do you want me to go out to my car and grab the breathalyzer? He has to be at least two times over the legal limit!"

"I don't think that'll be necessary right now Merle", Sheriff Preston replied.

"Breathalyzer", Brian said in a defiant tone. "I'm not drunk. If you don't believe me, just rewind the camera and play it back."

"That's a good idea", the Sheriff said. "Why don't we all walk over to the camera and take a look?"

The three men made their way to the camera.

"Do you know how to operate this thing?", Deputy Vickers asked Brian.

"I think so. It's a regular video camera."

Brian removed his gloves and put one in each of his jacket pockets. He pressed the stop button on the back of the camera. He held down the rewind button and the three watched the film speed backward. An intense bright blue-green light flashed by in the viewfinder. Brian kept rewinding until the light was gone. He pushed the stop button, followed by the play button.

The three watched and listened. The frantic voices of the participants boomed through the camera speaker. The light spun down over the circle. There were brilliant sparkles inside the orb. The screaming voices faded as the orb descended to floor level. The five holding hands were no longer visible. Flashing strobe lights were everywhere. Poof, the blue-green orb along with the four students and their professor were gone. The camera continued to run. They heard Brian's voice calling out for the others. There was no answer. He hit the stop button on the video camera.

"Holy mackerel, Sheriff, I don't believe what I just saw!", the Deputy said in amazement.

"I'm not so sure either Merle", the Sheriff answered.

"Brian, do you have the names of the students and their professor?"

"Yes."

"Would you mind giving me those names for investigative purposes?"

"Not at all", Brian said.

He walked over to where his yellow legal pad was lying on the floor. He bent down, picked it up and carried it back.

"You ready Sheriff?"

"Ready", Sheriff Preston confirmed.

Brian looked down at his list and began to read the names aloud. "Okay, there's Professor Donald Brammer, my fiancé, Brea Taylor, Josh Crenshaw, Terrance Bell and Cathy Reynolds."

The Sheriff was writing furiously. "Who'd you say before Terrance Bell?"

"Josh Crenshaw", sir.

"Got it."

"What'll we do now Sheriff", the Deputy asked.

"First, we're going to call Topeka for backup. We'll ask them to send all available personnel, including their canine unit. We need to contain this area and do a thorough search of the premises", the Sheriff finished.

"Brian, I need you to stick around here with me. Merle, I'll need for you to direct traffic outside should the media or members of the community catch wind of this."

"I'm on it Sheriff", the Deputy answered, in the solemn tone of a marine recruit.

CHAPTER FOURTEEN

"There is no certainty; there is only adventure."

Roberto Assagioli

Donald Brammer found himself lying on a large, oval rug. It felt as if he'd been hit in the head with a sledgehammer. The dimensions of the room seemed eerily familiar to him. He saw the portrait of a grey haired man hanging on one of the papered walls. The ceiling was neatly painted. A fire was roaring in the fireplace on the east wall. The east wall he thought, no, it couldn't be. However, the more he studied the room, the more the realization came to him. It was the living room of the McKenna farmhouse. However, the dilapidated, rundown farmhouse was now vibrant with life!

He slowly raised himself to his knees. He saw the others lying motionless in their same positions around the circle. The professor rose and made his way over to Cathy.

He shook her slightly while uttering the words, "Cathy, are you okay?"

She slowly started to gain consciousness. "Professor, what happened?," She asked, half in shock and half in disbelief.

"Let's make sure the others are all right and then we'll go over it."

"Sure", she said, walking over to check on Brea.

Brea was already shaking off the cobwebs. "Cathy, what happened, she asked?"

"I'm not sure yet", Cathy answered. "Are you okay?"

"I'm okay, just a little groggy."

Cathy lowered her right arm in order to help Brea to her feet. The two of them made their way over to Josh. He was sitting upright with his knees pointed toward the ceiling.

"You okay Josh?" Brea asked.

"I think so", Josh replied. "What the hell happened?"

"We're not sure yet", Brea responded.

At this point, Dr. Brammer and Terrance walked over and joined the other three.

"Professor", what happened, Josh asked?"

"This might sound really bizarre to all of you but the only explanation I have for what just happened is that we somehow created a precise amount of negative energy. I'm not a Quantum Physicist, but I believe the energy pulled us through a wormhole, you know, a time portal. Judging from the size of the room, I'd guess we're still in the McKenna living room. Unbelievable as it may seem to all of us, I think we just traveled back in time. One hundred and fifty years back in time!"

"Oh my God!", Brea blurted out. "You have to be joking. That's impossible."

"No way!", Terrance seconded.

Josh just shook his head and moaned, "I don't believe this at all!"

"Cathy, take a quick peek out the front window and tell me what you see?" Dr. Brammer asked, in a directing manner.

Cathy took the few short steps to the daintily draped window and pulled back the shade. She peered to the right and was startled.

"Dr. Brammer, there's a barn out there that wasn't there earlier!"

Terrance walked over to where Cathy stood in order to confirm her story. "Yeah, Dr. Brammer, there's a barn. Not only that, but there's a smaller sized red building about fifteen feet south of the front porch."

Brea began to cry. "I can't believe this is happening to us."

"Calm down Brea, everything will be alright", Dr. Brammer said in a soothing voice. "We're all okay and together we'll figure this out."

Looking out the front window, Cathy excitedly warned, Professor, there are two women walking toward the front of the house. They are dressed like the women on *Little House on the Prairie*. Behind them there appear to be two black men carrying something in glass jars."

Terrance interrupted, "The black men came out of the little red out building carrying those jars."

Cathy said in a whispering voice, "We need to hide, they're almost to the porch".

The five of them quickly scampered back toward the northeast corner of the living room. Josh opened the white door while the others followed. Josh shut the door, leaving a slight crack so he could see and hear what was going on.

Terrance shook his head in disbelief. He whispered to the others, "This is the room I peed in earlier."

Of course, when Terrance did his duty, the room was dark and filled with broken boards and crumbled plaster. Now the room was painted and furnished. The walls were light blue in color. There was a large cast iron bed located near the middle of the room. Covering the bed was a hand-embroidered quilt. Two wooden dressers adorned the east and south walls. One dresser had an old looking photograph of a woman. Seeing the photograph, Brea whispered, "I think that's Molly."

The front door opened and in walked the woman in the photograph. A younger version of her followed. They were both wearing long, cotton dresses. The younger woman had on a long, blue dress while the older one wore a long, green dress.

Peeping through the crack in the door just above Josh, Dr. Brammer whispered to the others, "The young woman is Sarah, the McKenna's daughter." He recognized her from their research photograph.

"Marcus and Samuel, would you please be so kind as to place the jars on the kitchen table, Molly asked? You two can join the men down by the barn when you're finished."

"Yes ma'am", both men chimed back. They headed across the living room in a northerly direction. Josh was sure they were coming to the bedroom, but the two made a right turn just north of the fireplace.

"Sarah, would you mind giving me a hand in preparing supper?"

"I'd be glad to mother", the soft-spoken voice responded.

The two women made their way to the kitchen, taking the same route the two young black men did before them.

"Dr. Brammer, what do we do now?", Brea asked.

"For one thing, we need to get out of this room as quickly as possible. At some point, someone is going to want or need something in here. Terrance, you mentioned that you saw a small out building?"

"Yeah professor, about fifteen feet or so away from the front porch."

"Okay everyone we need to sneak as quickly and quietly as possible out to that small building."

Cathy interceded, "They might kill us if they catch us!"

"That's a chance we're going to have to take", Dr. Brammer said, as if this were the only option.

"Is everyone ready, the professor asked?"

There was little reply from the bunch.

"The three men will lead the way and you two ladies follow. Try not to make any noise. Let's go!"

With that, Dr. Brammer opened the bedroom door and slowly began making his way across the living room toward the front door. Josh was stacked behind him, while Terrance followed closely. Cathy and Brea rounded up the back end of the line. As he got halfway through the living room, Dr. Brammer looked to his left down the hallway and saw the two women standing in the kitchen. Their backs were to him. He took his right index finger and pointed it in that direction, alerting the others that the women were there.

Donald Brammer put his hand on the front door knob. He gently turned the handle and pushed the door open. He stepped onto the porch. Josh followed right behind him. Terrance heard the faint sound of a voice and footsteps coming from the hallway. He took a quick peek behind him and saw Cathy and Brea scurrying back into the bedroom.

"Momma, can I wear Grandma's brooch, you know, the one I liked to play with as a child?"

"Sure Sarah", Molly replied. "It's in the keepsake box on my dresser."

Cathy noticed what appeared to be a small closet door on the west wall. Both women hurried toward it. Cathy opened the door and they piled in. It was completely dark inside. They stood motionless.

Sarah turned the doorknob and entered her parent's bedroom. She walked over to her mother's dresser and opened the wooden box. The two women heard her fishing through the box for the brooch. Sarah was happily singing. Finally, the shuffling stopped. She must've found the brooch, Cathy thought. From the closet, the two heard the box lid drop. Immediately, a pair of footsteps tapped their way to the door. Following, was the sound of a knob turning. A door opened and then closed. Cathy and Brea freaked out and were oblivious to the fact they were holding on to one another.

The three men made a mad dash for the small, red out building. Reaching it first, the professor opened the door. It was a very small room with sparse amenities. Straw covered the floor. Strewn on top of the straw were two blankets. There was a small, opaque glass window on each sidewall. He quickly deduced that this was where the two black men lived. He also noticed a trap door in the floor. Earlier, the men were carrying glass jars of food into the house. There must be a root cellar beneath the floor, he thought.

Josh and Terrance quickly followed the professor into the small room. The professor and Josh were panting heavily. Terrance was in much better shape than either Josh or the professor, so he caught his breath much quicker. Dr. Brammer pushed the door closed.

"This must be where the two young black men live", he said to Josh and Terrance. "They were carrying food into the house. This trap door in the floor probably leads down to a root cellar where the food is stored."

Josh and the professor were beginning to regain their breath.

"We can stay in this room, but we have to be careful and watch out for the two young black men. If they come this way, we'll need to head down into the root cellar."

"Okay professor", Terrance answered.

"Gotcha!'", Josh agreed.

"I hope the girls were able to scramble back into hiding", Josh said, with a bit of uncertainty in his voice.

Terrance tried to reassure the other two men. "When I heard footsteps, I turned and saw them running back toward the bedroom."

"I'm sure they're fine", Dr. Brammer added.

Terrance was looking out the small window on the east side of the building

"What now?" Josh asked in a lost way.

"What now?" Terrance repeated. "What now is the two men near the barn who are riding this way on a horse-drawn wagon? It looks like the two young black men are riding in the back of the wagon. They're sitting on something."

Josh and the professor joined Terrance at the window.

"This can't be happening", Josh said in disbelief.

"It's probably father and son, Alexander and Benjamin McKenna", Dr. Brammer said. He did so in the manner of a detective surveying a crime scene.

"Keep an eye on them Terrance. If they come this way we'll need to head downstairs."

"Will do professor", Terrance replied.

Brea and Cathy no longer heard the girl. Cathy whispered to Brea, "I think it's safe now."

"I don't know", she whispered back.

"We need to try and join the guys in the small out building". Cathy said this in an imperative voice that was a notch above a whisper.

"Okay", Brea responded.

It was pitch black inside of the closet. Brea felt for the door handle. She touched the outline of the handle and repositioned her hand for a better grip. Slowly, she opened the door wide enough to get a good look around the room. Cathy was right. The girl was gone. Brea was first to exit the closet. Cathy was close behind on her coattails. The two made their way to the bedroom door. Cathy moved in front of Brea and cracked the door open. Both stood silently, listening for voices or footsteps. It seemed quiet. Cathy looked at Brea and put her right index finger up to her lips in a signal motioning for quiet. Brea nodded her head in affirmation. Cathy carefully pushed the door open.

Now it was Brea's turn to follow on Cathy's coattails. The two inched their way across the living room. They were standing at the same spot where they first heard Sarah's voice. It was quiet. Cathy took a quick glance down the hallway toward the kitchen. It was clear. She grabbed Brea by the hand and led her to the front door. Both seemed to be regaining their confidence. Cathy turned the handle and opened the front door.

"Great", Cathy spewed in a low voice. She closed the door and looked back at Brea. She shook her head as well.

"What's wrong?" Brea whispered.

"There are two men in a wagon being drawn by a horse. The two black men are riding in the back of the wagon. They're down by the big barn and headed this way. We have to go back!"

Brea looked at Cathy in disbelief. Run back she thought, no way.

Cathy grabbed Brea's hand and both headed back to the bedroom. Cathy opened the door while Brea quietly closed it behind her.

"We need to get back into the closet", Cathy whispered.

"I don't want to go back in there!"

"If someone comes we won't have time to hide."

Cathy walked toward the closet, taking any other options out of Brea's hands.

The two women resumed their original positions in the dark, little room.

"They're getting closer", Terrance said to his two counterparts.

"Okay Terrance, let me know if they come this way", the professor countered.

Dr. Brammer brushed back the straw on the floor covering the trap door. He opened the door in anticipation of making a quick escape. It was completely dark below. He barely made out the top rung of a wooden ladder that descended into the darkness. The room smelled of musk and staleness.

"It looks like they're heading toward the house", Terrance said, with some relief in his voice.

The men, the horse and the wagon all continued their journey from the east, angling toward the house. Finally, they heard the older man shout, "whoa!"

The horse neighed and came to a sudden stop. The two men jumped down from either side of the wagon. The pair of young black men stood, but stayed in the back of the wagon. Terrance saw what appeared to be sections of trees in the wagon. Coming around the wagon, the younger man wielded a long handled axe. Terrance ducked down below the window out of view.

"I think they're going to chop firewood", Terrance whispered to the other two.

Josh and the professor nodded back in agreement. All three stood silently as they tried to concentrate on the conversation of the two men.

The booming voice of Alexander McKenna was hard to miss. "Son, why don't you let me take the first few whacks?"

"Father, I can chop the wood. Marcus and Samuel can stack it against the house."

Benjamin McKenna was in very good shape. The farm and its two hundred acres kept him physically fit. He was about six feet tall and weighed roughly one hundred and seventy pounds. He was wearing a pair of tan pants and a white cotton shirt. Over the shirt, he wore a tan, leather vest. His hair was shoulder length brown.

Alexander McKenna was fifty-three years of age. His hair was prematurely grey, most likely due to the stress and hardships involved in raising a family without the luxury of modern amenities. He was a stout man with a slightly pouched stomach. He weighed about two hundred and twenty pounds. He liked to smoke cigars. It was all too common to see him with one dangling from his mouth. He was wearing light grey colored pants and a matching jacket.

Benjamin led the horse and wagon closer to the front porch. He hitched the horse to the wooden porch rail. The two black men began to chuck tree sections from the back of the wagon onto the ground below. Each section of tree made a thud sound as it hit the ground.

Alexander waddled over to the front porch steps. He reached into his jacket pocket and produced a cigar and silver lighter. He spun the metal wheel with his right thumb, creating a large flame on top of the lighter. Holding the cigar firmly between his teeth, he leaned toward the flame and puffed mightily. He puffed several times on the cigar before it caught. Alexander returned the lighter to his jacket pocket. He coughed, and then comfortably sat on the second porch step.

The three men made little movement inside the small building. They were intent on not making noise or drawing attention to themselves.

Dr. Brammer's mind focused on his wife Patty. It was now two O'clock and he wondered what she might be doing. Was she doing laundry while watching television? Or perhaps, she was putting up the Christmas tree. She always started decorating by putting the angel on top of the tree.

He saw in his mind the delicate smile on her face as she chose spots on the tree for the ornaments. Even though it was an artificial tree, it had the aura of being real. A thought now crossed his mind and it scared him. Would he ever see her again?

"Whack", the sound echoed widely into the dense air as Benjamin began to chop the wood. He placed another section of tree onto the old tree stump and slung the axe down. Once again, "whack!"

CHAPTER FIFTEEN

"You don't know your own mind."

Jonathan Swift

Sheriff Preston took the hand held walkie-talkie from his beltline and raised it to his mouth. "One-eighty three to dispatch", he stammered loudly into the mouthpiece of the device.

After a couple of slight static discharges, the female voice on the other end answered, "Go ahead one-eighty three."

"Dispatch, can you connect me through to Topeka PD?"

"Sure, one moment please."

Thirty seconds passed when a male voice answered, "This is Topeka PD, Officer Williams speaking".

"Yes Officer Williams, this is Sheriff Preston from Floyd County."

"Yes Sheriff, what can I do for you?"

"We have a situation out here at the old McKenna farmhouse off of highway ninety-three. I'm going to need all the available units that you can spare, including your canine unit."

"What's the problem Sheriff?"

"A group of students and their professor were performing some sort of paranormal project out here. You know, the kind you see on television."

"Yes."

"Well somehow, and don't ask me how, they literally disappeared into thin air. I know it sounds crazy, but I watched it myself on the video camera they were using to record the event."

"Sir, I can send a couple of patrol units your way along with the canine unit."

"That would be much appreciated Officer Williams", Sheriff Preston thankfully said.

"You bet Sheriff", Officer Williams replied. "I'll get those units out to you as soon as possible."

"Sounds good, and thanks again", Sheriff Preston said. He twisted the little black button to the off position and holstered the radio.

Deputy Vickers opened the front door and yelled in, "Sheriff, we've got company."

The Sheriff walked over to where the Deputy was standing and saw a large white van with the letters "KTOP" in blue on the side. A large metal-coil antenna on top of the van was unwinding into the air in a corkscrew fashion.

"Good grief Merle, go out and head them off. Tell them that they'll need to park along the fence line next to the highway. Ask that they not approach within one-hundred feet of the house. If they have a problem, come get me."

"Yes sheriff", the deputy said, accepting the command. He began descending the porch while at the same time flagging down the driver. The van came to a stop. The Deputy approached the van as the front passenger's window began to lower.

"Is there a problem officer?", the well-dressed female smilingly asked. She was wearing eyeliner, make-up and blush. Her matching skirt and jacket were dark blue. She was wearing a white blouse under the jacket. The male driver was not so neatly dressed, wearing a pair of blue jeans and a light blue, long sleeved golf shirt. Lying next to him in between the seats was a brown leather jacket. Deputy Vickers assumed, and rightly, that he doubled as the cameraman.

"No, nothing wrong ma'am", the officer replied. "What brings you out here to the old McKenna place?"

The reporter hesitated for a second and continued, "We heard a report come over the police scanner, something about an experiment and some missing people. We wanted to come out and get the story for our viewers."

"I can't comment on what you may have heard over the police scanner", Deputy Vickers said.

"I am, however, going to politely ask that you park your van next to the fence line near the highway." He pointed to the west.

"Why's that?", she answered, in a somewhat perturbed manner.

"I'm just following orders ma'am."

"Whose orders?", she asked briskly.

"Ma'am, I'd appreciate it very much if you'd just cooperate. I'm also going to ask that you and your partner not come within one hundred feet of the house."

"Is this a crime scene or something?", she asked in a goading manner, trying to elicit more details from the Deputy.

"I'm afraid I can't answer any more questions at this time. Once again, please park your van where I directed. If the Sheriff wants to make an official statement I'm sure he'll come find you."

"Okay officer", she said acceptingly. She pressed the button and her window rose electronically. The driver shifted the van into drive and pulled it to where the Deputy requested. Deputy Vickers smiled and gave them a friendly wave. He headed back to his post on the porch. Glancing down at the watch on his left wrist, he saw that it was two-twenty.

"Brian, grab that flashlight and follow me", the Sheriff directed.

Sheriff Preston removed the flashlight attached to the right side of his belt. He flicked the button and a beam of light spurted out. Brian bent over and picked up the flashlight he'd been using during the experiment. He followed behind Sheriff Preston.

Sheriff Preston began to walk toward the northeast. He was about to enter the doorway when he said, "We need to be careful of nails and broken glass. Let's take a quick look around in here."

"Sounds good", Brian said. He smiled, and then thought to himself, this is the same room the cat came out of and Terrance went in!

Sheriff Preston cautiously took his first step through the doorway and into the dark room. He rotated shining his light, first at the ground and then around the walls. Beer bottles were lying about the room at random. The room had an eerie quiet about it.

"Are you with me Brian?"

"Yes sir", Brian responded.

"I have a question Sheriff?", Brian asked, in a conciliatory tone.

"What's that?", Sheriff Preston fully expected a question about the paranormal or missing people.

"Do you think that we can work something out regarding that ticket I got earlier today?" Brian used his most persuasive voice.

"Well, I tell you what", the Sheriff began. "If we can find your fiancé and the others, I think we can come to some arrangement regarding that ticket."

"Thank you sir", Brian said. He was now following closely behind the Sheriff, trying to avoid any loose or missing floor planks.

"We need to find them first though", The Sheriff said. He continued to move the beam of light around the room. "I don't think we're going to find them in here."

"Doesn't look like it", Brian said. He turned and headed back to the doorway and into the living room. Sheriff Preston followed right behind him.

As the men exited the darkness, they saw Deputy Vickers standing with four or five police officers in blue uniforms. One of the officers had a German Shepherd at his side, which he held onto by a leash.

"Sheriff, these are the Topeka officers that are here to help with the search."

"Excellent", he replied.

The officer furthest to his left stepped toward the Sheriff and extended his hand in a shaking gesture.

"I'm Ernie Green", the officer said, and shook the Sheriff's hand.

"Nice to meet you Officer Green, and thank you for coming."

The other four officers followed suit and introduced themselves to the Sheriff. The last one to do so informed the Sheriff that he was with the canine unit. He told him the dog's name was, "Bo".

"I appreciate all of you coming out on such short notice. The man standing next to me is Brian Foster. He was here when the experiment went south and the five people disappeared."

"Went south?", one of the officers asked.

"Yes, the five disappeared into thin air. Deputy Vickers and I both watched the whole thing on the video camera. I've never seen anything like it in my life. I think it'd be best for Brian to give you more details since he was an eyewitness to the event.

Brian cleared his throat nervously. "My fiancé Brea, her Psychology professor and three other students were conducting this experiment, like the Sheriff said." He swallowed hard. "As I'm sure you're all aware, there's a long standing mystery regarding the McKenna family who used to live here? There are many different theories about what happened to the family. Bottom line is they, two black workers and several Union soldiers vanished. Mind you, this was in the sixties, the eighteen sixties!"

The officers continued to train their puzzled expressions directly on Brian.

"To make a long story short, the experiment was designed to contact spirits or ghosts that may be in the house with the intention of shedding light on the mystery. That's when it happened."

"What happened?", one of the officers interjected.

"That's when the house started to shake violently. Then, an orb shaped, blue-green energy field descended over them. Sparks were flying everywhere and it was difficult to watch because of the brightness of the light."

"Sounds like something out of Star Trek", one of the officers quipped.

"Precisely", Brian answered. "Now it looks like we have a second mystery to add to the first."

"Bizarre", the canine officer replied. "How can we help?"

The Sheriff focused his line of sight on the canine officer, "I'd like for you men to take your cars to different sections of the farm and do a visual search for these people. Who knows, maybe that green orb carried them out to the edge of the farm? Anyway, I need you all to split up amongst yourselves and do a thorough search."

The men nodded and voiced their acceptance. The canine officer once again asked a question.

"That bottle sitting on the floor, was that used by one of the participants?"

"Yes, it was the professor's", Brian answered.

"I can try to use the bottle for scenting purposes, if that's okay? Bo here has a very keen smeller!"

"By all means", the Sheriff said.

"Thanks." The canine officer walked over and picked up the bottle. He ran it under Bo's nose several times. The dog seemed to get excited.

The officers decided among themselves which areas each would cover. As they were leaving, one of the officers remarked, "We'll let you know what we find Sheriff."

"Thank you all very much", the Sheriff said.

After the men left, Sheriff Preston signaled Deputy Vickers to come in. "Merle, I need you to keep directing traffic for me and to make sure that nobody enters the house".

"Yes sir", he responded.

"I'm going to take Brian with me and search an area just southeast of here."

"Sounds good."

With that, the three men made their way to the front porch. The Deputy remained on the porch, while Brian followed the Sheriff to his patrol car. Brian found the passenger's side door locked. He waited for the Sheriff to open it. The Sheriff flipped the electronic button on his key ring that opened all the doors. The two climbed in. Brian was somewhat fascinated, as this was his first time in a police car. Sheriff Preston put the key into the ignition and started the car. He backed up a bit and steered the car toward the southeast.

As Sheriff Preston started to the southeast, he heard the horn of the television van honking repeatedly.

"Just what I needed", he murmured, half under his breath.

He turned the car to the right and then to the right again. As he approached the van, the horn stopped honking. The passenger's side window lowered as he pulled along side of the van. The Sheriff lowered his window.

"Sheriff, can you give us any information at this time as to what's going on?" The words were coming to him from the well-dressed female reporter.

"Sorry, but I don't have anything for you at this time."

"How many people are missing?"

"No comment."

"Are you considering this a crime scene?"

"No comment. I'm sorry miss, but I don't have any details to provide to you at this time. If and when the time is right, I'll let you know and will give you a statement if necessary, okay?"

"Okay Sheriff, thank you", the woman said.

"Thanks for understanding", the Sheriff politely responded. He closed his window. After the window fully closed, he once again turned the car toward the southeast and began to drive.

"This is the part of our job that most people never see Brian", he said.

"I can see that it's not all about writing tickets", Brian answered.

"No, that's just a very small part of what we do."

As he headed to the southeast, Sheriff Preston waved to Deputy Vickers who was standing on the porch. The officer returned the wave.

The Sheriff pulled his patrol car near a cluster of trees. He parked the car. He and Brian climbed out of the car. The officer locked the doors to the car with his keychain remote. It made a much-abbreviated honking sound.

"Let's comb through these trees and this brush area Brian."

"Okay Sheriff", he replied.

The two men split up and walked in and out of the trees. Each was keenly focusing for any movement or disturbance in the snow. Neither man noticed any fresh looking tracks.

CHAPTER SIXTEEN

"Unrest of spirit is a mark of life."
KARL A. MENNINGER

The two young women stood still and quiet in the dark closet. The desperation of the situation was beginning to sink in. Although she could not see her face, Cathy realized that Brea was crying.

"It's going to be okay Brea, I promise", Cathy said. She reached her arm around Brea's shoulder and gave her a comforting squeeze.

"I'm scared and I miss Brian", Brea whispered, trying to choke back the tears.

They could see nothing, but their ears now acted as their eyes. Sounds resonated from the kitchen. They heard the clanking noise of what sounded like a cast iron pot hitting the top of the stove. There was conversation coming from the two women in the kitchen. It was too low and distorted for them to distinguish. In addition to the kitchen noise, there was the staccato of thump sounds coming from outside. Neither knew exactly what was causing the sound, but both were sure the men who rode up in the wagon were making it.

"I have a plan", Cathy said, in a voice lacking complete confidence.

"What's your plan?" Brea was now calming and the tears were no longer streaming down her cheeks.

"I noticed a window on the north wall of the bedroom. We need to try to open that window. Once we hear the thumping sound stop we can make our way around to the front of the house. When the coast is clear, we dash for the out building."

"Are you crazy?", Brea said, in total disbelief.

"Or, we can wait here in this closet until someone finds us?"

"Okay", Brea replied. "But not until we hear the noise from outside stop".

"Absolutely", Cathy confirmed.

Molly opened one of the glass jars and poured the contents into the cast iron pot. The white turnips and their juices made a small splash.

"Mother, how's the war going?" Sarah asked, in a concerned manner.

"Young lady you needn't worry yourself about such things. I'm sure that everything will work out just fine."

Sarah laid the freshly baked loaf of bread on the cutting board that sat on the table. She picked up a knife and began slicing it. The knife was very sharp and easily made its way through the crust. Alexander McKenna always liked to keep the knives sharp.

"Mother?", Sarah asked. She continued to slice the bread.

"Yes dear".

"Are Marcus and Samuel slaves?"

This question caused much consternation on Molly's part.

"Sarah you know better than that. You know that your father wouldn't keep slaves around. They're farmhands that help out with tending the fields and doing chores."

"But they don't get paid for their work?" Sarah knew she was pushing the issue, but her young mind and strong will couldn't resist.

"Sarah!" Molly paused for a moment as she stirred the turnips. "First of all, you don't know that they don't get paid. Secondly, even if they aren't getting paid in cash they're being provided room and board, free meals and clothing for their backs. I should say that is a pretty fair salary!"

"You're right, Mother. I'm sorry if my curiosity got the better of me!"

"Rest assured, those two men are well looked after."

"Yes mother." Sarah finished slicing the bread and put it on a plate.

While Sarah conceded the point to her mother, she wasn't totally convinced. She knew her father well. He was a businessman at the core. Making money was his prime objective. It consumed all of his time. Rarely, if ever, did he ask Sarah how she was doing. It was all about harvesting the crops and getting paid.

"Sarah, go check on the men and see how they're coming along? Tell them that supper is just about ready. The ham won't take me but a minute to slice."

"Yes mother", Sarah cheerily replied.

Cathy and Brea heard the patter of footsteps in the hallway. It sounded as though they were heading away from their direction toward the front door. They heard the front door open and then close.

"Father, Benjamin, mother said supper is about ready. Are you two almost finished?"

Alexander never started. He was still sitting in the same position on the porch step. Whack, the sound echoed as the axe blade separated the wood.

"Tell your mother that we'll be in directly, no later than ten minutes from now."

"Yes father", Sarah said reverently. She reversed her direction and walked back into the house. She passed the fireplace, which felt good on this cold day.

"Mother, father said they'll be no later than ten minutes."

"Thank you child", Molly appreciatively said to her daughter.

"You're welcome mother."

"Terrance, what's going on out there"?", the professor asked, with a sense of urgency in his voice.

"The young girl came out on the porch. She told the men that it was almost supper time."

"Great", the professor said, somewhat in disgust.

"What's wrong?", Josh asked.

"Well if they're going to eat soon that means the two young men will probably be eating as well. They won't be eating with the family. They'll be eating out here. We'll need to go down into the root cellar if they come out here with their food."

"Good point professor", Josh said.

"How're we going to meet back up with Brea and Cathy?"

"If we don't see Brea and Cathy soon, we may try to go to them." The professor knew this sounded like an off the cuff idea, because it was.

"They're in the bedroom," Terrance said. "We can't sneak past all of these men. Besides, someone will surely hear us walking through the living room.

"That's just it Terrance", the professor said, with a bit more confidence in his voice. "We'll wait until the men go into the house for supper."

"What about the two black men?" Josh asked. "If they aren't going to let them dine with the family, they may not even allow them inside. They may just hand them their food on the porch."

"We can work around that", Dr. Brammer replied.

"How"?, Terrance asked.

The professor continued with his impromptu plan. "When the two men are on the porch waiting for their food to be brought out to them, we'll sneak behind this building. When they come out here to eat, we'll make our way around to the back of the house."

"Sounds risky", Terrance said.

"I'm afraid it's all risky at this point", Dr. Brammer replied. "But I think we can pull it off. It's all about timing. We need to be ready when the door opens and the food is handed to them. That's when we make our break for the back of this building. Once we hear the door close, we make our way to the back of the house. Terrance, you'll be the lookout and let us know when they get their food."

"Gotcha'!"

The thumping sound of splitting wood came to a temporary halt. Terrance spied at the four men through the little window. All three smelled the aroma from the cigar that Alexander McKenna was smoking.

"I think it's time", Cathy whispered to Brea.

"Are you sure that we should try this?"

"I don't see any other option. Our best chance is to take a chance", Cathy said firmly.

"Okay", Brea hesitantly replied.

Cathy whispered, "I'll go first and you follow behind me."

"Sure thing."

Cathy turned the closet doorknob and gently pushed the door open. She stepped out into the bedroom and waited for Brea. Brea came out and closed the door behind her. The two made their way to the window on the north wall. Cathy gave an upwardly shove on the window, but it didn't budge. She took in a breath and tried again, nothing.

"Brea, help me push."

Brea lined up on the left side of the window with Cathy standing on the right. They each used both hands in an effort to create as much leverage as possible. The window didn't budge. Suddenly, the two heard a pair of loud footsteps coming from the living room. They sounded like men's boots.

"Back in the closet", Cathy muttered.

"Not again?"

Cathy was now pushing Brea in the direction of the closet. Brea opened the door and both slid into the closet. Cathy closed the door behind her. They once again found themselves in the familiar position of standing in the pitch-dark closet.

The two listened intently for footsteps. They didn't hear any. Cathy whispered to Brea, "They must've gone into the kitchen.

"Good", Brea said, letting out a sigh of relief.

"It sure smells good in here", Alexander McKenna bellowed.

"It sure does", Benjamin affirmed, in a hungry, working man's voice.

"You two go ahead and have a seat. Sarah and I will bring dinner to the table. Are Marcus and Samuel out on the porch?"

"Yes ma'am", Benjamin replied.

"Good. I'll have Sarah prepare them a bowl full of food each and take it to them." Molly was used to directing traffic in the kitchen, as this had become a daily routine.

Sarah filled two bowls each with turnips and a couple of slices of ham. She laid a slice of bread on top of each bowl. Picking up the two bowls, she began walking toward the front door.

"Professor", Terrance exclaimed excitedly.

"Yes Terrance."

"The two young men are waiting by the door!"

"We need to make our move now!" The professor said, without hesitating.

Terrance cracked the door open and saw the backs of the two young men standing on the porch. He quickly exited the small building. The professor followed right behind him.

To their bewilderment, Josh made a dash for the west side of the house. His concern for the two women outweighed his fear of being caught. He would soon join Brea in the bedroom closet while Cathy resumed her lookout from behind the door.

Both men were standing behind the small, red, out building. Terrance peaked around the corner of the building. He then whispered to the professor, "She's handing them their food".

"Okay", the professor followed in a low voice. "When we hear them enter the building and close the door we'll make our way to the back of the house. We need to be as quiet as possible. Get ready."

The two young men each took a bowl from Sarah. They smiled widely and Sarah returned one just as big. In their woolen pants and cotton shirts, they started from the porch, clutching the bowls as if they were gold bars.

Sarah stopped the two and quietly directed them into the house. She pointed to a spot behind the secretaire. Today, she thought, they'd eat supper inside, by the fire!

"We've got company", the professor said. He pointed to the east. Both men were shocked. Three Indians were emerging from the woods near the big barn.

"We need to hide over here", the professor implored. Terrance followed him to the west side of the red shack.

"We'll need to stay put here for now", Dr. Brammer told him.

CHAPTER SEVENTEEN

"Thought is action in rehearsal."

Sigmund Freud

"Here you are dear", Molly said in a polite voice. She passed a plate with several strips of ham on it to her husband.

"Thank you darling", the elderly McKenna replied. He set the plate down on the table in front of him.

Sarah took a small spoonful of turnips and juice from the bowl, putting them on her plate. She didn't like the taste or the smell of turnips. However, she knew she needed to take at least a token amount. She handed the white ceramic bowl to her father who was sitting at the head of the table to her right.

"Thank you pumpkin", he replied. On those rare occasions when he was in a good mood, Sarah's father would address her as "pumpkin" or "sweetie bird". Things must be going well today, she thought to herself. She cordially replied to her father, "You're welcome."

Benjamin was sitting at the opposite end of the table from his father. His mother pretty much awarded him that spot in recognition of the hard work he did around the farm. She also knew if anything happened to her husband, Benjamin would need to step right into his shoes.

"Before we start eating, let's say a prayer", Alexander said to the other three. They all took the hand of the person sitting next to them on their left and right. All four bowed their heads.

Alexander started," Dear Lord, we thank you for this food, which you have given to us. We also thank you for guiding and protecting this family, Amen."

An "Amen" followed from the others. No sooner had the handclasps been broken, Benjamin picked up a fork and began cutting the ham on his plate. The meat was tender enough and he was strong enough that he didn't like wasting time using a knife.

"This is delicious", he said, after swallowing his first bite.

"Thank you Benjamin", smiled Molly. "You can also thank your sister who helped prepare the meal."

"Thanks Sarah", he said, glancing her way.

"You're welcome Benjamin", she properly replied.

Alexander McKenna picked up the bowl full of turnips with his left hand. He took the large spoon in his right hand. He poured two heaping spoonfuls of turnips onto his plate. Alexander loved them. His mother had a special way of making them for him that Molly tried to copy. It wasn't exactly the same, but it was close.

"Brought up a cart full of wood that I'm going to chop after supper", Benjamin said, before tearing a large bite of bread off with his teeth.

"We can always use the wood", Molly answered, in a thankful tone. "Lord knows, it can get frightfully cold out here. Sometimes, when the wind blows it just chills me to the bone"

"Well, I'll keep the woodpile fully stacked mother."

"I know you will dear", she said, in an endearing fashion.

"Mother, why can't Samuel and Marcus eat with us?"

Sarah tried to contain herself, but she just couldn't seem to get out of her own way.

"Sarah, you know the answer to that question. We've gone over this time and time again. They have their own quarters where they like to eat and sleep. They value their privacy. We see them throughout the day and have plenty of opportunities to converse with them."

"It just doesn't seem right", Sarah followed.

Alexander lent himself to the conversation. "Sarah, we all know that you mean well. However, things have operated this way for a long time. We have to separate family from business matters."

"But they are like family", Sarah insisted.

"Yes, in many ways they are", Alexander assured her. "But it's proper this way."

"Besides, if we coddle them too much they won't want to do all of their chores", Benjamin chimed in.

"Enough on this matter", Molly interceded.

Sarah was trying to work her way around to the subject of paying the men. She'd never seen her father give them money for their work. It seemed wrong to her for the two men to work so hard for a bowl of food, some tattered clothes and a small shack where they slept. She was determined to find out the answer to the pay question.

Benjamin was the first to finish his meal. He ate faster than the prairie wind blew.

"I'm finished, may I be excused?"

"Yes you may", Alexander replied.

Ten minutes later, the sound of splitting wood came to an abrupt halt. Molly thought this strange. Benjamin had only been outside for such a short time.

The front door opened. "Mother, father, we have visitors", Benjamin called out toward the kitchen.

The sound of chairs scooting against the kitchen floor vibrated into the living room. Alexander and Molly walked down the short hallway to the living room.

"Would you men care for some supper?", Molly asked, with a smile.

"No ma'am", the Major replied. "But thank you kindly for the offer."

"How can we help you?", Alexander McKenna asked the Major.

"Sir, my name is Major Aaron Wilkerson and this is Corporal Livingston. We're here to investigate allegations that have been raised against you and your family."

"Allegations against me and my family?", he asked, in disbelief.

"Yes".

"What kind of allegations are you talking about?"

"Numerous sources have accused you and your family of harboring slaves."

Sarah walked from the kitchen into the living room and stood quietly next to her father.

"Slaves, that's outlandish!", Alexander McKenna spouted loudly.

"Marcus and Samuel work the fields and perform household chores. They're not slaves. They're like family."

"But do you pay them?", the Major asked.

"Listen here Major, you can't come into our home like this and make these kinds of accusations." Alexander paused while collecting his thoughts. Even though it wasn't hot in the room, he began to perspire.

"But are they paid?", the Major once again asked.

"Sir, I just told you that they are treated well. I pay them in kind. They receive food, clothing and a roof over their heads. Your charges are groundless, and insulting to my family and me. We're not on trial here!"

"Well sir, that's exactly what we're going to have here, a little trial!"

"You have no authority to do so", the elder McKenna said, his face flushed with anger.

"Mr. McKenna, we have the full authority of the government of the United States of America to investigate this matter. I strongly suggest that you and the members of your family fully cooperate."

Corporal Livingston studied the face of his good friend, Major Wilkerson. Looking into his eyes he saw a man that was about to snap. The bloody demons of the battlefield danced around in the whites of his eyes. Taking a deep breath, he waited for the Major's response.

"Sir, all of you have forfeited your rights by committing treason against your country!"

"All?", the elderly McKenna questioned. "My family has nothing to do with this matter. Take me back to the fort and try me if you must, but leave my family alone." He looked to put the responsibility square on his own shoulders. There was no more time for denying the allegations. It was time for him to protect his family.

"I've heard enough", the Major said. "Watch them, I'll be right back."

Major Wilkerson strode toward the front door. He opened it and walked out onto the porch. After completing the five-stair descent, he walked to his right where his horse was tied to the porch post. Opening the left leather saddlebag, he reached in with his right hand and pulled out a ten-foot long section of braided rope. He coiled the rope into a small circle and headed back into the house.

"Stand up and turn around!", he demanded of Alexander McKenna.

Alexander McKenna did as requested. He stood up and turned his back to the Major. Grabbing the sweaty right hand of the elder McKenna, the Major took the rope and fashioned a slipknot around his wrist. He brought his left hand to meet the right, and secured them both with a double cinch knot. After tightening the rope taught, he took the three-inch bladed knife from his belt and cut away the excess rope. He removed the blue bandanna from around his neck. Twirling the cotton kerchief, he reached around the face of Alexander McKenna and threaded it between his lips. Pulling back hard, he secured it with a double knot.

"You may sit down now sir", the Major said. He assisted him to a sitting position onto the divan.

"Please sir, please", Molly McKenna pleaded. "Is this really necessary?" She swallowed hard. "We're more than willing to dismiss the services of Samuel and Marcus."

"I'm afraid it's too late for that now ma'am", the Major answered, in a matter of fact way.

The noise of shovel blades penetrating the dirt continued to resonate throughout the house. All four holes had been outlined on the ground and the soldiers were about to complete digging the first hole. They rotated the digging between the three of them. Sergeant Blanks sat on a nearby wooden crate that he'd found. Every five or ten minutes, he'd turn his head to the left and spit a gob of brown, leafy juice onto the dirt.

Sarah, who'd been sitting quietly throughout this entire ordeal, now spoke to the Major. "Sir", she said in a begging tone, "I need to use the bathroom."

"Miss", you're just going to have to wait", the Major responded coldly.

"But I can't", she said, while batting her beautiful hazel eyes at him charmingly.

The Major thought for a moment. He relented, "Okay miss, but Corporal Livingston will need to escort you."

"Fine", she said thankfully. "There's an old pot on the bottom shelf in the kitchen that I can use."

"Very well Corporal, please accompany Miss McKenna into the kitchen."

"Yes sir", he responded.

Sarah stood from her chair and started down the hallway to the kitchen. The Corporal followed directly behind. She walked over to the cabinet beneath the sink and removed a copper bucket. Placing it on the floor, she looked up at the Corporal and demandingly asked, "Do you mind?"

"No ma'am", the Corporal replied, and turned his back.

Sarah faked the sound of wrestling with her dress. She scooted the bucket an inch or two against the wooden floor to cause another distracting sound. The Corporal didn't know that Alexander McKenna kept a pistol next to the pot. The Corporal loved his guns and knives. Quietly reaching to her left, she removed the revolver. Sarah lifted her dress and secured the gun underneath her corset. Smartly, she grabbed the opened bottle of wine sitting on top of the counter and began pouring it into the bucket. Corporal Livingston failed to recognize the deception.

After returning the bottle of wine to the counter, she placed the bucket into the sink. Again, she ruffled her cotton dress pretending to pull it up.

"I'm finished", she politely said.

Corporal Livingston turned to face Sarah.

"Thank you sir", she said, and brushed by him.

"You're welcome ma'am", he countered, while tipping the front brim of his blue hat.

The two returned to their positions in the living room.

Sarah tilted her head in an attempt to send a silent message to her brother. He saw her do this but was unsure what it meant.

By this time, the soldiers in the basement were digging the final hole. They'd worked up a healthy sweat. Tiring, their pace had dropped off dramatically.

"Let's wrap this thing up", Sergeant Blanks urged from his perch on top of the crate. He was anxious to finish this leg of the project so he could receive praise from his commander.

After they'd finished, Staff Sergeant Blanks led the three men loudly up the wooden basement stairs. After stepping into the kitchen, he extinguished the oil lamp and returned it to the kitchen table. Private Jenkins and the other two soldiers once again slung their rifles over their shoulders. They'd left the shovels in the basement.

"We're finished", Sergeant Blanks proudly professed to the Major.

"Very good Staff Sergeant", the Major replied, in a complimentary tone.

The living room was crowded with people. There was dead silence. After pacing like a cornered animal, Major Wilkerson broke the quiet.

"Let's review the facts", the Major announced. He quickly scanned the room with his eyes. "We've all seen the backs of these two young men." He pointed in the direction of where Samuel and Marcus were standing, motionless and speechless.

"They've been whipped severely about the back." He paused for effect. "We've heard from Mr. McKenna that these men were mistreated while living as slaves in the south."

Alexander McKenna tried to respond, but the gag in his mouth made it impossible.

"Mr. McKenna further stated that he bought the contracts of these two men in order to remove them from their hellish bondage. He'll have us believe that he brought them here to work the fields as free men. I ask you, where's the evidence of payment for their services? There is none. Not only is there no evidence of payment, we have two indentured servant contracts signed by Alexander McKenna himself." He walked over to the secretaire next to the fireplace. He picked up the two contracts. He pivoted in a semi-circle fashion while showing them to all in the room.

"So, we must decide whether these are truly free men or not." Once again, he paused for dramatic effect. Looking in the direction of the two black men he declared, "You're free men, you're free to go!" He pointed toward the men and then to the front door. Both men hung their heads, staring at the floor. Neither one moved.

"You can both go, go on!" Molly pleaded in a kind voice.

"Well, go ahead", the Major encouraged.

Both men shook their heads form side to side. "No sir", Marcus answered in a meek way.

"I must interpret this as a sign of control over these two men by the McKennas!" That crazed look returned to his eyes. The same look that Corporal Livingston saw earlier.

"As agents representing the United States of America we must find this family guilty of treason. Punishment will be death!"

"You can't execute all of us!" Benjamin blurted out as he stood defiantly. "My mother and sister had no knowledge of my father's actions. They're completely innocent of all charges!"

Corporal Livingston stepped forward, putting himself directly in the path between Benjamin and the Major.

Molly was now sobbing uncontrollably. Cathy stood as solid as a statue behind the bedroom door. Both Josh and Brea heard it all, but neither could believe their ears. Death, Josh thought?

"Private Jenkins!"

"Yes sir, Major Sir", Jenkins answered, as he came to attention.

"I need for you to get more rope out of the saddlebags. We need to tie the rest of these people up. On the quick step private!"

"Right away sir", Jenkins saluted, and then made haste for the front door.

Sarah knew she had little time to come up with a plan. The pistol she concealed was a Colt revolver. Thoughts raced through her mind. Could she remove it from her corset without drawing too much attention to herself? How many shots could she get off? It was imperative that the first bullet take out the Major. After that, she would just aim at blue and pull the trigger.

"Corporal, can you talk some sense into the Major, he's gone mad"?!, Benjamin said, pleading to the soldier that he felt might have some sway over the Major.

Still standing in a direct line between the Major and Benjamin, Corporal Livingston replied, "judgment has been passed and the sentences handed down. I'm afraid there are no appeals available to you or your family."

The front door flew open and Jenkins strode in carrying three long coils of rope.

"Here's that rope Major", he said.

"Very good Jenkins", the Major responded. "Start with the boy, then tie the women up as well. I want all of them gagged just like the old man."

"Very well sir", he replied.

Staff Sergeant Blanks stepped forward to assist Private Jenkins. Blanks grabbed Benjamin's right hand and turned him to face his father. Jenkins dropped two of the three-coiled ropes to the floor. He slid a knot over his Benjamin's right wrist. Blanks brought the other arm behind Benjamin's back to meet his right. Jenkins made a couple of spins and flips with the rope. It looked like he was roping a calf. Blanks removed the blue bandanna from his neck. He followed the same procedure the Major did with the elder McKenna. Reaching around him, he drew the twirled piece of cloth between his lips and then pulled tight. He applied a simple knot.

"Ma'am, I'm going to have to ask you to stand." Blanks said this in a half mumble through the chewing tobacco.

"You're a coward!", Molly screamed at the Staff Sergeant. She then spit into his face.

Blanks took his blue uniform sleeve and wiped it away. He pulled her up from the divan. After she stood, he shoved Benjamin onto the divan in the spot she just vacated.

Major Wilkerson stepped over to the secretaire in order to examine the indentured servant documents again. He did so in the arrogant manner of a cat that had just swallowed a canary. This was the ultimate power trip for him.

CHAPTER EIGHTEEN

Sarah stared at the Major who was standing no more than six feet from where she sat. She peeked over to her right and saw Blanks and Jenkins tying her mother up. It was now or never, she thought. She slowly slid her right hand down to her side. Ever so gently, she moved it up under her blue dress. She inched her hand over until she felt the cold, ivory grip of the Colt revolver. Private Jenkins bent down to grab another coil of rope.

Major Wilkerson straightened to an upright position. He was now facing Blanks and Jenkins. Blanks put the slipknot over Molly's left wrist and pulled it taught.

Sarah sprung to her feet. She rushed the Major. She saw the shock and fear written in his eyes. Things seemed to be moving in slow motion. He had no time to react. She raised the pistol and placed it flush against the middle of his chest. "B-A-N-G!!!!", the gun exploded with a deafening roar! The sound caused everyone in the room but Sarah and the Major to skip a heart beat. Sarah expected the noise, while the Major's heart had beaten its last beat.

Blood oozed out of the Major's chest and began to drizzle down the front of his blue uniform. His eyes rolled back into his head. The Major fell forward bumping into Private Jenkins. Instincts kicked in and Blanks dropped Molly's arm. He reached into his holster and drew his firearm. Sarah trained the pistol on one of the privates. Blanks bullet impacted the back of her head. A stream of blood shot out of the front of Sarah's head. She immediately fell to the floor. Molly ran over to where her daughter lay motionless.

"Oh my God!, Oh my God! Look what you've done!", she screamed in horror. She knelt next to Sarah and pulled her close. It was too late for Sarah. The other soldiers, including Corporal Livingston, pulled their weapons. Molly rocked and cried with Sarah in her arms. She was completely distraught. However, she did have the presence of mind to shift her body to conceal Sarah's weapon. The two McKenna men tried to stand and charge the soldiers. They knew it was futile, but at this point, they didn't care. One of the privates removed the rifle from his shoulder and jammed the butt of the gun into the side of Benjamin's forehead. Without hesitation, he did the same with Alexander McKenna. Both men crashed to the hardwood floor. This drew the attention away from the crying Molly for a few seconds.

Molly held the revolver firmly in her right hand. She let loose of Sarah so that she could steady the gun with both hands. Aiming the gun at Staff Sergeant Blanks, she repeatedly pulled the trigger. The first shot hit Blanks in the stomach, which caused him to spew his entire wad of tobacco. One shot missed, while the next two found their marks in his left shoulder and forehead. Blanks crumpled to the ground in a heap. Corporal Livingston aimed his revolver in the direction of Molly. He pulled the trigger three times. Immediately, she dropped the gun to the floor and her body slumped over the top of Sarah.

"Damn it!", Corporal Livingston shouted. His ears were ringing from all of the shooting.

"Did you hear that professor?" Terrance said, trying to keep his frantic voice to a whisper.

"Yes", Dr. Brammer replied. "Let me know if anyone comes out of the house. The Indians ducked back into the brush when they heard the gunfire. I'll keep an eye on them."

"Okay", Terrance answered. The gunshots took his mind back to being a twelve-year-old boy in Detroit. At that time, he was accustomed to it. He'd forgotten just how piercing the sound really was to the ears.

Dr. Brammer was right, the gunshots drove the Pawnee Indians back into the woods. He wasn't sure what kind of reaction this would draw out of them. In addition, the professor wasn't sure who'd been shot in the house. He prayed that his students were safe.

Corporal Livingston walked over to Blanks. He was dead. There was a pool of crimson blood on the floor around his head. His eyes were still open, so the Corporal bent down and closed them with his right index finger. He spun around and checked the two women. They were lifeless. Continuing on to the Major, he felt for a pulse. He couldn't find one. How ironic, Livingston thought. The Major was able to survive the bloody battlefield at Gettysburg's only to fall victim from a single gunshot of a teenage woman.

"Private Jenkins", the Corporal called out.

"Yes sir Corporal".

"Bring those two to me." He pointed in the direction of where Samuel and Marcus were standing near the Secretaire. Jenkins walked over and grabbed them. He escorted them back to the Corporal.

"I want you two to sit on this divan and not move. Do you understand?"

"Yes sir", they both said, at nearly the same time.

"Watch them Jenkins."

"Yes sir."

Corporal Livingston walked over to the McKenna men sprawled out on the floor. He now had the devil dancing in the whites of his own eyes. Still holding his pistol in his right hand, he leaned over and contacted the end of the barrel against Benjamin McKenna's head. Without hesitation, he pulled back on the hammer and squeezed the trigger. He did the same with Alexander McKenna. Blood began to pool on the floor around the two.

Josh covered Brea's mouth with his left hand. Sitting in the closet, he wasn't sure who was doing all of the shooting. He tried to calm Brea down the best he could. She was shaking. He found himself holding her with his right arm.

The living room floor was a red, slippery mess. Blood was converging in several different directions.

"You three men, I need you over here", Corporal Livingston barked.

The three men in blue uniforms carefully navigated around the blood and bodies.

"I need you to carry the McKenna bodies into the basement. You can rotate among yourselves so that the same two aren't doing all the lifting. Lay one body in each hole."

"Yes sir", Jenkins quickly responded. The other two shook their heads up and down in acknowledgement.

"Jenkins, when you have a body in each hole come and get me."

"Yes sir. What about the Major and the Sergeant?"

"We'll deal with them later. We'll tie their bodies across their horses and lead them back to camp."

"Yes sir", Jenkins replied.

Jenkins and one of the privates stood on either end of Molly McKenna. Jenkins lifted her by the arms while the other soldier lifted her legs. The third private made his way to the basement door. He opened it for the two. The two men slowly made their way down the stairs. Molly was very light. She weighed just over one hundred pounds. Carrying her to the second hole from the left, they dropped her body in. She landed on her back with a thump. Her eyes still wide open.

Marcus and Samuel sat silently on the divan. Neither one moved. Corporal Livingston holstered his pistol. He didn't expect any trouble from the two.

Over the next ten minutes, the soldiers carried the other three McKenna bodies into the basement. They'd rotated, carrying them as Corporal Livingston suggested.

Let's all head downstairs", the Corporal commanded.

One by one, they made their way to the basement. The three privates descended first followed by Samuel and Marcus. The Corporal was the last one down.

"Men, go ahead and fill those holes."

Jenkins and the other two privates walked over to the hole containing Alexander McKenna. Jenkins and one of the privates each picked up a shovel. They began the process of scooping dirt onto the bodies. The third private tamped the dirt down with his boots as sections of the hole filled. Before long, there was dirt over the entire hole. The two used the back end of their shovel blades to tamp the dirt down tight.

Cathy heard every shovel pass in the basement from where she stood in the bedroom. She was in shock. Her ears were still ringing. All of this could've been avoided, she thought. If only the Major hadn't gone berserk. It was her belief that the Major planned to execute the McKennas before leaving the fort. The war had changed him from being a soldier into being something else.

Jenkins handed his shovel to the next private. He stepped a few paces back as the other two soldiers continued to fill the next hole. It was Molly McKenna. He didn't sign on to kill women. Killing grey coats or Indians was one thing, but killing women. The Major had gone too far.

Corporal Livingston and the two young black men watched on in silence. Samuel and Marcus had no idea what fate had in store for them. However, after seeing what happened to the McKennas, both had an inkling that it wasn't going to be good.

Burying the McKenna children was the hardest. They, too, were victims of a Major who had gone completely psychotic. Corporal Livingston lost a dear friend in Major Wilkerson. He knew he'd been losing him for some time. His relationship with Blanks was not nearly as close. Still, he had to formulate a story for the base commander at the fort. One story that he couldn't use was the truth!

The last hole was filling up with dirt. The Corporal walked closer to inspect the graves.

"That's good", he said.

The men stopped shoveling. They carried the two shovels to the southeast and stood them up in the corner. After, they returned and stood next to the Corporal.

"If we all lift, we can carry that wine press over here and lay it across these graves". The Corporal said this as if they'd be carrying cotton balls. The three privates gave each other the eye. Jenkins wanted to get this whole thing over with as soon as possible.

The four soldiers walked over to the wine press. They tried to position themselves for maximum leverage. "On three", the Corporal said, "one, two, and three." They squatted and lifted in harmony. Each of them grunted and groaned. Slowly, they side- stepped the wooden beast a few feet at a time. They'd then set it down. Repeating this process several times brought them within five feet or so of the graves.

One more lift", the Corporal implored, while breathing heavily.

The men were all huffing and puffing. Each assumed his lifting position. Again, on three, they all lifted and carried it onto the freshly shoveled dirt. The wine press overlapped a small portion of the two outer graves. It completely covered the graves of Molly and Sarah.

"Good work men", the Corporal said, while catching his breath.

The other three leaned forward with their hands on their hips. They were trying to suck in as much oxygen as possible.

Cathy heard the sounds of boots climbing the basement stairs. The footsteps made their way down the hall.

"Men, we need to carry the Major and the Sergeant out to their horses. After we lay them across their horses, we need to rope them in. When we get outside, let's check to see how much rope's left."

"Yes sir", Jenkins and the other two replied.

Jenkins and the Corporal picked up the Major. The other two privates picked up the Sergeant.

"Be careful men, it's slippery in here", the Corporal warned.

The two teams of soldiers waddled their way to the front door. One of the privates laid Blanks left arm down so that he could turn the doorknob. He opened the door and re-gripped the Sergeant. They carried him out onto the porch. Jenkins and the Corporal weren't far behind with the Major. Marcus and Samuel stood and watched. They were the last to leave the living room.

CHAPTER NINETEEN

Patty Brammer lifted the lid on the white Maytag washing machine in the utility room. She pulled out a load of wet, white clothes. She turned to her left and dropped the bundle into the matching Maytag dryer. They weren't new machines, but they were reliable and efficient. Reaching into a white cabinet above the dryer, she ripped a sheet of fabric softener from its box. She dropped it on top of the white clothes that she'd just loaded. Turning the metal dial, she stopped at the forty-five minute setting. Closing the lid, she pushed in on the round sliver button located on the back panel of the machine. Almost instantly, she heard the sound of clothes tumbling.

It was now two forty-five in the afternoon. Patty walked through the kitchen and into the living room. Earlier that morning she'd carried up the Christmas tree and a large box containing the lights and decorations. It took her about fifteen minutes to assemble the tree. She grabbed the television remote and turned on the television. She punched in the numbers for a local station, two-one-seven. It was almost time for the Oprah Show.

Before stringing the lights, Patty always liked to plug them in first to make sure that none of the bulbs had burned out. She was pleasantly surprised to see all of them glowing. Unplugging the string of lights from the wall socket, she began the task of draping the green cord of lights around the tree. Her starting point was in the back of the tree near the top. She evenly wrapped the strand in a downward spiral until the male end of the plug was lying on the floor. Again, she plugged the two prongs of the cord into the wall socket. The sparkle from the tree lights made her smile.

Patty took a swig from the coffee cup she'd set down earlier on the end table. She was wearing blue jeans with a red sweatshirt. On her feet, she wore a pair of white cotton socks. She didn't like to wear shoes inside.

After setting the coffee cup down, she started filtering through the large box of ornaments. She pulled out a medium sized box that held six, blue, glass ornaments. These were among her favorites. Reaching back into the box with her right hand she pulled out a small packet of metal ornament hooks.

Brad Pitt was the guest on Oprah today. The two of them were having a lively discussion. It was nothing too personal, mostly about the current project he was working on. Suddenly, the television screen cut away from Oprah to a red background displaying the words, Breaking News.

"Hello once again everyone, this is Karen Adams from the two-seventeen newsroom."

Patty fitted an ornament hook into the ring atop one of the bright blue ornaments.

The female news anchor continued, "We want to get you updated on a story that we first brought you about an hour ago. Let's go live on the scene to Christy Simmons. Christie, what do you have for us?"

Patty stood up from her kneeling position on the floor and reached out to hang the ornament onto the tree.

"Well Karen, as we first reported to you, there are a group of people missing out here at the Old McKenna farmhouse."

"C-R-A-S-H!!", Patty felt the ornament slide out of her hand and heard it hit the hardwood floor. It shattered into about fifty tiny fragments. "Oh my God!", Patty shrieked. She felt queasy in her stomach. Missing people..... McKenna farmhouse.....that was Donald and his team of students. She felt a wave a panic flow through her body.

Patty blankly stared at the television screen as the reporter continued. "I have here with me Floyd County Sheriff Mark Preston." The cameraman panned back a bit so that he could get the Sheriff into the shot as well.

"Sheriff, what can you tell us about these purported missing persons?"

He looked into the camera as she held the microphone up to his mouth.

"So far, all we have is preliminary information to report. A professor and four of his students were conducting an experiment out here at the old McKenna place. Somehow, during their paranormal investigation.....he then paused...they all disappeared."

She pulled the microphone back for a second and asked, "Disappeared?"

"Yes, disappeared. We're not exactly sure at this time how it happened. They were sitting in the living room of the house in a circular formation when an unidentified light source descended upon them. Ten seconds later, they were gone."

"Gone, you mean as in an alien abduction?"

"We aren't certain at this time as to the cause of the disappearance. We do have several members of the Topeka PD who are here helping us search the farm property. In addition, the Topeka canine unit is on site. Hopefully we'll have more information once they've completed their searches."

"How long do you expect that to take?" She looked back into the camera as she moved the microphone toward him.

"At this point there's no time frame regarding the search. We'll do a complete and thorough search of this property. If needed, we'll extend our search to surrounding properties."

The news reporter graciously thanked the Sheriff for his time in doing the interview.

"You're welcome", he courteously replied. "If we have anything to add or update I'll let you know."

"Thank you Sheriff", she said. She then sent the camera feed back to Karen in the newsroom.

The camera lights dimmed as she made her way toward the van and into warmth.

The Sheriff headed east down the hill to the farmhouse. Two of the three Topeka PD cars sat in front of the house. The canine unit hadn't returned. He carefully climbed up the porch steps, avoiding the missing step. As he entered the living room, he saw Merle, Brian and the Topeka officers huddled around one another.

"What do we have so far?", the Sheriff asked.

Topeka Officer Green replied, "We searched the north and west ends of the farm and came up empty". He said this with a tad bit of disappointment in his voice.

"That's okay", the Sheriff positively responded. "We can eliminate those areas from our search grid for now."

"Officer Green, do you think Topeka can spare us three units around the clock tonight?"

"I'm sure that we can Sheriff. I'll call down to headquarters and make the request."

"Thanks", he said.

"Merle, do you mind taking Brian with you to round us up some coffee and donuts?"

"Sure thing Sheriff", the Deputy responded.

Sheriff Preston reached into the back left pocket of his pants and produced a black leather billfold. He pulled out two twenty dollar bills and handed them to Deputy Vickers.

Brian and the deputy went out the front door to his squad car. He started it up and headed toward the main entrance onto County Road.

"Sheriff, good news", Officer Green said, and smiled. "I got a hold of the Captain down at headquarters and he said the three around the clock units should work out okay. If something does come up he may need to pull one of the units for a period of time."

"That's great", Sheriff Preston offered back. "If possible, I'd like two of your units to run a checkpoint at the main entrance of the farm at County Road. Now that this has gone out over the television, we may get some curious onlookers. We'll need to keep everyone away from the farmhouse if possible."

Patty Brammer broke her mesmerizing gaze from the television screen. She picked up the television remote and pushed the off button. Her mind was racing quickly. She tried to organize her thoughts. It was difficult. She couldn't focus away from the image of Donald in her mind. What had happened? Where was he? She thought back to earlier in the week when he told her not to worry. She could still hear his voice speaking the words, "nothing has ever happened in the past and nothing will happen at this experiment either".

She hurriedly put on her coat and tried to calm herself down. "Everything is going to be alright", she said aloud. She walked back into the kitchen and grabbed her purse, car keys and garage remote from the table. "Slow down, everything is going to be alright", she once again reassuringly told herself. She started to cry, but tried to fight the tears. "Come on Patty, be strong", she told herself, and then walked out the front door. She closed and locked it behind her.

One of the officers signaled with his hand for the car to stop.

It did, and the officer approached the driver's side window.

As the window slid down, he saw an attractive, blonde haired woman crying. She looked much shaken.

"Ma'am, can I help you?", the officer asked.

Patty Brammer tried to get the words out but stuttered. Finally, in a frantic manner, she said, "Officer, my name is Patty Brammer. My husband is Dr. Donald Brammer who was leading the group of students in the experiment up at the McKenna farmhouse. I heard on the news that he and his students are missing. I need to see for myself what's going on."

"One moment", the officer calmly said. He took the two-way radio from his belt and pushed the talk button. "Sheriff Preston, I have a lady out here at the front gate that seems pretty shaken up. She said her name is Patty Brammer and that her husband was leading the experiment up at the house."

The officer took his finger off the talk button and heard the Sheriff's voice, "go ahead and let her through. "Have her park up by the house, next to the other cars. I'll meet her up here."

"Ten-four!"

The officer instructed Patty Brammer to drive up to the house where the Sheriff would be waiting for her.

"Thank you officer", she said. Patty took her right hand and wiped away the tears streaming down her left cheek. She proceeded to drive her Accord up to the house as directed.

By this time, Sheriff Preston had already made his way down the porch steps to where Patty Brammer was parking her car. She turned off her car engine and removed her seat belt. After opening the car door, she quickly exited.

"Mrs. Brammer?"

"Yes officer."

"My name is Sheriff Mark Preston with Floyd County. I'm in charge of the investigation and search for your husband and the four students. Please follow me up to the house if you will."

The Sheriff turned and started toward the porch steps. Patty Brammer was not far behind him.

"Watch you're step ma'am, there's a step missing."

"Okay Sheriff", she responded.

The two of them made their way across the small porch and into the house.

"I recognize Donald's equipment", she told the Sheriff.

"Yes ma'am", he responded.

"I want you to look at something for me if you will?"

"Sure", Patty said. She followed him to where the camera and tripod stood.

He pushed the rewind button on the camera and let it roll until the blue green aura passed. He pressed the stop button. Next, he pushed start. He motioned her over to the camera's viewfinder as the professor began to ask his question. She watched in disbelief as the swirling blue-green aura descended upon the group. In a matter of a few seconds, the aura was gone as were the five sitting in circular formation.

"Have you ever seen anything like this before Mrs. Brammer?", the Sheriff asked.

"Oh my Gosh no", she replied. "What happened? Where did they go?"

"We aren't sure ma'am, but we're going to find your husband and his students. You can count on it!"

"I sure hope so", she said, and started to cry once again. The Sheriff put an arm around her shoulder in a comforting fashion.

"We will", he reassured her.

Deputy Vickers pulled his patrol car up to the entrance of the McKenna property where the two officers were standing. The same officer that spoke with Patty Brammer just minutes before approached his car window.

The window started to slide down and Deputy Vickers handed him a box full of donuts. The other Topeka officer joined them. Deputy Vickers took two coffees from the tray Brian was holding and handed them one at a time the officers.

"Thanks Deputy", the two officers quipped.

"Thank you both for all of your help", the Deputy responded.

He slid his window up and began the short drive to the house. After the Deputy parked the car, Brian slid out of the passenger's seat carrying the tray with two large coffees. He looked down at them as he walked. He still saw remnants of the mustard stain on his brown jacket. Deputy Vickers held a box of donuts in each hand as he made his way up the porch stairs. The deputy held the front door for Brian who followed him in. They both walked over to where the Sheriff and Patty Brammer were standing.

"Mrs. Brammer, I'd like for you to meet Deputy Merle Vickers and Brian Foster. Brian is the fiancé of one of the students who was participating with your husband in the experiment."

"Nice to meet both of you", she said.

"Would either of you like a hot cup of coffee?", Brian asked. He held the carrying tray out in front of him and extended it toward the two of them.

"Thank you", they both said. Each twisted a cup full of coffee from its mooring in the tray.

"We have some donuts too", Deputy Vickers offered.

"Thank you, but none for me", Patty replied.

"I think that I might have one later", the Sheriff said.

"We've got the Topeka units on a twenty-four hour basis for now", the Sheriff said to his partner.

"Good deal", Deputy Vickers replied. "With all of this help I'm sure we'll find them soon." He said this in his most reassuring voice while smiling in Patty Brammer's direction.

CHAPTER TWENTY

*"It is an ironic habit of human beings to run
faster when we have lost our way."*

ROLLO MAY

"Did you hear that?", Dr. Brammer asked Terrance.

"Hear what?"

"The soldier's horses, they were neighing."

"Yeah?"

"They're also stirring around."

"Okay", Terrance replied. He wasn't quite sure where the professor was going with this line of questioning.

"Come over here for a minute Terrance".

Terrance walked over to where the professor was standing near the east side of the shack.

"Take a real good look over there. What do you see?"

Terrance did as requested. "I don't see anything", he replied.

"Keep looking", the professor implored. "Watch carefully around the tree line."

Terrance refocused his sight on that area. He still didn't see anything.

"Did you hear that crow call out about five minutes ago?", the professor asked.

"Yes", Terrance said. "But I don't see it."

"Look just to the right of the barn."

Terrance now steadied and noticed some movement in that direction.

"I think something moved".

"Keep looking", the professor urged, as both trained their eyes to the east.

"Oh my God", a startled Terrance exclaimed. "I just saw an Indian move between those two trees!"

That's what I saw earlier", Dr. Brammer affirmed.

"Look, that Indian has a black nose!" Terrance pointed to where the Indian was standing in the snow.

"He sure does", the professor agreed. "It also looks like he has a couple of black feathers sticking up out of the back of his hair. See the way he's directing the movements of the others. My guess is he's their leader."

"Look's like it", Terrance said.

"I think there are several of them. They're probably here to trade goods with the McKennas. When they saw the soldiers horses tied to the porch, they no doubt went into stealth mode. We need to be sure they don't sneak up on us.

"Right", Terrance replied.

Turning toward the professor he added, "We have to warn Josh and the girls!"

"I'm afraid we can't do that Terrance. They'll spot us for sure!" Dr. Donald Brammer normally had an answer for every contingency. He now, however, found himself with a helpless feeling in the pit of his stomach.

"Yeah", Terrance said. "What're we going to do professor?"

"I'm not sure yet", he responded. "But something is going to have to happen soon."

Terrance said, "If I didn't think it would cause a loud ring, I'd call Brea's cell phone."

"Wouldn't work ", Dr. Brammer said, like the professor on *Gilligan's Island*."

"We can't get a signal out here?" Terrance figured there wasn't a cell tower in range.

"No, that's not it", the professor answered.

"What is it then?", Terrance asked, with the look of a person who'd covered all his bases.

"The phone", the professor said.

"The phone?"

"Yes, the phone. It hasn't been invented yet!"

It finally dawned on Terrance that it was 1864 and not 2011!

"Professor, look". Terrance pointed toward the soldiers on the porch.

"It looks like two of them are either wounded or dead."

"Yes, and we're not the only ones watching", Dr. Brammer said, as he pointed to the southeast where the Indians were hiding.

The two teams hoisted the dead soldiers on top of their respective horses. They fashioned slipknots out of the remaining rope and secured each of them across their horse.

"Jenkins, go back and get their hats", the Corporal ordered.

Jenkins sprinted back up the porch steps and into the house. He grabbed the smaller hat of the Sergeant with his left hand. He walked a few feet further, then bent over and picked up the Major's hat with his right hand.

Brea was now tired and stiff. She and Josh both switched from standing to sitting some time ago, but now sitting in the closet was getting old.

"I need to stretch my legs", she whispered to Josh.

"No, he quietly pleaded with her".

Josh warned Brea they needed to be still and motionless. Brea didn't listen. She raised herself up to a standing position. What she hadn't expected was that her equilibrium was off. She lost her balance and fell into the right wall of the closet. Thump, the sound was audible to Cathy. In addition, Jenkins heard the dull noise and drew to a sudden stop. The sound came from behind him. His first thought was a mouse or even the wind. Why not take a quick peek, he thought to himself? Cathy heard the sound of boots walking in her direction.

Jenkins turned the doorknob and pushed open the door. Cathy held her breath as the door swung inward and covered her position. The soldier took two steps into the bedroom and looked from right to left. He stood still and listened for the noise again. Nothing, it was probably the wind, he thought. He grabbed the door handle and pulled the door shut. Cathy heard him walking toward the front of the house. Cathy, Brea, nor Josh moved a muscle. Finally, they heard the front door open and close.

Cathy made her way to the closet. She opened the door.

"What the heck happened in here", she whispered.

"I couldn't sit in that position any longer", Brea squeakily said in her own defense.

"Brea you could've gotten us killed", Cathy scolded her as a mother would her own daughter.

"Let's forget it you two", Josh interceded. "It's a non-issue. We need to concentrate on meeting up with Terrance and the professor."

"You're right", Cathy conceded.

All three were standing in the bedroom. Josh quietly closed the closet door.

"Let's sneak up front and see what they're doing", Cathy said, encouraging the other two.

"Not so sure that's such a good idea", Brea said.

"It's risky", Josh added.

Cathy shook her head and flipped her bangs back with her right hand. "If someone comes, we can always run back in here or downstairs."

Josh and Brea stood silently.

"Okay, I'll go up there by myself. I don't need you two chickens to tag along."

Cathy opened the door and made her way to the front window. She saw the soldiers making their last rope ties on the two dead men draped over their horses. Out of the right corner of her eye, she caught the sight of something she wasn't expecting. She saw one of the Pawnee braves scampering between two trees.

She hurried back to the bedroom to summon Brea and Josh.

"Come on you guys, you need to see this." Cathy called for Josh and Brea to join her at the window. The two slowly made their way to the window. Cathy then pointed toward the big barn and asked Brea and Josh to watch.

"I don't see anything, Brea said.

"I do", Josh said. I just saw an Indian over by that clump of trees.

"What?" Brea asked in disbelief.

"I saw an Indian. Look at the trees directly across from the barn."

Brea focused and saw the Pawnee Indian.

"Oh my God, she exclaimed!" We need to get Terrance and the professor in here now so we can try to summon up that blue-green orb. We may not have another chance. One of us will need to sneak onto the porch and signal them."

We can't".

Why not Cathy", Brea asked.

"Between the soldiers and the Indians someone will see them running up to the house from the shack."

"You said earlier that taking a chance was our best chance."

"Forget what I said earlier. This is way too risky."

"I agree", Josh added. "Besides, look what the soldiers are doing."

Brea and Cathy refocused their sites on the soldiers. They couldn't believe what they saw. Two of the privates were stringing ropes over the branch of an oak tree. Two ropes with a noose each dangled side by side.

The hanging branch was about ten feet above the ground. "Look girls", Josh said. "The two black men have their hands tied behind their backs."

"Oh my God!", Brea gasped. "They have two large sections of tree below the ropes. Both tree sections are standing upright."

Terrance and the professor were watching the same horror, only from a slightly different angle. The Pawnee leader was starting to sneak closer to the front of the big barn. The other braves were edging a little closer as well.

"Professor, they're putting those ropes around the necks of the two black men. We have to do something!"

We can't", the professor insisted.

This wasn't the tree in the back yard that the Major originally wanted to use. However, the Corporal was tired after helping lift the wine press and then the Major. He was ready to finish the task and make the trek back to the fort.

The two black men stood as still as they could on top of the tree blocks. All three of the privates turned their attention to the Corporal. They were looking for the signal to kick the trees blocks out from under the two men.

The professor and Terrance watched from the red shack. Josh, Brea and Cathy watched from their perch inside of the front window. None of the five wanted to watch.

An object flew from near the barn in the direction of the Corporal. At first, Dr. Brammer thought it was a bird. Looking over at the Corporal, he realized there was an arrow sticking out of both sides of his neck. The Corporal grabbed it and tried to pull it out. His effort was to no avail. He crumpled to the ground.

"Pawnee!", Jenkins shouted to the other two soldiers.

The braves were running at full speed toward them. Jenkins sprinted for his horse. The other two privates kicked the tree blocks out from under the black men. The two men dropped about three feet and hung.

Jumping up into his saddle, Jenkins never saw the tomahawk coming. It lodged deep between his shoulder blades. He leaned forward, falling out of his saddle to the ground. The remaining two privates shouted at their horses. "Get!, Get!", they screamed. They rode west as fast as the horses would take them. Four or five braves kneeled about fifty feet from the soldiers. Each brave had his bow stretched out in front of him and an arrow loaded in the string.

They let loose of their strings and the arrows flew true to their mark. Three arrows ripped into the blue shirt of one soldier. The other private caught one arrow in his chest and another in the side of his head. Both flipped off their horses. The horses continued galloping west without their riders in a ghostly fashion.

The braves dropped their bows and ran toward where the men were hanging. They drew knives from their waistbands and climbed up on the tree logs, cutting both ropes loose. They removed the ropes from around their necks. The men were motionless. The Pawnee braves stood over them in a semi-circular alignment. Suddenly, Marcus gave out a gasping cough. Thirty seconds later Samuel did the same. They were alive. They'd survived.

The Indian with the black nose and two feathers in the back of his hair approached the group. He surveyed the scene and called out orders to the other braves in Pawnee. Two of the Pawnee braves picked up the black men. They slung them over their shoulders and carried them toward the big barn.

Other braves ran through the snow where the privates were laying. They drug them through the snow and to the remaining horses. They threw Jenkins on top of his horse. The other two privates were piled one each on top of the Major and Blanks. They took the horse reins in their hands and headed toward the barn.

The professor and the students directed their attention to the black nosed Indian. He leaned over the Corporal. Although the arrow penetrated his neck, the Corporal was not yet dead. The Indian unsheathed his knife and cut a circle around the top section of the Corporal's scalp. The Corporal let out a blood-curdling scream. The black nosed Indian grabbed the bloody hair of the Corporal and held it high in his left hand. The Pawnee mimicked the Corporals blood-curdling scream. He attached the Corporal's hair to his belt. The other braves brought the horses around. The Corporal had no life left in him. They lifted his limp body and threw it on top of Jenkins.

They all made their way toward the big barn. Two braves opened the large wooden doors. They threw the soldiers bodies into the barn. One of the braves used a flint stone to try to start a fire in a pile of hay. He was able to create a spark, making the dry hay flame. Another brave shut the doors. The barn was fully engaged in flames. The Indians danced around the burning barn.

"This is our chance", the professor whispered to Terrance.

Before Terrance could give his opinion, Dr. Brammer started running toward the porch. He tried to stay low to the ground. Terrance was just leaving the side of the shack as the professor approached the front porch. Cathy opened the door. Brea and Josh encouraged the professor.

Terrance started to climb the porch steps. Reaching the next to top step, he slipped and fell. The motion and sound of his fall against the wooden porch step caught the attention of the Pawnee leader. Pulling his bow from over his shoulder, he drew an arrow from his quill. He aimed quickly and let the arrow fly. Terrance regained his footing on the porch. He felt an intense burning sensation in his right calf. Looking down, he saw an arrow sticking out of his leg. Josh and the professor ran across the porch to the top stair. They dragged Terrance inside of the house. The Pawnee leader gave out a yell. He raced toward the house. Other Pawnee braves joined him in the chase. They were all loudly screaming a war cry!

"Girls, take your positions around the circle!" , Dr.Brammer yelled out with angst.

Cathy and Brea dashed for their spots. Brea was the first to reach her spot and quickly sat down. Cathy reached her spot but slipped on a pool of blood once belonging to Staff Sergeant Blanks. Her feet went out from under her and she landed on her rear. Both her boots and jeans were blotched in red crimson. Not hesitating, she quickly scooted toward the perimeter of the circle.

Terrance loudly moaned as Josh and the professor dragged him between Cathy and Brea. His face grimaced in pain. Brea saw the arrow sticking out of his right leg for the first time.

"Oh my God!", she screamed.

The moment seemed surreal to Brea. Just three days earlier, all four of them were having a beer down at Bruno's. The blood was beginning to soak through the dark sweatpants that Terrance was wearing. His breathing became shallow and labored.

"Hang in there Terrance", the professor urged. This was no longer an experiment, he thought, this was a nightmare.

Josh and the professor assembled Terrance into an upright position. "Grab his hands and hold him up girls", Dr. Brammer instructed. Brea and Cathy grabbed a hand each trying to balance Terrance. Josh ran behind Brea to his position in the circle. The professor trailed right behind. Josh dropped to the floor into a sitting position. He took his left hand and connected it with Brea's right.

Donald Brammer reached down onto the surface of the secretaire and snatched up the two indentured servant contracts. In nearly the same motion as taking his position, he slid the two papers underneath his green sweatshirt. Cathy and Josh each reached out and took a hand of the professor. Terrance was screaming and writhing in pain. This, however, was muffled by the high-pitched screams of the Pawnee warriors nearing the house.

From his sitting position, Dr. Brammer saw the braves approaching. They were about thirty feet or so from the porch. He saw the leader's face, the one with the black nose. There was intense rage on his face. The black nose intensified his dark, piercing, brown eyes.

All five were holding hands around the circle. Most of the connected arms were shaking with fear. The two girls did their best to steady Terrance. Brea and Josh closed their eyes. Dr. Brammer said a prayer to himself. He asked God to protect his students and to forgive him for putting them in jeopardy. At this point, he wasn't concerned about his own safety.

The screams coming from outside were growing louder and louder. Dr. Brammer thought this must be a similar fear that pioneers felt when being attacked.

"Come on, come on", Cathy implored. She thought back to earlier in the day when the blue-green orb first appeared. At that time, she tried to fight it. This time, she wanted to embrace it.

A sudden jolt shook the living room. The house began to sway. The five of them once again felt the sensation of a tremor.

"Hang on everyone!", The professor was hoping to see the green-blue spinning light soon. There wasn't much time. He peeked toward the front door and saw two of the braves starting up the porch steps. The angry one with the black nose held a large knife in is right hand. He would later learn that this was the Pawnee Chief, Two Crows.

The Chief and the other warrior tried to steady themselves on the porch. The house was rocking violently. Professor Brammer looked up at the ceiling and prayed for a miracle. He could barely believe his own eyes. Slowly descending from the ceiling was the blue-green orb. It was spinning and rotating like a top. Brea and Cathy were both screaming and crying. Josh had a small tear in the corner of his right eye.

Reaching out with his left hand, Chief Two Crows opened the front door. It was like a whirlwind inside of the living room. The portrait of the grey haired man that hung on the wall sailed across the room. Much of the furniture was overturned. The blue-green orb was just above the circle.

Looking at the Pawnee Chief, Donald Brammer sensed a bit of uncertainty in his eyes. The Chief was no doubt expecting to see Union soldiers. He wasn't prepared for five people wearing unrecognizable clothing. The Chief took one step inside of the door, but it was his last. The blue-green orb was too bright for his eyes. The intense sparkles shot out of it like a giant fireworks display on the Fourth of July. The light and concussion from the spinning orb blew him back through the front doorway and onto the porch. Dr. Brammer watched as he knocked the other brave over in bowling pin fashion.

The blue-green orb was spinning at floor level. The five hung on to one another's hands with a tight grip. The two Pawnee tried to regain their footing, but were unsuccessful. They watched from a kneeling position as the brilliant blue-green orb spun out of the house and up into the sky. In seconds, it was gone. The shaking ceased. Gaining their feet, the two Pawnee charged through the doorway with weapons in hand. They were completely stunned. The five beings in strange clothing were gone.

The Chief looked back at the brave standing behind him. "Chingawa!" (Evil Spirits) , he shouted. The brave knew all too well what this meant. The two descended the stairs and met with the other braves who'd made their way to the house.

"Chingawa!", the Chief once again shouted at the top of his lungs. Looking past the braves, he saw the big red barn fall into itself in a blazing heap. He also saw that several of his braves were protecting the two young black men.

"Ban- co- check" (We must go) the Chief told them. The four made their way through the thin snow to the barn. The barn was still full of fire and generating a large tower of black smoke. The Chief signaled for the braves to put the two black men on top of the Major' and Corporal's horses. They were now part of the Pawnee nation. Going forward, they'd be treated by the Pawnee nation as one of their own.

The group of Pawnee warriors and the two black men made their way east. They headed back to their village along the river. It'd be just four months later that the entire tribe would march northwest to Wyoming. Chief Two Crows didn't want to test the power of the Chingawa.

CHAPTER TWENTY-ONE

"Change starts when someone sees the next step."

William Drayton

The blonde haired television reporter was getting restless sitting in the van. Her partner quietly read a Stephen King novel. She watched as the Topeka PD canine unit pulled up to the house. The officer opened the back door. Out jumped a well-groomed German Shepard. The dog followed the officer onto the porch and into the house.

"Anything?", Sheriff Preston asked the canine officer.

"I'm afraid not Sheriff."

"We really appreciate your effort and that of officer "Bo"."

"You're welcome Sheriff."

"Why don't you and Bo go home and get some rest. We may need you both again in the morning."

"We'll do that Sheriff. Say goodnight Bo", the officer said to Bo in a stimulating manner. "Ruff, ruff", Bo answered on cue.

"Smart dog", Patty Brammer complimented.

"Yeah, sharp dog", Brian concurred.

The officer and Bo quickly made their way to the front door and onto the porch. They exchanged greetings with Deputy Vickers as they descended the stairs. Moments later, the police car was heading toward the checkpoint at the front gate. He waved at his fellow officers and made a right turn onto County Road.

"Ma'am, would you like Deputy Vickers to follow you back home? It's cold out here with no real good place to sit."

"I'm fine Sheriff", she insisted. "I want to be here just in case something does happen. I'd be a nervous wreck at home alone worrying about Donald."

"I understand", the Sheriff replied.

Sheriff Preston, Brian and Patty Brammer stood along the north wall of the living room. It was very close to where Brian originally took his notes.

On the other end of town a telephone rang.

"No Finer Diner", Madge cheerfully answered.

"Madge, this is Sheriff Preston."

"Sheriff Preston, how are you?"

"Good Madge", he replied. "I need for you to do me a huge favor."

"Sure Sheriff, what do ya' need?"

"Can you fill up a couple of those large thermoses that you have in the kitchen with coffee for me?"

"I'd be glad to. Do you want me to run them out to you?"

"No, that won't be necessary Madge. I'll send Merle down in a few minutes to pick them up."

"Sounds good Sheriff", she said.

"Thanks a bunch Madge, I owe you big time."

"You don't owe me a thing Sheriff, I'm glad to do it."

"Thanks again Madge, bye".

"Bye Sheriff", she heard the sound of the phone click in her ear.

. "Marty", she hollered out toward the kitchen. "Can you find me those big thermoses that we have in the back?"

"Sure thing", Marty bellowed. He began to look in the lower cabinets under the sink. They weren't there. He opened the two wall cabinets next to the refrigerator. There he saw two large thermoses, one red and one green. Reaching up with his right arm, he lowered the green one and then the red one. Taking each in a hand, he walked them to the sink and rinsed them out. He dried them with paper towels.

Pushing the swinging door open with his body, he stepped to where Madge was standing behind the counter.

"Here ya' go Madge", he said pleasingly.

"Thank you honey", she said, as she took the containers from his hands.

"Sure thing Madge", Marty said, and then returned to his station in the kitchen.

She took one thermos and filled it up with regular coffee. She took the other and did the same. At first, she was going to fill one of them with decaffeinated coffee, but decided the situation called for full strength. After filling both, she screwed on the lids and set them down on top of the counter.

"How about a refill?", She asked the two men sitting at the counter.

"Sounds good to me", both salty looking men replied. Gil Cramer and Russ Zimmerman were long time regulars of the diner. Gil and Russ owned adjacent tracts of farmland. They'd been neighbors since they were kids. They both farmed the same land their grandparents did during the darkest days of the Depression.

Madge looked up at the clock on the wall. The time was two thirty-five. The lunch crowd had pretty much come and gone. There'd now just be the occasional straggler coming in before dinner.

"Breaking news, everyone!" Cindy excitingly said. Madge trained her eyes up at the television. Marty walked out from the kitchen to look at the television as well.

"Good afternoon everyone", the well-dressed woman said with a smile. "This is Karen Adams for T.V. 217. We have some breaking news to bring to you. Our reporter Christy Simmons is standing by in the field. Cindy what do you have for us?"

The screen cut to the shot of a woman standing in the snow wearing a large blue coat. She had a blue headband around her ears, which pushed up her blonde hair.

She raised the microphone to her lips. "Good afternoon Karen", the energetic voice boomed. "We have what appears to be a developing situation out here at the old McKenna place off of highway ninety-three. From what we've been able to gather thus far, five people are missing. As you can see behind me, the Sheriff's Department is on the scene." The cameraman panned above her left shoulder to the porch of the house where Deputy Vickers was standing.

"The woman behind the news desk asked, "Christy, do we know the names of the missing persons?"

"No Karen, police aren't releasing any details at this time. It appears that a search is under way. We're going to stay with the story and let you know details as they become available."

The television screen swung back to the woman in the studio behind the desk.

"Thank you so much Christy. We look forward to your updates".

The camera briefly scanned back to the reporter standing in the snow. "You're welcome Karen."

Karen Adams picked up a couple of pieces of paper and tapped them against the top of the desk. "Once again, for those of you just joining us, there's been a report of missing people out at the old McKenna farmstead. We'll bring you further details when they become available."

The screen flashed the words, Breaking News. Without a blink, Ellen was now dancing down the aisles in her studio.

"Wow, how do you like that?", Cindy uttered.

"It sounds a bit creepy if you ask me", Marty said.

"Yeah, it does sound creepy", Madge concurred. "There hasn't been anyone living out there for years. I wonder what the heck those people were doing out there."

"Don't know", Cindy answered. "I guess we'll have to keep an eye on the news for an update."

"The world has gone crazy I tell ya'!", Gil said. He was wearing a red flannel shirt tucked under his blue jean overalls.

"You aren't just kidding", Russ followed. I pray for the families of these poor people."

"I hear ya' Russ", Madge said in agreement.

Cindy was standing just to the right and behind the two men. She was shaking her head in agreement.

Gil, who was usually short on words, shook his head and commented, "I think either this economy is making people snap or these people aren't taking their med's?"

Russ answered Gil's rhetorical question. "People survived the Depression without snapping. I have to believe that there are more mentally ill people walking the streets than ever."

"I think that's it", Madge agreed. "It's scary out there."

The two farmers meandered over to the cash register. Cindy quickly followed them from behind the other side of the counter.

"How was everything fella's?'", Cindy asked, in her charming Midwestern drawl.

"Good as always darlin'", smiled Gil.

Cindy proceeded to ring both men up. Before leaving the counter, each man turned the small dial on the clear plastic toothpick holder. Each picked up a toothpick and placed it in his mouth.

"See ya' all later", Russ said. He and Gil walked toward the front door.

"You fella's take care. See ya' soon!" Madge said.

Thirty minutes or so elapsed when Deputy Merle Vickers pulled his police car into the parking lot of the diner. He parked in the same spot he'd vacated earlier in the day.

Deputy Vickers cautiously made his way down the neatly shoveled sidewalk to the front of the building. Reaching out with his right arm, he grabbed onto the oblong metal door handle and pulled it open.

Upon walking into the restaurant, a cold, chilling breeze followed him.

"Hey Deputy", Madge greeted him with her usual upbeat and charming voice.

"Come on in and grab a seat. Warm your bones for a minute."

The Deputy slowly made his way to the front counter.

"I don't really have time for that", he replied in his monotone voice. Taking a quick look around the diner, he saw that it was nearly empty. There was a group of five or six teenagers sitting around a table. They were laughing and joking among themselves. He figured school closed early because of the snow and that they were probably out sledding.

"I can understand", Madge said. "I saw you on television".

"You did?"

"Yes. You were on the news update. I saw you standing on the porch out at the old McKenna place."

"Yeah, I'm headed back there from here."

"That's really strange those people disappearing." She was now trying to bait him into a conversation.

"We don't have any answers yet", the Deputy said, in an attempt to cut her off at the pass.

"I'm sure you and the Sheriff will figure it all out soon."

"We're sure gonna' try", he answered.

Madge reached out with both hands toward the counter and grabbed a thermos in each. She slid them in front of the Deputy. After, she turned and walked back to the coffee maker. She grabbed a nearby stack of white Styrofoam cups packaged inside of a clear plastic sleeve.

"Here's that coffee the Sheriff wanted", she said.

"What do I owe you?", he asked.

"You don't owe me a thing darlin'", she said, shooting him a warm smile. "You just work on finding those missing people. Get them back to their families."

"We'll do our best", he said.

"I know you will."

"Thanks again Madge", he said, then picked up the stack of cups and two thermoses.

"Be careful out there", she wished him, as he turned around and made his way toward the front door.

"Will do", he lobbed back in her direction. Putting both containers and the sleeve of cups in his left arm, he pulled the door open with his right hand. Once again, this ushered in the cold.

Chapter Twenty-Two

*"He that is good with a hammer tends
to think everything is a nail."*

Abraham Maslow

"Did you feel that?" Brian asked a bit startled.

"Feel what?", said Patty Brammer.

"Feel the floor shaking."

"I didn't feel anything", the Sheriff remarked.

"I could've sworn I felt a tremor", Brian said.

"Probably just nerves", the Sheriff said. "We're all a bit on edge right now."

No sooner had the Sheriff finished his statement, Brian once again felt the house rock. This time the house shook a little harder.

"I felt that one", Patty exclaimed.

"I did too", the Sheriff said.

The house began to shake more violently. The two officers at the checkpoint felt the ground move, as did the reporter and the cameraman in the van. Deputy Vickers held on to the front wall of the house for support. Patty Brammer started to lose her balance, but Sheriff Preston helped steady her against the north wall. Brian was lying on the floor at the mercy of the rocking house.

The green-blue orb appeared below the ceiling. Brian looked up and recognized the twirling object from earlier in the day. It seemed even brighter and intense to him this time.

"What in heaven's name?", Patty shouted out.

"I'm not sure ma'am, but hold on tight", the Sheriff instructed.

"Okay", she said. Her voice was barely audible as the spinning orb was creating a deafening noise.

"It's the blue-green orb", Brian shouted toward the Sheriff.

The orb was twisting fast. It was dropping closer to the floor. The three tried to watch it, but the light was too bright. Sparkles were flashing throughout the room.

Merle Vickers slowly fought his way to the front door. He opened the door and was stunned. There was the blue-green orb that he saw earlier in the day through the camera lens. Only this time, it was real. The force of the wind from the orb blew him across the porch. He laid there motionless waiting to see if the tornado would subside.

"Did you see that?", the television reporter asked her partner.

"See what?" he asked, not taking his eyes away from the book he was reading.

"Over here Jim, damn it!"

"He lifted his eyes and looked toward the house. "What in the hell is that?"

"I don't know, but we need to get our gear out and get a shot of it."

Jim set the book down and ran to open the back doors. He removed the camera and shoulder harness. He flipped the camera on and turned toward the house. Adjusting the viewfinder, he zeroed in on the house. It was gone. He couldn't find the blue-green orb.

"Where'd it go?", she yelled out of the passenger's window to her partner.

"I don't know, it disappeared", he said, with the awe of an eight year old watching a card trick.

Deputy Merle Vickers staggered through the open front door and into the house. "What the ......?" He didn't finish the sentence. Looking around the room, he saw chaos. The Sheriff and Mrs. Brammer were huddled on the floor next to the north wall. He saw Brian sprawled against the east wall. To his shock, there were five bodies lying near the center of the room in a circular formation. He saw blood stains on several of them. It can't be, he thought to himself. There was an arrow sticking out of one of them. Blood was trickling out of the wound and down his leg.

"Sheriff, you okay?", Deputy Vickers called out.

"I think we're fine over here Merle. We need to check the others."

Sheriff Preston helped Patty Brammer to her feet. "Are you alright ma'am?"

"I think so", she said in a disheveled manner. She was now regaining her wits. Patty ran over to the spot on the floor where her husband lay motionless. She dropped down on her knees and started to shake him.

"Donald, Donald, are you okay?" Patty was crying hysterically. "Talk to me Donald!"

The professor slightly opened his eyes. He was extremely confused. "Patty, what're you doing here?'

"You were all missing", she stammered, as the tears streamed out of her blue eyes and down her cheeks. "We didn't know where you were. All of a sudden, a blue-green light came into the room. It dropped all of you down like rain from a cloud."

Dr. Brammer pulled himself upright. "Terrance", he yelled.

Sheriff Preston and Deputy Vickers were already standing over Terrance.

"Merle, run out to your car and grab the first aid kit. We need the tourniquet to stop the bleeding."

"Right away!" He quickly made his way out the front door.

Brian regained consciousness. He saw Brea lying on the floor near the south end of the room. There was a smidgeon of blood on her jeans.

"Brea, are you okay?", He called out, making his way to her location. He snatched her up into his arms. Her eyes were open, but she wasn't moving.

"Brea, Brea!", he screamed, gently shaking her body.

Brian noticed a twitch in her left arm. She was beginning to snap out of it.

"I think I just got hit by a train!", She said to him, with a dazed expression on her face.

"Thank God you're alright!", He smiled, while squeezing her tight.

Dr. Brammer stood. Patty was holding him close. She was still crying. "I was so scared!"

"I know baby", he said, trying to calm her down. "I'm alright. We need to check on the others."

Donald and Patty walked to where the Sheriff was attending Terrance. Terrance was moaning in a great deal of pain.

"My leg, my leg", he cried out.

"Hang in there son", the Sheriff encouraged.

"Here's the first aid kit", Merle said, handing the box to the Sheriff.

"Thanks Merle. Merle, call nine-one-one and get an ambulance out here as soon as possible." Sheriff Preston opened the medical kit and removed a blue strip of rubber. It was similar to those used when drawing blood.

"Professor, I need you to check on the others." All of those years of training for emergencies were now kicking in. The Sheriff took the piece of rubber and tied it around the leg of Terrance to slow the flow of blood.

"An ambulance is in route Sheriff."

"Good Merle", the Sheriff replied.

Patty Brammer checked on Cathy. She was sitting up, but clearly disoriented.

"Who are you?", she asked.

"I'm Dr. Brammer's wife, Patty."

"What happened?"

"It's kind of a long story. Are you hurt?"

"Just a little bruised", she replied.

Patty Brammer extended out her right hand. Cathy grabbed hold and pulled herself up. She remembered scattered details. The shooting, the bloody bodies sprawled on the floor. They were gone. It became clear to her that she was still in the McKenna living room. However, this time it was in the old, dilapidated one.

Josh was trying to shake off the cobwebs.

"You okay Josh?", The professor asked with concern.

"I think so professor?, How is Terrance?"

"They're working on him now. I think he's going to be all right. He's in a lot of pain though."

The sound of sirens grew louder. As the ambulance approached the front gate, one of the Topeka officers drove his car up to the house in an escorting fashion. The other officer stayed in place, minding the entrance.

All in the room now focused their attention on Terrance. Blood ran down the backside of the Sheriff's right hand. He had a firm grip on the right leg of Terrance.

Two paramedics dressed in dark slacks and light blue shirts entered the room. They were on either end of a gurney. They rolled it next to the Sheriff.

"We've got it now", one of them told the Sheriff as she kneeled next to Terrance.

"Hunting accident?", she asked.

"Something like that", the Sheriff nervously responded.

"We're going to need you and the other officer to help us lift him up onto the stretcher."

"Sure thing, Merle, you get over on his left side."

Merle quickly made his way to the left side of Terrance. The male paramedic grabbed hold of Terrance's feet. Sheriff Preston and the female attendant took one shoulder each.

"On three", the female paramedic barked out. "One, two, three!", She said.

Josh steadied the stretcher as all four lifted Terrance. They gently laid him onto the gurney.

"We'll need your help getting him down the stairs as well".

"No problem", the Sheriff quipped to the male paramedic.

Terrance groaned in agony as they rolled him over the front door threshold.

"Watch out for the broken step!", Deputy Vickers alerted.

Soon they were on the snow and at the back of the ambulance. The two paramedics lifted and slid Terrance in. One of them hopped into the back while the other closed the doors and whisked around to the driver's door. Siren blaring, they hastily made their way through the checkpoint and toward the highway.

The Topeka police officer who escorted the ambulance to the house asked the Sheriff, "What can I do to help?"

By now, the Sheriff caught a glimpse of the female reporter and cameraman headed down the snowy hill.

"Can you stop those reporters and tell them that I'll have a statement for them in a little while. I just need a little time to collect my thoughts?"

"Sure thing Sheriff."

The officer waved his arms over his head in a halting signal. "Stop", he called out to the two. They came to a standstill. The officer approached.

"I need for you two to stay back", he ordered.

"Can you tell us what happened?", The female reporter asked, in an inquisitive fashion.

"Ma'am, I have no comment at the current time. However, the Sheriff would like to make a statement in just a bit. If you go back to your van he'll let you know when he's ready."

"Okay, thank you officer", they both responded.

"You're welcome", the officer said, with a slight smile.

The two turned around and made the slow trek back to the van. The officer retreated to the front porch. He would use this position as his lookout.

"Is everyone okay?", the Sheriff asked loudly.

He received either a verbal yes or a positive nod from each of them.

Dr. Brammer spoke up, "What hospital are they taking Terrance to?"

"They're taking Terrance to Memorial Hospital", the Sheriff said.

"If it's okay with you Sheriff, my wife and I would like to be with him at the hospital. We want to make sure he's alright."

"That's fine", the Sheriff replied. "As for the rest of you, it would be a great favor to me if you'd stick around here and give a full statement. I'm going to need as much information as possible regarding what just happened. I know you've all been through a lot, but this is necessary."

"Does anyone have my cell phone number?", Dr. Brammer asked.

"I do", said Brea.

"Good, Brea, call me when you're finished. I want to make sure that everyone gets home safely."

"Okay Dr. Brammer."

"Merle and I will make sure that all of your students are returned home safely Dr. Brammer."

"I'd appreciate that Sheriff."

With that, the professor and his wife walked out the front door. They quickly made their way to the white van.

"Okay everyone, I know this is going to be difficult, but we'll go slow and take our time. Deputy Vickers and I will be taking down notes. I'd like for you to speak one at a time. If anyone has anything to add later, that's fine. Before we start, why don't we all take a minute to regroup? There are some donuts and coffee over there." The sheriff pointed to the west wall where two boxes of donuts and two thermoses of coffee sat.

"Thanks Sheriff", Brian said.

"You're welcome. The rest of you please help yourselves."

The group thanked the Sheriff and made their way over to the west wall. Brian began pouring coffee while Josh held the cups.

Cathy picked up a box of donuts and held it out to Brea. "Here Brea, you pick first."

"Thanks Cathy", Brea smiled.

Brea naturally went to the glazed donut with chocolate icing. Anything chocolate was her favorite. She took a large bite.

Cathy pulled a glazed donut from the box. She looked at Brea and said, "See, I told you it was going to be alright!"

"Yeah, you were right Cathy. I was so freaking scared!"

"We all were Brea. But I'm proud of you for staying strong." Cathy said this in a genuine way. She was no longer envious of Brea being Dr. Brammer's favorite.

"Thanks Cathy", Brea said, as she took another bite of the donut.

"Here's a cup of coffee", Josh said, handing it to Brea.

"Thanks Josh".

"You're welcome."

Josh rejoined Brian and they poured another cup full of coffee.

"Here ya' go Cathy", Josh handed her the hot cup of coffee with a warm smile.

"Thanks Josh", she said.

"You're welcome."

The two poured a couple more cups of coffee for the officers. After pouring a cup, Josh handed it to one of the officers. Each time, the officer thanked him.

Finally, Brian poured two cups of coffee, one for Josh and one for himself. They made their way to the donut box that Cathy was holding in her left hand.

"Here ya' go Josh", Cathy said, handing him the box of donuts.

"Thanks", Josh replied. He took the box and put it in between himself and Brian. Josh was hungry and the donuts looked good. He snapped up two glazed donuts and handed the box to Brian.

"Thanks", Brian said, accepting the donuts form Josh.

Brian chose a donut and walked the box over to the Sheriff and Deputy.

"Here ya' go Sheriff", Brian said, handing him the box.

"Thanks Brian. Why don't you all relax for a few minutes? Calm yourselves down. Merle and I are going to do the same."

"One other thing, Sheriff?", Brian asked.

Automatically, the Sheriff's mind envisioned a picture of him handing that parking ticket to Brian earlier in day. Before he could get a word out, Brian broke the silence.

"I want to thank you for all of your help, you too, Deputy."

"You're welcome", they uttered and nodded simultaneously.

"Oh yeah, Brian, remember that traffic ticket?'

Brian looked up at the Sheriff in a guilty fashion. "Yeah, I remember."

The Sheriff flashed him a huge grin and said, "Well, I don't!"

Both men chuckled. Even Deputy Vickers snickered.

Brian returned to Brea and the group. He wanted to get another cup of coffee inside of him. Like the Sheriff, he was anxious to find out exactly what had happened.

CHAPTER TWENTY-THREE

*"Free yourself from the rigid conduct of tradition
and open yourself to the new forms of probability."*

CARL ROGERS

A very light snow fell as Donald Brammer turned on the windshield wipers. He spun the lever located on the left side of the steering wheel. The wiper blades swung back and forth across the glass at their lowest intermittent setting. In addition, he flipped on his left turn indicator. Looking north and then south, he saw no cars in either direction. He pulled the white van from County Road onto highway ninety-three. Twenty minutes and they'd be in Topeka.

"Donald, what happened to you and the students? Where did you go? What did you see?" Just like the Sheriff and Brian, Patty wanted to know.

"Honey, I can tell you but it's an unbelievable story. I don't want to scare you." He knew this wouldn't be enough to appease her, but he wanted to try to soften the blow anyway.

"Tell me Donald. I believe you. You know that you can trust me. We've been together for nearly thirty years."

"Babe I'll tell you. I'll start from the beginning. Remember though, some of what I tell you may shock you."

"That's fine. I am a big girl."

"Okay." Donald continued to steer the van south. He kept it in the right lane so that faster traffic could pass on his left.

"You pretty much know the basics. The students and I set up the equipment in the living room of the run down house. We formed a circle and held hands while taking turns asking questions of the spirits. At first, we received a light indication, such as a tap on the wall. After one question, a white cat sprung from the darkness of the next room and startled us all. It came out almost on cue. Running around and through the group it hissed loudly. It eventually ran back into the dark room."

Patty was deep in thought listening to her husband. She loved it when Donald told stories to her. He had a knack for it. Her gut feeling was that this story would be unlike any other he had told. At least she already knew the outcome. Donald and the students were safe. Still, she braced for the parts that she didn't know.

"We identified the presence of a spirit. She said her name was Molly. If you remember correctly, Molly was the wife of Alexander McKenna." He shot a brief glance her way.

"I remember", she said. Donald had told her about the McKenna family during their Spaghetti dinner Monday night.

He once again focused his sight through the front windshield and onto the highway.

"Skipping forward a bit, I asked the spirit, Molly, did something bad happen in this room". It was shortly thereafter that the old house creaked and rocked. The blue-green orb came down from the ceiling. It was spinning like a tornado. The light was blinding."

"I know", Patty interrupted. "I saw that same blue-green light just before you and the students reappeared. The house rocked and shook just like you said."

"Well, the force from the object was intense. I've never felt that kind of gravitational pull. It was stronger than any roller coaster I've ever ridden on. There was a sense of lost time. The next thing I remember is waking up in the middle of the living room floor. Only this time the living room was warm and vibrant. The old house was clean and neat. It was wallpapered and the ceiling was neatly painted. I couldn't believe it Patty, but we were still inside the McKenna farmhouse..... Only it was eighteen sixty-four!"

"Oh my gosh", Patty gushed. "That's impossible."

"Normally, I would agree with you. However, this was anything but normal. All five of us regained consciousness. None of us was hurt badly. I asked Cathy to look out the front window. She told me that two women were approaching. They turned out to be Molly and her daughter Sarah."

"Wow", Patty said with amazement.

"At first, we all hid in the adjoining bedroom. It was the bedroom of Alexander and Molly McKenna. The room was small. There were no real good hiding spaces for all five of us. Cathy had a decent spot behind the door. Josh and Brea could possibly hide in the closet. I thought it best at the time that all five of us make a break for the shed if the opportunity presented itself." The wiper blades squeaked against the glass windshield as the snow began to taper off. Donald didn't mind the noise, it acted as a timing device for telling his story.

"What happened next?"

"We all tried to sneak across the living room. Just as Terrance was about to reach the front door we heard footsteps and voices coming down the hallway toward us. The three of us men made it out to this little shed, but Brea and Cathy had to run back into the bedroom. Eventually, they hid in the bedroom closet." Donald glanced out the corner of his right eye and noticed a thin, green, oblong highway sign. The top line read, "Topeka - 6". The lower line read, "Kansas City - 67".

"So, you and the two young men are in the shed and the girls are in the bedroom closet. Then what?"

"A wagon slowly rolled up the snowy hill from the east. Sitting in the front were Alexander and Benjamin McKenna. A load of tree pieces they intended to cut into firewood was in the back. So were two, young black men."

"The alleged slaves?", Patty inquired.

"Yes. Benjamin, the McKenna's son, chopped wood for a while as the two black men stacked it against the house. Alexander McKenna sat on a porch step and smoked a cigar. Fifteen minutes or so went by when Sarah McKenna, the daughter, came out onto the porch and requested that the men come in and eat. I knew this wasn't a good hiding spot for the three of us."

"Why not?"

"This was eighteen sixty-four and the young black workers wouldn't be allowed to eat with the family. I also noticed old blankets lying on the straw covered floor. It became apparent to me that the two men slept in the shack. No doubt, they ate in the shack as well. A trap door in the floor led to a root cellar. We could've chosen to hide down there but it would've been risky.

If the two men didn't leave the shack again after eating, we could've been trapped down there all night."

"What did you three do?"

"By now, we were all on the west side of the small shack. For some reason, Josh decided to make a dash for the back of the house. It was a risky move, but he made it.

"Good", she said.

"Well, not that good", Donald replied. "A group of Indians showed up from the east. They were near this large barn.

Donald and Patty saw the outlines of the taller buildings in downtown Topeka. They were getting closer to the hospital.

"How did Terrance end up with an arrow in his leg?"

"I'm getting to that sweetie. I'll try my best to cut to the chase."

Donald adjusted his sitting position behind the steering wheel. He continued.

"Benjamin finished eating first and went back to chopping wood. It ended up being the quiet before the storm."

"Storm?", Patty asked.

"Not long after going outside to chop wood, Benjamin returned inside the house. With him were the two black men along with six Union soldiers who'd shown up. From the side of the shack, we heard the boom of gunshots. I wasn't sure who was doing the shooting. I prayed that my students were safe. Donald took exit 3A into downtown Topeka. He turned right on Summit Avenue. The hospital was located three miles west on Summit Avenue.

"Anyway, the Pawnee braves continued to lurk around the tree line near the big barn. They must've noticed the soldier's horses tied to the front porch rail. My guess is that they were there to trade goods with the McKennas. The Pawnee didn't want anything to do with the soldiers. Like us, they became silent spectators."

Donald slowed the van to a stop for a red light. They were at the intersection of Sixth and Summit Avenue. The hospital was another six blocks. Patty was in awe. She was right. This was unlike any story that he'd ever told.

"Let me try and wrap this thing up before we get to the hospital." The light turned green and he lightly stepped on the gas pedal.

"Ten or fifteen minutes passed. It seemed like hours. I watched the Pawnee while Terrance kept an eye on the house. The front door to the house opened and four of the soldiers came out with the two black men. Two of them tossed ropes over the branch of a large oak tree. Another carried blocks of chopped wood to the tree and set one under each rope. Patty, this is the scary part. Are you sure that you want me to go on."

"Yes, I'm sure. I need to know what happened."

"Okay", he answered. "The soldiers put the nooses over the necks of the two black men." He could see her pupils dilating. She covered her mouth with her right hand.

"The Pawnee attacked the soldiers. One of them, their leader, fired an arrow. It went through the neck of one of the soldiers. The soldier tried to remove it, but couldn't. He collapsed to the ground. Two of the soldiers kicked the wood stocks out from under the black men. They dropped about three foot and hung. The Pawnee made quick work of the remaining three soldiers. In addition, they rushed to the tree and cut down the men."

Donald saw the hospital. It was just to his right. The emergency entrance was at the rear of the building.

"The Pawnee loaded up the dead soldiers onto their horses and walked them down to the big barn. Two of the warriors slung a black man each over his shoulder. The others followed them to the barn. After loading the barn with the dead soldiers, they set it on fire. All of them danced and chanted around the burning barn. I knew this was our chance. I made a dash for the front porch and Terrance followed behind me. Unfortunately, Terrance slipped on the snow covering one of the top porch steps. The Pawnee leader, who by the way had his nose painted black, noticed Terrance stumble. Pulling his bow from over his shoulder, he drew an arrow from his quiver. In a blink, it was sticking out of Terrance's leg. Josh and I drug Terrance into the living room. We all took our original places around the circle. Just before doing that I picked these up." He reached his right hand under the green sweatshirt he was wearing and pulled out the two documents. He handed them to Patty.

"Oh my God, they were slaves", Patty exclaimed, as she continued reading down one of the documents containing the words, Indenture Servant Contract, plastered near the top.

"Finally, we all held hands and prayed for the blue-green orb to show. Just as the Pawnee leader opened the front door, it appeared. Once again, it was very bright and rotated fast. It knocked the Pawnee leader back and into another brave. The next thing I remember I was lying on the floor asking you what you were doing at the McKenna place."

Donald navigated his way to the back of the hospital.

"Look", Patty said. "There's the ambulance". She pointed to the semi-circular drive beneath the "Emergency Room" sign. She handed the papers back to her husband. He stuck them under his sweatshirt.

Donald parked the van. He and Patty got out and walked through the sliding glass doors into the emergency room area. To their right, they noticed a woman sitting at a desk. She was behind a half wall. "Excuse me ma'am", Donald said in a rushed voice. I'm Dr. Donald Brammer and one of my students just arrived. His name is Terrance Bell.

The woman looked up at the professor. "Yes, Mr. Bell did just arrive.

"When can we see him?"

They took him straight back to surgery. The surgery should take about an hour. I'd allow another hour for recovery. My best estimate is that you'll be able to see him in about two hours. If you'd like to have a seat in the waiting area I'm sure that the doctor or nurse will give you an update as soon as possible.

"Thank you", Donald replied.

He and Patty took a seat next to each other. There were a couple of other people waiting as well. He took out his cell phone to make sure that he hadn't missed a call from Brea. There were no messages.

Donald fixed his gaze on the television hanging on the almond colored wall. It was a news update from the McKenna farm. He noticed an orange truck with the words, Wayne Construction on the side.

"Patty?"

"Yes dear."

"It's been a long day. Why don't I drop you off at home so you can get some rest? I need to go back to the McKenna farm and give the Sheriff our statement. Afterward, I'll swing by and pick you up. Terrance should be out of recovery by then."

"Now you want to go back. You're mind is always thinking, isn't it

Donald. It's always analyzing, plotting, trying to manage every minute of the day."

"Patty, I can't stop now. The truth's been waiting out there for one hundred and fifty years. It's time to unveil it."

To be honest I am kind of tired. I could use a short nap. It sounds like a decent plan."

"Thanks Patty." You know I'm not very good at sitting still.

She smiled and said, "I know."

"Donald, you call me. I don't want to be up all night worried sick about you."

"I will baby."

"Donald Brammer?", the nurse called out.

"Right here nurse", Donald said.

"I was told to give this to you. It's the arrow taken from Mr. Bell's leg. The Sheriff specifically requested that you receive it."

She handed him the wrapped arrow.

"Thank you nurse."

"You're welcome. Well, I need to get back to the surgery room. Things are going well. Someone will contact you when he's out of recovery."

The nurse smiled, turned, and headed down the tiled hallway.

Donald Brammer removed the cell phone from his pocket. He pushed the contacts icon. Scrolling down, he stopped at the name Chuck Weston. He pushed the green button labeled call.

"Hello", the deep burly male voice answered on the other end.

"Dr. Weston?"

"Yes."

"This is Donald Brammer, Psychology Professor down at the college."

"Oh yes, how're you doing Donald?"

"I'm doing fine, thanks."

"I've been watching clips of the news coverage. That was something out there at the old McKenna place."

"Yes", that's the reason for my call. I know that you're one of the leading experts in Native American Indian tribes of the Midwest. I also know you've been on several digs that found artifacts left behind by these tribes." Donald paused for his reaction.

"Yes", I've been on a few digs".

"Well, I have a big favor to ask of you."

"What would that be?", Dr. Weston asked.

"You mentioned watching the news clips today from out at the old McKenna place. It's my belief that the family was buried in their basement. The Sheriff and a group of construction workers are at the house as we speak trying to locate and uncover their graves. Your knowledge and experience would be of great value in identifying any remains found. Would you be willing to take a ride with me out there?"

"Sure, I'd be willing. I'll be glad to help in any manner possible."

"Good, thanks Dr. Weston."

"Call me Chuck."

"Okay, Chuck. How about I drive by your place and pick you up in about twenty minutes?"

"I'll be ready."

"That sounds good."

"I'll see you in a few. You know where I live, right?"

"Yes, you're about five miles south of me. You live on North Chestnut, correct?"

"Yeah, I'm at 516 North Chestnut, which is in the middle of the block."

"I'm on my way."

"Okay." Donald Brammer heard the phone click in his ear. He pressed the "off" button on his cell phone.

CHAPTER TWENTY-FOUR

"Difficulties strengthen the mind, as labor does the body."

Seneca

Deputy Vickers turned toward the Sheriff and handed him his note pad. Sheriff Preston flipped the already turned pages around so that he could start reading from the beginning. He quickly scanned the first page. It mentioned the blue-green orb. Near the bottom of the first page, two words caught his attention, "Civil War".

He stopped scanning and began to read more carefully. Next to the word, Brea, he found the following. *She awoke dazed and confused. Cathy walked up to her. She asked Cathy what had happened. Cathy asked if she was okay. She told her that she was fine, just a little shaken up. Shortly thereafter, the three men joined them. Dr. Brammer said he thought that they'd traveled through some sort of time portal. It sounded impossible. Then again, they were in the McKenna living room. Only this time, it was vibrant with life. There was even a fire going in the fireplace.*

So all of you woke up in the same place, only everything was neat and tidy", the Sheriff asked.

"Yeah, Josh said in his high pitched voice. "We woke up one hundred and fifty years ago."

"Why that's impossible".

"No sir, it's the truth", Josh insisted.

"You two young ladies agree?"

"Of course", Brea replied.

"That's exactly what happened", Cathy said in an unwavering manner.

Sheriff Preston shook his head and continued reading the Deputy's notes. He flipped to page two. Two more words caught his eye, "Union soldiers".

"Union soldiers", he barked aloud. "The Union Army disbanded in the late eighteen hundreds."

There was no reply from the four sitting on the floor. Deputy Vickers kept a solemn face as his counterpart continued reading his notes.

In the middle of page two, he found a section that sounded surreal. *Sarah held the gun to the Major's chest. She pulled the trigger and we all leaped at the loud booming noise. Blood trickled down the front of his blue shirt. He collapsed and fell to the ground. Another soldier shot Sarah in the head. Molly ran and held Sarah. She was dead. Molly picked up the gun and shot the soldier several times. The Corporal then shot Molly. They were both dead. The two McKenna men lay on the floor tied up. The corporal shot them both in the head. The soldiers dug graves in the basement and buried the four members of the McKenna family. They lifted and carried a heavy object and laid it on top of the graves.*

"Who's going to believe this?" the Sheriff asked incredulously.

"It's the truth", Cathy implored. "Anyone who believes in the truth will believe it."

He continued to read the rest of page two. *The four remaining soldiers carried the two dead soldiers outside. They also tied up the two young black men. After tying the dead soldiers across their horses, the soldiers took some rope and made two nooses. They hung the two black men.*

Mark Preston had read some bizarre stories as a child, but nothing to the extent of what he was now reading. He shook his head sideways a couple of times. He turned to the third and final page of notes. *An Indian shot an arrow into the Corporal's throat. He died. They killed all of the other soldiers too. Two of the Indians ran and cut the black men down. They were still alive. The Indians took the dead soldiers and threw them in the barn. After closing the door, they set the barn on fire. It burned and collapsed to the ground. Dr. Brammer and Terrance made a dash from the shack to the house. The professor made it fine but Terrance slipped. The angry looking Indian with the black nose shot him with an arrow. We dragged him inside and then formed a circle. The blue-green orb brought us back.*

"This is how Terrance got the arrow in his leg?", the Sheriff asked.

They shook their heads up and down.

"Not possible", he said. There haven't been any American Indian tribes in these parts since the Pawnee left. That was just after the Civil War."

Deputy Vickers looked at the four of them and said, "Do you all know what perjury is? There are laws against perjury."

"We know what perjury is", Brea shot back. "You can believe us or not. But that's what happened."

Sheriff Preston paced the floor a bit. "Okay, we have your statements for now. I'm going to ask Deputy Vickers to drive you back to your homes. We may have some further questions for you later."

They all nodded affirmatively.

"Sheriff?", Brian asked.

"Yes Brian."

"Is it alright if I take Brea home? I'd like to stay with her for awhile until she settles down."

"That's fine Brian. Also, I tore that little piece of paper up."

Brian knew he was referring to the speeding ticket.

"Thanks Sheriff."

"You're welcome Brian."

Brea shot Brian an inquisitive look.

"I'll tell you about it on the way home", he said.

Josh and Cathy stood and followed Deputy Vickers to the front door.

"Call me Cathy", Brea shouted.

"I will", Cathy replied.

"Do you need us to stay Sheriff?" Brian asked.

"No, that won't be necessary. Take your time and be careful driving home."

"Yes sir", Brian politely responded.

He and Brea walked across the scuffed wooden floor and out the front door. Sheriff Preston found himself standing alone in the living room. There's one more thing that I need to do, he thought to himself.

Plucking the flashlight from the right side of his belt, he made his way down the narrow hallway. He saw a doorway to his left. It appeared to him that the door had been missing for many years. Shining his light into the darkness, he noticed an old set of stairs leading down. Cautiously, he navigated his way into the basement. It stunk. Years of rot and neglect filled the air.

It also smelled as though several varieties of animals now called the basement home. He pointed his light toward the east wall. Various items of trash and other long-ago abandoned items strewn about the wall. Then he saw it. It looked like a giant soapbox derby wreck. Even in its advanced state of decomposition, he could clearly identify the wooden creature. It was a wine press!

Brian Foster slowly turned his red Mustang into the apartment complex parking lot. He found a spot close to Brea's unit. After shutting off the engine, he quickly made his way around the back of the car. Brian opened the passenger door for Brea.

"Thanks", she said in her high-pitched squeaky voice.

"Sure babe", he replied.

He wrapped his left arm around her small frame. They made their way down the snowy walkway and to her apartment door. She took the key from her front jeans pocket and inserted it into the lock. With a quick twist, the door opened. Both rushed inside from the cold. Brian closed the door and locked it behind him.

Brea took her coat off and slung it down on the wooden rocking chair next to the brown sofa. Walking into the kitchen, she flipped on the light switch. She tossed the key onto the kitchenette table.

"I don't know about you Brian, but I need a drink." She was already opening the kitchen cabinet that contained a bottle of whiskey and a bottle of rum. She reached up and pulled down the one with the Captain Morgan label. She set it on the table.

"Yeah, I could use one as well sweetie", he said. "I forgot my notes out in the car. I'll need them to write my article."

"Sure thing", she said. "I'll have the drinks poured when you get back."

Brian turned and made his way to the door and back out into the cold. Brea grabbed a couple of glasses down from the same cabinet that held the liquor. She set them on the table. She stepped over to the refrigerator and opened the door. Reaching out with her right hand, she pulled out a large bottle of Coke. She closed the door to the refrigerator with her right foot.

Brea heard the front door open and shut. She could see Brian from her vantage point in the kitchen. He turned the silver knob and locked the door. Carrying his tablet and pens, he walked to her computer and set them down next to it. He quickly removed his coat and tossed it across the room toward the rocking chair. It landed on top of hers.

Brian walked into the kitchen. Brea was filling both glasses with ice cubes from the freezer. She walked to the table and set both of them down. Brian walked up to where she was standing and held her tight to him. Their eyes locked onto one another. He leaned in and gave her a soft kiss on the lips. She tilted her head and kissed him passionately. Her arms draped over his shoulders. It was a long kiss. They both let out a deep breath as they separated.

"I love you Brea", Brian said, looking directly into her eyes.

"I love you too Brian", she said.

She picked up the bottle of rum and poured each glass about one-third full. After, she filled the glasses full with Coke. Taking a spoon form the drawer, she stirred both drinks.

"Here ya' go babe", she said. She then handed him one of the glasses.

"Thanks sweetie." He took the glass from her in his right hand. With his left hand, he pulled out a chair. He sat down and took a healthy swig from the glass. Brea did the same.

"I still can't believe what happened today", Brian said in a puzzled way.

"I can't either", she responded. "But it happened. I don't care what that dumb Deputy thinks."

"I believe you", he affirmed. "All of those people getting killed must've been horrible. Not to mention Terrance being shot in the leg with that arrow."

"It was", she said, and took another drink. "I didn't think we were going to make it back!" At this point, she started to quiver a bit and tears began to well up in her eyes.

"Its okay baby, it's okay". Brian slid his right hand on top of her left hand.

"Are you hungry?" he asked.

"I'm kind of hungry", she replied.

"Why don't I call and order us a pizza", he offered.

"That'd be super", She said, and smiled. "Can you order a dozen chicken wings too?"

You've got it", he said in an upbeat fashion. "Do you want mild or hot sauce with those?'

"Mild".

He pulled the cell phone from his front pants pocket. He flipped it on and tapped the contacts button. Brian ordered pizza often enough that he saved the number along with those of his friends.

He called and ordered the pizza. "Babe, do you mind if I use your computer and start writing my article?"

"Go right ahead. If it's okay with you Brian I think I'll rest on the couch until the pizza gets here."

"Sure", he said. "I'll be right over here at the computer if you need anything."

"Thanks", she replied. He sat in the chair in front of the computer. She picked up her drink and meandered over to the couch. Brea set the drink down on a small, wooden end table. She pulled the blanket from the back of the sofa down over her. The feeling of relief was instantaneous. Brea's head rested gently on the sofa pillow. She closed her eyes.

Brian began to look over his yellow legal pad at the notes he had taken earlier in the day. He picked up his cell phone and dialed Dr. Brammer's number that he took from Brea earlier.

Dr. Brammer's cell phone rang.

"Hello", he answered.

"Dr Brammer?"

"Yes."

"This is Brian Foster".

"Hey Brian, are you and Brea doing okay?"

"Yeah professor, we're doing fine. Brea is resting on the couch."

"Good", Dr. Brammer answered.

"Dr. Brammer, can I ask you for a huge favor?"

"Sure Brian, what do you need?"

"I'm preparing to write an article based on the events surrounding the experiment today. It's mostly verbal recollections from the students. I was just wondering if you were able to hang on to the arrow from Terrance's leg.

"Funny you should mention that Brian. The surgery nurse just handed me the arrow."

"Do you think you could take a picture of it with your cell phone and email it to me?"

"Not a problem. Let me get a piece of paper and a pen so that I can jot down your email address. Hold on a second Brian."

Brian heard a shuffling noise in the background.

"Okay Brian, go ahead."

Brian rattled off the email address to the professor.

"Got it", Dr. Brammer said. "I'll also send you pictures of the Indentured Servant Contacts."

"That would be great", Brian replied. "I really appreciate this professor."

"No problem Brian. You should have those pictures shortly"

"Super", Brian said, in an excited tone. "How's Terrance doing?"

"He's still in surgery but the nurse said it was going good."

"Good", Brian said. "I won't keep you professor. Thank you for all of your help."

"You bet Brian. If you don't have the pictures in your email within an hour give me a call."

"I'll do that."

"Good luck on writing that article."

"Thanks again Dr. Brammer. You take care."

"You do the same."

Both men hung up their cell phones. Brian felt more confident and energized. With the pictures of the arrow and the contracts, it would be much more difficult to dismiss the story as a hoax.

CHAPTER TWENTY-FIVE

According to the clock, it was now three-fifty. Vera shook her shoes on the small red carpet just inside the front door. The diner was nearly empty, but this didn't surprise her too much. The weather was bad and it was still early.

"Hey Vera", Madge said, while greeting her with a smile.

"Hey Madge, how's your day going?", she asked.

"To be honest with you Vera it's been a bit weird around here today."

Vera slid a hanger under her coat. She hung it up on the metal bar of the large coat rack near the front window.

"How so?", she asked.

"Well, earlier today the Sheriff and Deputy were in for lunch as usual."

"Yes."

"Next thing you know, I see both of them on the news!"

"What were they doing on the news?"

"I guess some people were missing out at the old McKenna place", Madge said.

"I thought that place was vacant?"

"Well, it is. But according to the television interview that the reporter did with the Sheriff, there was supposedly a professor and a group of his students performing some kind of experiment out there."

"That's odd", she said.

"Tell me about it", Madge followed. "I guess Topeka PD is conducting a search."

"These days nothing much surprises me", she said. "I heard on the radio earlier where some nut-job in a clown suit shot a bunch of people in Los Angeles."

"Wasn't that just horrible?"

"Yes", Vera replied. "Some woman and her young son witnessed the whole thing."

"I know."

Marty opened the kitchen door and made his way out into the diner.

"Hey Vera", he said.

"Hey Marty, how are you?"

"I'm doing okay Vera." He walked toward the fountain dispenser and picked up a glass. He hit the ice button and filled it. Tapping the black handle under the little square that read Coke, a stream of brown liquid filled his glass.

He took a sip and walked back through the swinging door to his private domain in the kitchen.

Madge stepped to the west end of the dining counter. Sid Hollister was still working on his bowl of chili. He was another lifelong resident of the area. He managed to survive the Great Depression as a teenager. He owned four hundred acres of farmland about five miles west of town. Using his age as a teenager during the Depression, Madge figured old Sid was around ninety. Other than not hearing well, he looked to be in good shape. He drove an older model Ford pick-up truck. There were signs of rust around the wheel wells. Heck, there were signs of rust around Sid. Sitting on the barstool next to Sid was a green John Deere hat. He rarely went anywhere without it. With the weather being what it was, she was somewhat surprised to see Sid today. Maybe he was just lonely, she thought. He'd been a widower now for nearly twenty years.

"You doin' alright Sid?", Madge asked in an endearing fashion.

"I'm still above ground", Sid blurted back. This produced a chuckle from Madge. Sid smiled and took a sip of coffee. He liked to use somewhat odd and funny sayings. On one occasion, Madge was sure that Sid had lost his mind. It was a rainy spring day. A slightly soggy customer came through the front door and stood near the counter, three stools down from Sid. He shook some of the moisture out of his umbrella onto the floor. He folded it and laid it on the footrest under the counter in front of him. Sid kind of sized the man up and told him that he had one fine bumper-shoot. He looked at Sid as if he were crazy. He didn't have a clue what Sid was talking about. The bumper-shoot, Sid said again, while directing his gaze at the man's umbrella. Sid made the hand gesture of a parachute opening up on the back of a racecar. "Oh umbrella", the man replied. Sid nodded his head in affirmation.

"Let me fill that coffee up for ya' Sid".

"That'd be wonderful darlin'", Sid appreciatively said to Madge.

Vera walked over to a booth near the front window. The man sitting there was dressed in black slacks and a black jacket. Under his jacket, he was wearing a black shirt with a white square covering his Adam's apple. He wasn't a regular.

"How're you today Father?", she asked, flashing him a smile.

"It's Reverend", he responded, as he raised his eyes from his newspaper and looked up at Vera. "I'm doing well thank you. The weather could be a little more cooperative, but this is December."

"That it is Reverend", Vera replied. "Can I get you a cup of coffee or something else to drink?"

"A cup of coffee and a slice of pie sound good. What flavor pies do you have?

Vera thought for a second. "We have Blueberry, Cherry and Apple."

"Why don't you bring me a piece of that Apple pie?"

"Sounds good, I'll be right back."

Vera turned and crossed the tile floor. She walked to the coffee machine and poured a cup of coffee into a porcelain cup. A refrigerated metal cabinet with a clear sliding door was anchored to the wall just left of the coffee maker. She slid open the door and pulled out the Apple pie. Laying it on the countertop, she noticed that one piece was already missing. Vera took a nearby spatula and laid a piece of pie on a white ceramic plate. She returned to the booth where the man of the cloth sat.

"Here ya' go", Vera said politely.

"Thank you dear. What's all the fuss about over there?" He shifted his gaze in the direction of the wall-mounted television. Vera followed his eyes to it.

"Oh my goodness, that's Sheriff Preston. I'll run over and turn the volume up a bit."

"Sounds good", he said.

Vera made her way behind the counter. She picked up the black remote that was lying on the stainless steel countertop. Something just didn't seem right about the man having coffee and pie. His eyes looked hollow. He seemed out of place. What was he doing at the diner in such bad weather?

Holding the volume button down on the remote control with her right index finger, the sound grew louder on the television.

"Turn it up a little more", Sid barked, from his perch on the barstool.

"Will do Sid". Vera watched as the green volume bar on the bottom of the television screen filled in further to the right.

"That's good", Sid bellowed.

Sitting behind the news desk was the well-dressed news anchorwoman from earlier in the day. The bottom of the screen carried the banner, "Breaking News".

"Good afternoon everyone, this is Karen Adams from the "217" news desk. We want to bring you an update regarding a story that aired earlier. There are five people reported missing at the old McKenna farmhouse. Let's go live on the scene to Christy Simmons. Christy, what do you have for us?"

The television camera cut away from the anchorwoman to a young female reporter. She was standing a distance from the old McKenna house. However, the cameraman was able to get the front porch of the house in the shot.

"Thank you Karen", the young, sweet sounding voice replied. She was wearing a large coat and had a sweatband around her head that covered her ears.

"Earlier, we brought you the story of a professor and several of his students that were reported missing. They were conducting some type of paranormal experiment out here at the old McKenna farmstead." She turned slightly to her right.

"I'm pleased to have Floyd County Sheriff Mark Preston standing next to me." Just moments ago, we saw an ambulance take away what appeared to be one of the students. Is this correct?"

Christy extended the microphone toward Sheriff Preston.

"That's correct. The Psychology professor and the students are doing fine at this time."

"Do you have any updated information regarding the injury to the student?"

"I don't wish to comment on that at this time." Sheriff Preston tried to convey a reassuring tone in his body language and facial expression.

"Can you tell us what happened?", The female reporter asked.

"As I said in my previous statement, earlier today there was an unidentified orb that seemed to pick up the professor and his students. At this time, we're gathering more details from the students and the professor. We aren't sure what the bright blue-green light was, nor do we know where it took them."

Everyone in the diner was watching the television monitor intently. Even the well-dressed stranger seemed to take a special interest in the proceedings.

"The Sheriff sure does know how to handle himself", Vera quipped.

"He's a true professional and we're lucky to have him as our Sheriff", Madge added, with a sense of emphasis.

"Damn right!" Sid loudly confirmed. I've known Mark since he was a little boy. He's a hard worker. Smart too!"

"That's for sure", Vera agreed.

All eyes once again focused on the television and the young female reporter.

"Sheriff, do you expect to bring charges against the professor and the students?"

"Absolutely not", Sheriff Preston replied, with a choke of resentment in his voice. "These people were conducting a class experiment. They had the full permission of the current owners. No one is being investigated at this time."

"Can you give us an estimate as to when you might be finished interviewing the students."

"We have no set time table. We plan to take as much time as needed to gather all of the details for our investigation."

"Well, I want to thank you for your time Sheriff."

"You're very welcome". The Sheriff turned from the reporter and started to walk back to the house.

"There you have it Karen", the young reporter said, looking directly into the camera lens. She had a glimmer in her eye.

"Thank you so much Christie for your report. We look forward to any future updates that you may bring us." The anchorwoman paused. "Well, it sure has been an interesting and unusual day out at the old McKenna farmstead. Please stay tuned to "217" news for developing details", she said.

The camera shot faded out and local broadcasting resumed.

Madge grabbed the remote and turned the volume down.

"Something just doesn't seem right about those people being out at the old McKenna place", Sid said, in his usual booming voice. "There were rumors about the McKennas when I was a boy."

"Come on Sid, everyone is aware of the tall tales regarding the McKennas. It's the past and nobody knows for sure what happened to them. Let's not get all worked up over it".

Sid Hollister took his last sip of coffee. He picked up the check and started toward the cash register. "I'm not going to say anything Madge. Everyone has their own opinion and theory regarding the McKennas."

"I agree one hundred percent." She took the green and white slip of paper from his hand. "That'll be three dollars and forty-two cents please."

He reached into his back left pants pocket and pulled out an old leather wallet. His hand trembled slightly as he opened it long ways. Sid licked the ends of his right thumb and index fingers in order to get a better grip on the green bills. Madge watched astonishingly as he thumbed nonchalantly past several one hundred dollar bills. Finally, he plucked out a five-dollar bill. The bill was new and crisp. "Here's a brand new Lincoln for you!", he chuckled, handing Madge the bill with the portrait of President Abraham Lincoln.

She tried to work up a not so phony sounding laugh. This wasn't the first time, or the second, or the third time that he'd used this line. It probably wouldn't be the last either, she thought.

"Sure is a shiny new Lincoln", she said, in a patronizing way.

"You keep the rest Madgey". Madgey was his pet nickname for her.

"Thank you much", Madge said and smiled at him. "You be darn careful out there in this weather."

A grin came across his face. "At my age, I have to be darn careful about everything I do."

Sid twisted the toothpick holder and snatched the little pointed wooden object from the clear plastic tray.

"She ya' all later", he said, as he turned his back and began a slow shuffle to the front door.

Vera went to check on the Reverend who'd ordered the Apple pie and coffee earlier.

"How's the pie?", she asked.

"It's wonderful", he replied. He reached out with the fork in his hand to take another bite. As he did so, his jacket sleeve shortened up a bit. Vera noticed a faded looking tattoo on the back of his wrist.

"Army?" she asked, looking at his arm.

"Yes, Cavalry."

"Wow, I didn't know the Cavalry still existed."

He finished the next bite and focused his steely eyes upon Vera's. He didn't say a word. This made Vera feel very uncomfortable.

"Okay", she said. "I'm going to leave you the check for when you're ready. If you need anything else just holler. My name's Vera."

"I'll do that Vera", he said, half-grinning back at her.

Vera made her way back behind the dining counter. Earlier she had an odd feeling about him. This last conversation only served to intensify it.

CHAPTER TWENTY-SIX

"Knowing your own darkness is the best method
of dealing with the darkness of others."

CARL GUSTAV JUNG

"Sheriff Preston, this is officer Dixon at the perimeter", the voice crackled over the hand held radio.

Mark Preston lifted the radio from his side. "Come in Dixon".

"Sir, I have three gentlemen in an old blue pickup truck out here. The driver claims that he owns the place."

"Send them on up to the house Dixon."

"Ten-four", the officer answered. He ended the connection.

Sheriff Preston hooked the radio back onto his belt. He walked to the front door and watched as the blue pickup truck approached. It stopped and three burly men exited the truck. They quickly made their way up the porch steps.

After opening the door, Mark said, "I'm Sheriff Preston".

The older man in between the two younger men said, "I'm Abe Cauffield, Sheriff. These are my two sons, Robert and Perry. I'm the owner of this property.

"It's nice to meet you Mr. Cauffield", the Sheriff said, as he gestured for the men to enter.

The elder Cauffield looked at the Sheriff and said, "we were watchin' the news earlier today and it looked like all hell was breakin' loose out here. What in 'tarnation is goin' on?"

"Well, there was an incident that happened with that group of people who asked for your permission to use the house."

"Yeah, I remember signin' that paper."

"Some strange things happened. Those people are all okay, but we're still investigating the situation."

"I see", he replied, as he combed his straggly brown beard with his left hand.

"I'm afraid that I'm going to have to ask you to sign another paper as well."

"Sign another paper?" He asked in a confused manner.

"Yes, I would like to have your permission to search the basement. We may need to dig around a bit as well."

"That's fine with me Sheriff", he said. The two young men stood like columns on either side of him.

"Let me write up a couple of sentences and I'll have you look it over and sign it."

"Okay."

Sheriff Preston walked over and picked up the tablet from the floor that contained Deputy Vickers notes. He tore a page out from near the middle. Quickly, he printed two sentences. The first asked for the owner's permission to search the residence. The second stated that the Sheriff and Floyd County wouldn't be held liable.

"Here you go", the Sheriff said. He handed it to the elder Cauffield.

Abe Cauffield didn't even try to read the words on the page. He handed it to his son Robert who was standing to his immediate left.

"Robert, read that back to me", he ordered.

The young man slowly read the two sentences aloud. He was careful to articulate each word. When he finished, he handed the paper back to his father.

"You got a pen Sheriff?" The old man asked.

"Right here", the Sheriff answered. He removed a pen from his shirt pocket and handed it to him.

Abe Cauffield took the pen firmly with his right hand. He was very deliberate. After finishing, he handed the paper and pen back to the Sheriff.

"Thank you sir", the Sheriff said. Sheriff Preston looked down at the signature on the paper. It wasn't legible. He knew, however, that this man's word was his bond.

"We'll keep you posted Mr. Cauffield", the Sheriff said, in a manner suggesting that the conversation was ending.

"I'd appreciate that sir", the elder Cauffield replied. The three men turned and made their way back to the old pick up truck. As the engine turned over a loud backfire kicked out of the tail pipe.

They drove to the front entrance. Deputy Vickers passed them in the opposite direction. It was no longer snowing. The sky, however, was getting darker. He looked down at his watch as saw that it was five-thirty. After parking, the Deputy climbed the porch stairs and entered through the front door.

"They're all home safe", he informed Sheriff Preston.

"Thanks Merle", he said thankfully.

"No problem Sheriff."

"Hey Merle."

"Yeah Sheriff."

"Does your brother-in-law still own that construction company?"

"He sure does Sheriff. The boom times are over, but he still manages to scratch out a living."

"Is he real busy this time of year?"

"No, can't do much building in this weather."

"Do you think he'd be willing to lend us some equipment and maybe a couple of his employees?"

"I don't see why not", the Deputy said. "Why do we need them?"

"After everyone left earlier I walked down into the basement."

"Yeah".

"Guess what I found down there?"

"I give up."

"I found the wine press!"

The Deputy's eyes lit up. "Wow, you found the wine press." Merle still wasn't buying into the students story. "Maybe those students found it before conducting their experiment? That would explain how it wound up in their story."

"I don't think so Merle", the Sheriff answered while shaking his head back and forth. "They didn't have any reason to explore the basement."

"I don't know Sheriff", the Deputy said with uncertainty.

"Do you think that your brother-in-law will be willing to help us prove the kids wrong?"

"I think so", Merle replied. "I'll give him a call and see what he says."

"Thanks Merle", the Sheriff answered. He patted the Deputy on his left shoulder.

About forty minutes elapsed when a middle-aged man walked through the front door.

"Hey, Merle".

"Hey, Wayne. Sheriff, this is my brother-in-law Wayne. Wayne, Sheriff Preston."

"Nice to meet you Sheriff", he said with a smile.

"Likewise", the Sheriff responded.

"I appreciate you coming out Wayne. What I need is for your men to excavate an area along the east wall in the basement."

"Alright", Wayne replied.

"We may need to move some debris from the area. There's also an old broken wine press that needs to be moved."

"Show me what ya' got Sheriff."

With that, Sheriff Preston led the men into the basement. "See that wine press over there?"

"Yeah, I see it Sheriff", Wayne responded.

"We were given information today that the McKenna family members might be buried underneath that wine press."

"Well, if they are, then we'll dig them out."

"Thanks Wayne."

"You bet Sheriff."

Wayne and his employees walked upstairs to retrieve their equipment. Two of the men manhandled a jackhammer down the stairs.

"Do you think that jackhammer is necessary?" The Sheriff posed this question to Wayne.

"We may need it Sheriff. That ground is quite solid. We'll mostly use it to break the surface area. The real digging will be done with picks and shovels."

"Sounds good", the Sheriff shot back. "If they're buried under there we want to try and keep whatever is left in tact."

"We'll be careful", Wayne assured the Sheriff.

The loud roar of an electric generator pierced the air. One of the men hooked a pneumatic hose to the end of the generator. He attached the other end of the hose to the jackhammer.

"I'ill be upstairs", Sheriff Preston yelled over the groan of the power equipment.

"Sounds good Sheriff", Wayne yelled back.

CHAPTER TWENTY-SEVEN

*"Confidence, like art, never comes from having all the
answers; it comes from being open to all the questions."*

Diogenes Laertius

Donald Brammer pulled his white van up in front of 516 North Chestnut. Daylight was fading and Dr. Weston had his porch light on. Donald briefly met Dr. Charles Weston at a couple of teacher conferences. He seemed nice, but a bit introverted. Then again, most college professors Donald knew fit this bill. The front door opened and out stepped Dr. Weston. He was wearing heavy work boots. Standing about five feet, six inches tall "Chuck" was a stout man. He wore a brown coat and a hat that reminded Donald of Indiana Jones.

"Hey Don", Chuck Weston said, as he opened the passenger's door to the van. "Some weather we're having."

"That's for sure. How're you doing?"

Dr. Weston climbed into the passenger's seat and closed the door. He reached over his right shoulder and grabbed the hanging seat belt strap. Pulling it out as far as it'd go, he stretched it around his plump waistline and clicked it into place.

"I'm fine. It look's like you had one dozy of a day though".

"Unlike any other day that I've ever had", Donald said, shaking his head. "I don't know how good the light is in here but I want to show you something." Donald Brammer merged the van onto highway ninety-three.

I'd like for you to take a look at this", he reached behind him with his right arm and grabbed the wrapped arrow. He handed it to Chuck Weston.

Dr. Weston meticulously rolled back the wrapping. He noticed blood stains on the wooden stick. The two, black crow feathers at the opposite end also seemed to fascinate him. Finally, he looked the wooden shaft over closely.

"Wow, he said in awe. "This is one fine handmade arrow. It looks a lot like some of the Pawnee Indian arrows we uncover on our digs. This arrow was definitely not purchased at K-mart."

"No, I can assure you of that", Donald Brammer answered.

"Where'd you come across it?", Chuck Weston asked.

"Today, at our experiment, one of my students was shot in the leg with it."

"It's hard to believe a hunter would be using this type of an arrow."

"It wasn't your average hunter."

"Really?"

"This hunter was an Indian."

"That's surprising. Not too many Indians left in these parts."

Donald saw the exit coming up on his right. The large, green highway sign said "County Road - exit 3A". He turned left and drove the short distance to the front entrance of the McKenna property. Donald lowered his window. A Topeka police officer stood next to his car. He walked over to the white van.

"Can I help you fella's?"

"Yes officer, my name is Dr. Donald Brammer. Some students and I performed an experiment up at the old farmhouse earlier today. I need to speak with either Sheriff Preston or Deputy Vickers.

"One moment please". The officer pulled the hand held radio from his belt.

"Sheriff Preston, this is Officer Peters out at the main gate."

The Sheriff removed the radio from his side and walked out onto the front porch. There was too much noise inside for him to hear clearly.

"Yes, Officer Peters."

"I have two gentlemen out here in a white van. The driver claims to be Dr. Donald Brammer. He said that he was out here with some students earlier today conducting an experiment."

Sheriff Preston saw the white van from his vantage point on the front porch.

"Send them on up to the house Officer Peters."

"Will do Sheriff", the officer in blue uniform instructed Donald Brammer to drive up to the house.

"Thank you officer", Donald offered.

"You're welcome sir."

Donald drove the one hundred yards or so up to the house. There were several news vans sitting up on the west hill. He parked the van and the two men exited the vehicle.

"Dr. Brammer, what brings you back out this way?"

Donald Brammer and Chuck Weston began to climb the porch steps.

"Careful of that missing stair", Donald warned the History expert.

After successfully navigating the five stairs, Donald extended his arm in a gesture to shake the Sheriff's hand. The Sheriff shook his hand firmly.

"Sheriff Preston, I'd like you to meet Dr. Charles Weston. He's a professor at the same college where I work."

Both men shook hands and exchanged pleasantries.

"Why don't you two gentlemen follow me", the Sheriff said.

The two professors followed Sheriff Preston through the living room to the basement door. The three men descended the wooden stairs into the basement.

"Your timing is impeccable", Sheriff Preston said. "Dr. Brammer, one of your students claimed that the McKenna family was buried along the east wall of the basement. How she knew that, I don't know. Anyway, we moved an old wine press out of the way and began to dig. At first, we used a jackhammer to break the frozen, top layer of dirt. The men dug deeper with pick axes and shovels. About thirty minutes ago we hit something solid in the far corner." Sheriff Preston pointed to the northeastern corner of the room.

"Dr. Weston, you may want to take a look at this yourself."

The three men walked over to the corner. A small pile of bones was lined up around the edge of the hole. The men were digging with hand spades in an attempt not to compromise the deteriorated remains.

Dr. Weston kneeled down to get a better look at the bones. He picked up one of the bones with his right hand and examined it.

"I believe this is a middle aged male", he said.

"How can you tell?", asked the Sheriff.

"This is the pelvis bone."

One of the men digging in the hole excitedly exclaimed, "I've got something for you Wayne."

Wayne Barnett stepped over to the man. He handed Wayne a gold pocket watch.

"Looks like this probably belonged to the owner of the house. My guess is this is the body of Alexander McKenna."

Wayne passed the watch to the Sheriff for his examination.

"Wayne, this is Dr. Brammer and that's Dr. Weston.

"Nice to meet you both", Wayne replied.

"Wayne is the brother-in-law of my Deputy, Merle Vickers."

"Nice to meet you", both men answered.

Sheriff Preston handed the watch to Dr. Weston. Chuck Weston looked over the round, golden piece of metal closely.

"You don't see these very often", he remarked. "It's an 1850's Verge Movement watch. The face is cracked, but if you look closely, you can see where a key would be inserted near the center dial." He took his finger and pointed to the spot.

"This is incredible", the Sheriff remarked. These people have been buried here undisturbed for roughly one hundred and fifty years. I'm not one who believes much in the supernatural, but the accuracy of the stories that your students told us are amazing."

"I was there too Sheriff", Donald Brammer reminded him. "This was a bloody day for all those involved."

"Check this out Sheriff." Wayne approached, holding a cracked human skull with both hands. It was missing a portion on the top front where the forehead normally would be located.

"Which hole did this come out of?", he asked.

"Third one down", he answered. "Look's like there are small fragments of blue material in there as well."

"Do you mind if I take a look at that skull?", Dr. Weston asked the Sheriff.

"By all means", the Sheriff replied.

Taking the skull from the Sheriff's hand, Chuck Weston examined it closely. Dr. Weston noticed a flat hole about half an inch wide on the back, left side.

"Judging by the entry wound, it appears that this person was shot with a large caliber weapon. My guess is a forty-four caliber revolver. Many members of the Union Army carried forty-four caliber Colt revolvers. They were six shooters. What made me think that it might be a Colt revolver are the pins above the handle. These pins held the stock of a rifle for longer-range shots. The larger stock steadied the aim of the shooter."

"I can tell you there were Union soldiers present that fateful day in eighteen sixty-four", Dr. Brammer said.

"How do you know that Don, Chuck Weston asked?"

"I was there", Donald Brammer said with conviction.

"That's impossible. These people have been dead for over one hundred years. The last Union soldiers died in the nineteen thirties."

"Well, these soldiers were very much alive. They had a vindictive purpose."

"Sheriff, Chuck, take a look at these." He reached under his sweatshirt and produced the two indentured servant contracts. Both men eyed the parched documents. He handed one to each.

"Oh my word", Sheriff Preston uttered. "You want us to believe that you brought these back with you from some sort of time travel?"

"I can't tell you what to believe Sheriff. I'm just showing you the documents."

Chuck Weston perused the contract in his hand. This thing looks authentic enough. It has the state seal of Alabama. I don't know if we have any other documents signed by Alexander McKenna that we can compare these signatures against?"

"Maybe in some of the old property records that the county keeps?, the Sheriff offered. "I'm not sure how far back they go, but it might be worth a shot."

"Good suggestion Sheriff", Dr. Weston replied.

"Well Sheriff, Dr. Weston and I will let you and your men continue your excavation. Donald Brammer reached into his back jeans pocket and pulled out his billfold. Inside one of the compartments, he removed a business card with his name and phone number at school.

"Do you have a pen handy Sheriff?"

"Sure do", he said. He unclipped the ballpoint pen from his front shirt pocket and handed it him.

Donald Brammer jotted down his home telephone number and cell phone number near the bottom of the card.

"Sheriff, if you need anything please call me. This has been a trying day for all of us. I think I need to get something to eat and then some rest." Donald handed the business card to the Sheriff.

"I understand", the Sheriff said. "It was nice to meet you Dr. Weston. I may have a question or two for you, depending on what we find here."

"It was nice to meet you to Sheriff. If something comes up just give Don a call and he'll get a hold of me."

"Super", the Sheriff said.

Donald Brammer and Chuck Weston made their way from the basement to the van. Both men climbed in from the cold. Donald started the engine and flipped on the headlights.

"This is incredible stuff", Chuck Weston commented to his colleague. "I'm afraid that I'm still trying to get my arms around the time travel part."

"Chuck, do you remember any of the Pawnee Indian Chief's names back around the time of the Civil War?'

"Yeah, there were two major leaders of the Pawnee tribe before they migrated to Wyoming. The first great leader was Sky Chief. He led the tribe up until about 1860. He appointed his son as Chief when he became old and infirmed."

"What was his son's name?", Donald asked.

"His name was Two Crows. Wait a minute, are you telling me that the arrow belonged to Chief Two Crows?"

"Do you have an idea of what he looked like?", Donald asked.

"Yeah."

"What if I could give you some unique detail of his appearance? Would that help convince you?"

"Sure it would, there were only a handful of photographs taken of Two Crows. As a matter of fact, I have one of only two books published that contain a photograph of him."

Donald waved at the Topeka police officer as he drove through the checkpoint. He made a right turn and drove to the four way stop. He looked both ways but didn't see any headlights coming in either direction. Pausing, he looked at Dr. Weston and said, "He had a black painted nose."

"Oh my God, only a handful of people know that", Chuck stammered. How could you possibly know that?"

"I know because I watched him shoot that arrow." He reached back and handed the arrow to Dr. Weston once again.

"Unbelievable", the History professor sighed. He took a closer look at the arrow. The black crow feathers didn't throw up any red flags the first time he looked at it. Now, he saw the faint etchings of what appeared to be four bird feet on the wooden shaft.

"Donald, are you familiar with the story of John Brown?"

"Vaguely Chuck."

"Since we don't have much time, let me give you a condensed version."

"That sounds good."

"Well, in the mid 1850's, John Brown and about twenty-five of his men showed up on the doorstep of a farmstead owned by a family named Doyle. The Doyle's were pro-slavery. Brown and his men gained entrance to the house and drug the Doyle men out. History has it that the Doyle men were hacked to pieces. This is where the event gets its name, the Pottawatomie Massacre."

"Wow, how awful", Donald replied.

"Yeah, it was a bloody time here in Kansas during the Civil War years. Most people associate the war being fought in the south, but some of the bloodiest and most heinous acts occurred right here!"

"Thanks for sharing that with me Chuck."

Donald Brammer made a right hand turn onto highway ninety-three. There was silence inside of the van. Dr. Charles Weston seemed to be at a loss for words.

"So the Union soldiers killed the McKennas because they owned slaves?"

"Yes, Donald Brammer replied." Alexander McKenna purchased the indentured servant contracts of the two men without the knowledge of his family. He treated them for all outward appearances as if they were paid labor. Some of the residents caught wind of his buying the contracts. They informed the Union soldiers. The soldiers who came out to the McKenna place that day sought vengeance. Many of the soldiers that they'd fought side by side with died on the bloody battlefields. They were so adamant about stomping out slavery that they lost control when they found the contracts. All four members of the McKenna family were executed."

Donald made a left on North Chestnut. Dr. Weston lived two blocks down.

"So why did the Chief shoot an arrow into your students leg?"

"To make a long story short, he and I were hiding outside of a little red shack. The Pawnee burned down a big barn with the soldiers bodies in it. They were dancing and chanting around the fire. It was a chance for us to reunite with the other three students in the house and try to recreate the time portal. I made it up the porch okay, but Terrance slipped on the next stair from the top. Chief Two Crows caught this out of the corner of his eye. He instantly reached back in his quiver for an arrow and launched it toward Terrance. It hit him in the back of the leg."

The van was pulling up in front of Dr. Weston's house.

"How'd you escape the Pawnee attack?"

Donald Brammer parked the van, but left the engine running.

"Just before Chief Two Crows and one of his braves reached the living room, the blue-green orb brought us forward in time."

"Thanks for bringing me in on this one", Chuck Weston said. Do you mind if I hold on to this arrow for a bit. I'd like to do some research on it if I can?"

"Donald Brammer smiled as he made direct eye contact with his History counterpart. "You keep it!""

Chapter Twenty-Eight

"A pessimist sees the difficulty in every opportunity;
an optimist sees the opportunity in every difficulty."

Winston Churchill

Donald Brammer and his wife Patty returned to the hospital and sat in chairs near where they did earlier.

"Honey, would you like a cup of coffee?" Donald Brammer asked his wife.

"That would be nice dear", she replied.

He rose from his chair and took a couple of strides across the thin, blue carpeting. The vending machines were up against a wall near the front desk. On the left was a candy machine. Flush against it stood a beverage machine. To the right of that was a small counter. A two or three foot tall brown machine sat on top of the counter. Near the top of the machine was the word "Coffee". He looked over the selections and chose decaffeinated. He slid three quarters into the slot and pushed the red button. A paper cup dropped from a hole and landed upright at the bottom. He heard the clicking sound of a small condenser. Dark brown liquid squirted into the cup. Steam puffed for several seconds. Donald removed the cup with his right hand.

Walking back to his wife, he saw the back of a man dressed all in black. He was leaning on the desk talking to the woman behind the counter. Donald heard their voices but couldn't make out the conversation.

"Here you go honey", Donald smiled, then handed the hot cup of coffee to his wife.

"Thank you babe", she said.

"Careful, it's hot", he warned.

She nodded her head in an acknowledging manner. She held the cup, but didn't take a sip.

Donald noticed that a nurse had joined the man in black and the woman behind the counter. The nurse was wearing modern type scrubs. She had on a pair of blue cotton slacks. The top was white and covered with colorful designs. They appeared to be flowers or fish.

The nurse turned from the desk and began walking down the aisle to the right of where Donald was sitting.

"Follow me Reverend Wilkerson", the nurse sweetly said.

"Thank you nurse", he replied. He carried a red covered Bible in his left hand.

The two were getting close to Donald. The nurse gave him a quick little smile as she passed him. The Reverend took a brief glance at Donald. He refocused his sight on the nurse walking in front of him.

At first, Donald didn't think much of it. The Reverend passed and Donald heard two pairs of shoes clacking their way down the tile hall.

He gave Patty a perplexed look.

"What's wrong Donald?", she asked.

"I don't know for sure", he said. "Something just seems a bit strange."

"What seems strange?"

"The Reverend, did you notice him?"

"Yes", she replied.

"Something isn't quite right about him."

"What do you mean Donald? You're starting to scare me. It's been a trying day and your mind is probably working overtime."

"Maybe", he said.

Donald took his right index finger and brushed it across his mustache.

"No, it can't be", he said.

"Can't be what?"

"The Reverend's voice.....his last name."

The wheels in his head were now turning swiftly. First, his mind processed the name, Wilkerson. He knew that name. It was familiar to him. However, he couldn't quite place it. The Reverend's voice brought the image in his mind into complete focus. He could see the McKenna's and the Union soldiers standing in the living room. He remembered Molly asking the man if he was hungry. The man said no. Then, the soldier introduced himself. "My name is Major Aaron Wilkerson and this is Corporal Livingston", he said. The voice was identical to that of the Reverend.

"Oh no, it can't be!" Donald shouted loudly as he popped up out of his chair.

Before Patty could get a word out, Donald was racing down the hallway.

"Donald, Donald", she yelled, but he didn't turn around. Patty watched as he reached a set of double wooden doors. He pushed a metal button on the left side and the two doors opened inward. She saw Donald hurry to a square area surrounded on all four sides by long counters. The two doors closed and Patty could no longer see her husband.

"Sir, can I help you?", the nurse offered.

"The nurse and the Reverend?", Donald asked.

"Yes sir".

"Which room did she take him too?"

"Sir, this is the surgery recovery room. You shouldn't be back here."

Donald noticed a room chart sitting on top of the desk next to the nurse. It was facing upside down. He tried to make out the names. No, no, no he thought. Yes, he spotted the upside down name of Terrance Bell. The room number was 801. He quickly turned the numbers around in his mind, "108".

Donald raced down the small hallway to his left. He glanced at the room numbers as he went. One hundred two, one hundred three, one hundred four.....the numbers grew larger as they progressed to his right.

"Sir, come back. You can't go down there", the nurse insisted.

Donald ignored her plea and made a right turn down the next bank of rooms, one hundred six, one hundred seven, finally one hundred eight. The curtain was drawn. He took his left hand and swiped back the multi-colored draping. What he saw stunned him. The Reverend stood with his back to Donald. He was ranting and raving in the direction of Terrance. There was a red book lying open on the tray next to the bed. The book was drilled empty of pages. It was a concealed carrying case for a gun. The Reverend was pointing a silver revolver directly at Terrance.

"Wait!", Donald shouted at him.

The Reverend turned around with his steely dark eyes and stared a hole through Donald.

"You're all going to die!", the Reverend said in a psychotic manner. "You shouldn't have disturbed the dead."

Donald knew he wasn't bluffing. Reaching out with his right arm, he grabbed onto the barrel of the gun. He quickly pointed the weapon to the side. Both men wrestled for control of the gun. Terrance watched in horror. He was unable to move.

Patty Brammer started the long walk down the empty hallway toward the recovery room. Her heart was beating hard and loud. Every step seemed labored. She could only imagine what awaited her behind the double wooden doors.

Terrance slid his left hand down to his side and pushed the nurse call button.

The Reverend freed the weapon from Donald. He took the butt end of the gun and slammed it into his forehead. The professor gave out an audible cry and grabbed his head. He felt queasy. His focus was fading in and out. Once again, the Reverend trained the pistol on Terrance. Donald shook off the blow and grabbed the Reverend around his waist. He tackled him into the wall just to the left of Terrance. A loud shot rang out. Donald felt for the revolver tucked in between the two of them. They both struggled fiercely. "Bam!", a second shot went off.

Donald Brammer felt the resistance on the other end of the gun give way. He leaned back and saw blood seeping from the black shirt. Reverend Wilkerson gave him a starry-eyed look. The professor scooted back on his bottom a couple of paces. Sparkles started to surround the Reverend. A blue-green orb descended over his body. It twirled and tightly rotated. In an instant, the Reverend was gone. The orb took with it all of the blood, the gun and the red Bible.

"You okay Terrance?" Donald asked. He made his way next to the hospital bed.

"I'm fine professor", Terrance offered up with one of his patented grins.

"Thank God", Donald said, breathing a heavy sigh of relief.

A security guard in an all brown uniform brushed past Patty Brammer.

He reached out and tapped the silver "Open Door" button. She followed right behind him. The nurse behind the desk saw the officer. "Over there", she shrieked, pointing in the direction of room 108.

As he rushed into the doorway, the officer saw Donald Brammer standing beside Terrance. The professor was holding his head where the Reverend hit him with the butt of the pistol.

"You okay?" the security guard nervously asked Donald.

"Fine", the professor replied.

"What about those gunshots?"

"What gunshots?" Donald asked innocently.

"The two gunshots", the officer said.

"There were no gunshots, officer. I tripped and crashed into the adjustable standing tray, knocking it down." He pointed to it. "I fell and hit my hit against the front of that chair. I must be getting old", he said, apologizing to the officer.

Patty Brammer walked into the room. She stopped next to the security guard. "Donald, what happened?" She was a notch or two below hysterical, but certainly on edge.

"Everything is fine honey", Donald told her reassuringly. "I'm so clumsy. I tripped over the tray and collided with that plastic chair over there. Didn't I Terrance?"

"Yeah", Terrance said meekly. Patty and the officer looked at both of them but sensed there was more to the story than the two were leading on.

"But there were gunshots, I heard them", she said to her husband.

"No that was just me tumbling out of control. Want me to show you?"

"No", she commanded him. Patty walked over to her husband. She removed his hand from his forehead.

"Your forehead is all red. It's going to bruise and swell." She half turned to the guard, "Can you get him an ice pack please?"

The security guard stood stunned for a couple of seconds. He was still trying to digest the scene. This couldn't be, he thought. How can a fall sound like a gunshot?

"Please, hurry", Patty encouraged the officer.

"Ma'am, I'll get the nurse and be right back."

Still in shock, the officer left the room and headed down the corridor to get the nurse.

"I got here as quickly as I could", Patty said, looking up at Donald. "How're you doing", she asked Terrance.

"I'm doing fine ma'am. I'm just in a little pain."

"Where is the Reverend?", she asked her husband.

Before he could answer her question, the security guard and the nurse entered the room. The nurse was carrying an ice pack.

"Here you go", she said, and handed it to Donald.

"Thank you", he said.

The nurse looked the professor up and down. "Who shot the gun? Where is the Reverend?" She asked both of these questions in rapid succession.

"I tripped", Donald said, sticking to his story. The loud noise was me knocking over the tray and hitting my head on that chair." He pointed to the chair with a serious expression on his face.

"Well, you scared the living daylights out of us", she clamored. After saying this, she walked to the opposite side of the bed from where Donald and Patty were standing.

"And how are you feeling young man?", She asked Terrance with a slight smile.

"I'm doing okay", he responded. "I still have quite a bit of pain."

"I'm sure that you do", she answered. "Fred, thanks for coming down, but I think we have things under control now", she said to the security guard.

"You're welcome. That's why I'm here." He took one last astonishing look around the room, shook his head and left.

"Okay, I'm going to need you two to leave the room for a few minutes while I check his vitals and give him some more pain medication.

"Of course", Patty said. She and Donald started toward the opened sliding glass door.

"If you'll stay a few minutes in the waiting room, I believe the doctor would like to speak with you."

"We appreciate that", Donald replied. "Terrance, we'll check in on you before we leave."

"Sounds good professor", Terrance chirped back.

The nurse escorted the two down the hallway of the recovery room. Donald and Patty took a right through the double doors. The nurse swung to her left. The nurse fully focused on getting pain medicine for Terrance and taking his vital signs.

Patty Brammer bent down and picked up the cup full of cold coffee. She walked it over to the sink next to the coffee machine. Pouring it down the drain, she turned on the water to help wash it down.

"Do you want another cup, Donald asked?"

"No, not right now", she answered.

There were now several more people in the waiting room than earlier. A young female was trying to settle down her young toddler. It wasn't going so well. The child was obviously tired and cranky. Patty smiled at the woman and her daughter. Across the room sat an elderly couple. They both looked worn out. She felt bad for both of these families.

Donald sat down in one of the light blue, cushioned chairs. He held the ice pack against his head. What an unbelievable day, he thought to himself. First, the blue-green orb carried them back in time one hundred and fifty years. The Union Soldiers murdered the McKennas. The narrow escape from the Pawnee warriors was harrowing. This most recent incident with the apparition of Reverend Wilkerson may have topped them all. Donald had interviewed serial killers and psychopaths. However, in his twenty-five years of being a psychologist, this one easily topped the cake.

A tall man in his mid forties entered the waiting room. He wore wire-rimmed glasses. His hair and eyes were brown. A long, white lab coat covered his shirt and the top part of his grey slacks.

"The family of Terrance Bell, he called out?"

"Right here", Donald said, as he stood up from his chair. Patty rose from her spot next to her husband.

"I'm Dr. Fadoni", he said to the Brammers.

"I'm Donald Brammer and this is my wife Patty."

"Glad to meet you", he said. He shook their hands. "There's a small conference room around the corner. Do you mind following me?"

"Not at all", Patty replied. Dr. Fadoni led the way. They followed him to a small room. There was a round table in the room with four chairs. Otherwise, the room was bare.

"Terrance is a very lucky man", the doctor said in a somber tone. "The arrow barely missed the main artery in his leg. The tourniquet that was applied helped slow the bleeding."

"He is going to be alright, Patty asked?"

"I believe that he'll make a full recover", Doctor Fadoni answered. "We carefully removed the arrow tip. We cleaned the wound thoroughly and applied antiseptic to prevent infection. It took twelve sutures to cover the wound. The doctor paused. I think it best that we keep him here for a couple of days to ensure that there's no infection. This will also give him a little time to gain back some strength."

"Makes perfect sense", Donald said.

"Do you have any questions, the doctor asked?

"No, no questions at the moment. Thank you so much doctor for all of your help", Donald offered.

"You're very welcome." Doctor Fadoni stood, as did both of the Brammers. Patty and Donald exited the room. Dr. Fadoni flipped off the light switch and closed the door.

"Is your head okay, Dr. Fadoni asked? Donald was still holding the ice pack against his head.

"I'm fine. I just tripped and hit my head."

"You might want to get that looked at", said the doctor.

"If it doesn't heal soon I will do that, thanks."

Donald and Patty returned to the waiting room.

"Okay dear", Patty said with a smile. "It's late and I think it's time that we home.

"I agree, Donald said. They both made their way out to the white van.

CHAPTER TWENTY-NINE

*"Courage is the display of a decision to let go of
the familiar as you explore the unknown."*

David L. Hanson

Brian heard the knock on the front door of Brea's apartment. He walked to the door and took a quick glance through the peephole. It was the pizza delivery person. He opened the door and asked the young man to come in out of the cold.

"What do I owe you, Brian asked?

The thin kid wearing a baseball cap looked down at the receipt and said, "Twenty dollars and twenty-one cents. Brian pulled out his billfold and removed a twenty and a five.

"Here ya' go", he said, as he handed him the two bills. "The rest is yours."

"Thank you sir", the young man replied respectfully. He opened the red, square canvas bag and removed two cardboard boxes. He handed both boxes to Brian, one large, thin box containing the pizza and a smaller, taller box with the chicken wings.

"Thanks again", Brian told him.

"Thank you sir and have a wonderful evening." The young man reached out and took hold of the door handle. As soon as he was outside of the apartment, Brian locked the door.

"Brea, the pizza is here", he said.

She didn't respond. She was asleep. He walked over to her and stuck the pizza box under her nose. She smiled and opened her eyes.

"Everything smells really good", he said. "Let's eat while it's hot."

"I'm on my way", Brea said sleepily.

Brian carried the two boxes to the kitchen and set them on the table. He reached up into the cabinet behind the stove and pulled down a couple of paper plates. Walking back to the computer, he picked up his empty glass. Time for a refill, he thought.

Brian took another giant bite of pizza. It was a supreme, his favorite. He was on his third slice while Brea was working on her first.

"What's wrong Brea?" he asked.

"Nothing's wrong Brian. I'm just still overwhelmed with everything that happened today. I can hear the screams and gunshots in my head. It was horrible." She laid down the slice of pizza she was eating and shook her head. Brian saw the tears begin to well up in her eyes.

"I know it was awful", he said. "I can't imagine how scary it must've been. I'm so proud of you for being brave and doing what you needed to do to survive."

"Thank you Brian for understanding."

"You're welcome. Take your time and eat what you can. When you're finished, why don't you lie back down on the couch and rest for awhile I write my article?"

"I think I will", she said.

"I'm going to get started on my article. I told Janet Krigle down at the Reporter that I'd have an email to her no later than eight o'clock."

"That's fine Brian. I hope this article gives you a boost. What about Hank? Why isn't he reviewing your work?"

"Oh, Hank took a few days off. He's probably doing some Christmas shopping with his wife."

"I see", she said. "I'm going to go lay down again. Wake me up if you need anything."

"All I need is for you to be safe and to be with me."

Brea smiled. "I love being with you." She walked across the small living room and plopped down onto the sofa. She pulled a blanket down over her.

Now for the high wire act, Brian thought. It was bad enough that he skipped the beauty contest for the experiment. Now he had to write an article that was truthful, yet believable. He had the pictures that Dr. Brammer emailed to him. Those would serve as hard evidence. Sure, some may question their authenticity, but what great story didn't have its own built in conspiracy theory?

The first step was choosing a title for the article. It needed to sound interesting, yet not too fantastic. He thought for a minute, what about, "The Untold Story of the McKenna Mystery." It had a nice ring to it, but sounded more like a book title than a newspaper article. What about, "Experiment sheds light on one hundred and fifty year old McKenna mystery, he thought." That had a solid ring to it and just enough information to whet the appetite of the reader. So, in bold letters and large font he typed it into the top portion of the blank word document. He looked down at his watch and saw that it was six-thirty. Next, he took his cell phone and UBS cord. Plugging one end into the side of the laptop, he hooked the other end into the phone. A blue square popped up on the screen informing him that there were digital images available. The file name was the date, December 17, 2011.

Brian took a sip of his rum and coke. He stared blankly at the Microsoft Word document that sat in front of him. He had a title for his article regarding the disappearance of the McKennas. Now, Brian thought, to write this incredible story with enough truth and fact to capture the interest and belief of the Reporter readers.

He glanced over at Brea. She was exhausted and deep asleep on the couch. She, the professor and the other three students survived something akin to an H.G. Wells novel. He had a little over one hour to compose his thoughts and email them to Janet at the Reporter before his self proposed eight o'clock deadline.

Where would he begin? How would he describe the blue-green orb? Through whose eyes would he tell the gruesome tale? One nice thing about a word processor program is that you just start typing, he thought to himself. Correcting errors was easy. How did the great writers of the past do it without this technology?

Brian started typing into the laptop keyboard. He had a mental outline of what parts of the story he wanted to emphasize. Letting his mind relax, he typed what came into his head.

He first described the experiment. Professor Brammer and the four Psychology students doing a research project into the McKenna mystery.

They were trying to find some answers using paranormal and telepathic techniques.

Brian briefly gave an example or two of the types of questions they asked of the spirits. He described the fury of the spinning blue-green orb after Dr. Brammer asked his second question. His next lines were hard hitting:

"The house began to shake violently. It felt like an earthquake or a tornado had hit. Actually, it felt like both. The blue-green orb spun down from the ceiling and covered the members of the group who were sitting in a circle holding hands. I couldn't look directly at them. It was like looking directly into the sun. There was a deafening quiet. Then, the five of them were gone. I called out to them but got no answer. I walked over to where they had been sitting. I stuck my hand out into the path that the orb had taken. I felt nothing, no heat, no vibration, nothing.

Brea stirred a bit on the couch. She slightly opened her eyes.

"Brian, I'm kind of scared. Will you stay with me tonight?" She asked him in a sensitive and sympathetic way. Her hazel eyes looked at him with a sense of vulnerability. She felt frightened and feared having nightmares. Her mind was still trying to digest all of the trauma and horror of the day

"I was planning on it Muffin", Brian said, with a calm and relaxed voice. "You just rest and don't worry about anything. I'm right here."

Smiling at him, Brea said, "Thanks babe". She wrapped up in a cocoon shape underneath the blanket. He noticed that she was stretching her legs. A moment or two later, her hand appeared from underneath the blanket and tossed her jeans onto the floor.

Brian was not sure how much detail to share in the article. He did have one thing on his side. The public shock factor was broken earlier with the television news coverage. That was the good news. The bad news was that they only reported the missing person's side of it.

He decided to go for broke. If Janet didn't like the stunning details, she would edit them out or maybe even ax the entire story. Taking a deep breath, his fingers started to type out the bizarre string of events. First, he described the professor and his four students traveling back in time. How they used the bedroom and the little red shack as hiding places. Without going into graphic details, he told the readers how the Union soldiers murdered the McKenna family. He emphasized Alexander McKenna buying the slave contacts of the two men. He described it as a business deal that Alexander McKenna kept hidden from his wife and children.

Finally, he spoke of the Pawnee Indians. He mentioned that they were most likely friendly traders with the McKenna family. Most importantly, Brian told of how the Pawnee saved the two young black men from hanging. Next, he described the arrow penetrating Terrance's leg. Finally, Brian ended the article with the depiction of the blue-green orb bringing them all back.

Brian opened up his email account. He clicked on the button that read, "compose a message". Brian attached the Microsoft Word document containing his article. Next, he added the two pictures using the attachment feature, first the photo of the indentured servant contract and then the photo of the arrow. In the body of the email message, he wrote:

> *Dear Janet:*
>
> *Please find attached to this email the article that I have written regarding the paranormal experiment that took place at the old McKenna farmhouse today. You may have caught a glimpse of television news reports covering the incident. I know the story sounds unbelievable, but I'm hoping that the two attached pictures will add credibility. Please call me with any thoughts or questions that you may have.*
>
> *Sincerely,*
> *Brian*

He looked down at his watch. It was ten after eight. Brian stood and walked to where Brea was sound asleep on the couch. He nudged her but she didn't wake. "Brea", he whispered her name lightly and shook her again. Her hazel eyes opened.

"Come on babe, let's get you to bed". Brian reached out with his right hand to help her up. The blanket fell on the living room floor as she stood. He wrapped his left arm around her shoulder and escorted her to the bedroom. She was so light, so delicate and so beautiful. Brian gently lowered her onto the bed. He covered her with the large, green comforter that draped the bed. Brian kissed her on the forehead and then left the room.

CHAPTER THIRTY

*"There seemed to be endless obstacles... it seemed
that the root cause of them all was fear."*

MARION MILNER

One more hour, Madge thought to herself. It'd been a long day. Moreover, it'd been a weird and wacky day.

"Order up", Marty hollered from the kitchen, as he rang the little sliver bell." He, too, was ready for the day to end. In his mind, he envisioned himself kicking off his shoes and walking through his apartment door straight for the refrigerator and a beer. Looking down at his right hand, he could almost feel the television remote in the palm of his hand. It was Thursday night and he liked to watch the forensic crime shows. He was fascinated at how they could determine so much about a person from a sample of their DNA.

Vera ambled to the rectangular hole between the kitchen and the front of the diner. She saw Marty standing in front of the grill tending to a couple of burgers. Vera picked up the two glass plates sitting on the stainless ledge. She carried one in each hand as she cut through the open path that separated the two, long countertops. Her eyes looked through the clear glass windows in the front and out into the cold, dark sky.

"Nooooooooo!!!!", she screamed, as the two plates dropped simultaneously from her hands. The loud, stinging sound of the ceramic plates crashing against the tile floor immediately brought her all of the attention in the diner.

Marty took the two hamburgers that he was cooking and quickly moved them to the very edge of the grill where they would get less fire. He pushed the swinging door open. Madge was already on her way to Vera.

"Vera, you alright sugar?" Madge asked in a very caring and concerned tone.

Vera was shaking. Her eyes were still looking through the front window glass. Spattered about her feet were the remnants of two dinners.

"Come sit down Vera. Marty, grab a large glass of water, would you hun'?"

"Sure thing Madge", He made his way over to the dispenser and clicked the lever filling the glass full of water.

"Here you go Vera", Marty said, as he handed her the water. Marty was also concerned. He was accustomed to Cindy dropping plates every so often, but not Vera. If it were football, Vera would be the trusted receiver.

Vera gazed out into the cold, dark night. She took a sip of water.

"I'll run grab the mop and bucket", Marty volunteered.

"Thank you sweetie", Madge said.

Vera set the glass down onto the countertop.

"It was him, she said in disbelief. It was him."

"It was who?" Madge replied.

"The Reverend, he was in earlier today. He sat in that booth over there and ordered a cup of coffee and a piece of Apple pie."

Marty rolled the plastic, yellow mop bucket between the break in the counters. He took the mop with both hands and cut a wide swath through the culinary jigsaw puzzle on the floor. After, he dunked the dirty strands of the broom into the bucket. He put the mop into a squeezing device to wring out the excess water.

"The Reverend, Madge asked curiously?"

"Yes, I'm sure that you saw him. He was dressed all in black and had a red bible with him."

Madge looked around the diner and saw two of her regulars looking on from a booth on the west end of the diner.

"Jerry, Glen, can you two fella's run outside real quick and see if someone is loitering around?"

"You bet ", Jerry replied, as both men stood and made a brisk beat for the front door.

"Madge it was him....I swear...it was him!" Vera was still somewhat hysterical and shaking profusely.

"Settle down Vera", Madge implored. "If it was him, Jerry and Glen will find him. You just calm yourself down."

"You saw him Madge. You saw the Reverend earlier today."

Madge had no clue regarding the Reverend who Vera described. Except for a five-minute break here or there, Madge had worked the front of the diner the entire day. Sure, she was tired, but she would've noticed a man of the cloth.

A cold breeze swept the diner as the two men returned from their scouting mission outside.

"Not a single soul, nobody", Jerry said, shaking his head.

"Thank you for looking fella's", Vera replied, while smiling at the two. Both men made their way back to the booth where they'd been sitting.

"Madge, he stared right through me", Vera rattled. There was a stream of blood running down the front of his black shirt."

Madge thought to herself for a moment. What would be the best way to handle this situation? Marty continued to mop up the remaining remnants of food.

"Hey Marty?"

"Yeah, Madge."

"This was Jerry's and Glenn's order. Can you do me a huge favor and remake it for them."

"Of course", Marty replied, as if speaking endearingly to his own mother.

"Folk's, I'm sorry for the interruption in your dinner. I would appreciate it if you'd bear with us for a few minutes." She then raised her voice to a half yell, "Jerry and Glen, Marty is remaking your order now. It should be right out."

"We understand, no problem Madge", Glenn said in his burly voice.

"Thanks sweetie."

Madge took Vera by the hand and led her through the swinging door and into the kitchen. She set her down in the corner chair where Marty would sit when not busy.

"Take another sip of water dear", Madge persuaded her.

Vera took a healthy drink of the water. She set the glass down. Her face told the whole story. She was still in shock.

"It was him Madge. Just above his wrist, he had a tattoo. He told me that he served in the Cavalry. The red bible sat on the table right next to him."

"Well sugar, Jerry and Glenn searched around the building and nobody was out there. Maybe you saw a reflection from something. Lord knows it has been a screwy day with those missing people and all."

"It wasn't a reflection Madge. I recognized that beady look in his eyes. Most preachers have a soft, gentle look to them. This man looked hardened, more like a soldier than a preacher."

"Vera, we believe you honey", Madge reassured her.

"Yeah, we believe you Vera. He probably ran when the two of you made eye contact", Marty said.

"Honey, I want for you to sit back here and take it easy for the rest of the night. We have about forty-five minutes until close. I doubt if we'll get many customers between now and then. You'll be safe back here with Marty. He and I will handle the rest of the shift."

Vera had a glazed look in her eyes. "Okay", she responded more in the fashion of a robot than a person.

"Good", Madge said, and gave her an affectionate squeeze on the wrist.

"But Madge, he really was here."

"We know Vera, just relax", Madge coaxed.

I need to speak to Marty up front for just a second hun'. Then we'll be right back here with you, okay?"

"Sure", she responded with little conviction in her voice.

Madge gave Marty a look, and they both walked through the swinging kitchen door into the diner. Madge signaled him over to a booth in the corner of the restaurant.

"Marty, I need to ask you for a favor."

"Sure".

"Will you follow Vera home after we close. Can you make sure that she gets into her apartment safely?"

"Absolutely", Marty replied. I'll be glad to."

"Thanks Marty, I'm not sure what I'd do without you." Madge said these words with meaning. She knew inside that she couldn't run the diner alone. Marty was in a way a surrogate for her late husband Jim.

"That was a nice thing to say Madge". Marty tried to keep from blushing. Madge was somewhat of a mother figure to him. His own mother passed away when he was in grade school. In some respects, Madge put discipline and security into his life.

Marty began to rise from the booth.

"One other thing", Madge said to him. "This is just between you and me". She gave him the look of one CIA agent passing classified information to another.

Marty stopped. He was standing just outside of the booth. Leaning toward Madge, he was anxious to hear what she was about to tell him.

"You know when Vera said that she served the Reverend a cup of coffee and a piece of Apple pie?", Madge whispered.

"Yes", Marty whispered back.

"Well, we don't have Apple pie today. All we have is Blueberry, Cherry and Strawberry Cheesecake!"

Marty felt a shiver run up and down his spine. He gave Madge a blank look. "I'll be sure and follow her home tonight. I'll walk her to her door."

"Thanks Marty", Madge said.

Just south of the diner at Memorial Hospital, the two twenty year olds stepped up to the information desk. There was a woman sitting behind the desk who appeared to be in her seventies.

"We'd like to know what room number Terrance Bell is in?" Cathy asked.

"One moment please".

The woman typed a few keystrokes into her computer keyboard.

"Terrance Bell is in room two twenty-one", she said. "Remember that visiting hours end at nine o'clock."

"Yes ma'am, thank you", Josh replied politely.

"Please use the elevators just beyond and to the left of the cafeteria sign."

"Thanks", they both chimed back.

Cathy was the first to walk into the room. Josh was right behind. Terrance was watching the news on the television hanging on the wall directly across from his bed.

"Hey there "T", Cathy said with a smile, "How're you doing?"

Terrance looked at both of them and offered up a smile. "I'm doing fine, my leg is a little under the weather though."

"I bet it is", Josh answered. "It won't be long that you'll be up and running again chasing some more spirits."

"Don't say that Josh. The thought of it makes me cringe."

"I was just kidding with you, trying to lighten the mood."

"I know, Terrance said". He smiled at Josh.

"Are they giving you the good pain medicine?" Cathy asked.

"That they are", Terrance replied. "See this machine here", he pointed to the upright object standing next to his bed.

"Nifty", Cathy sparked. "Just be sure that you don't give yourself too much."

"I can't, Terrance said. It only delivers a shot every eight minutes."

"Well, look who has visitors, the nurse brimmed." She was in her mid to late twenties and beautiful. Next to her on wheels was a small, box shaped apparatus. "It's time for vitals."

"Do you need for us to leave?" Cathy asked.

"No, you two are just fine. I won't be but a minute." She took the foot long green sleeve and wrapped it around the right arm of Terrance. After pushing a green button, the sleeve began to inflate. Finally, it deflated on its own. "Blood pressure looks excellent", she happily said. "Let me get your temperature and I'll be out of the way." She placed a white pen shaped object under Terrance's tongue.

"It looks like you're getting well cared for here", Josh said with a hint of jealously in his voice. "I wonder if they have any vacancies on this floor."

Terrance laughed, but managed to keep the thermometer under his tongue. Cathy gave Josh a somewhat cross look. Men, is that all they think about, she thought.

"Temperature is normal. If you need anything, just push down on the nurses' button.

"I will", he replied humbly.

The nurse turned and wheeled her machine into the hallway. She was just out of sight when Josh said, "Dang Terrance, you might be laid up for a little while?"

"Come on Josh", Cathy scolded him.

"Well, what I meant was that we want you fully healed before you leave."

"We know what you meant Josh", Cathy said, and shot him a look.

"I've been watching the news tonight. Our experiment is all over the local news. I saw the ambulance hauling me away and everything."

"I know", Cathy, said. "I'm not so sure if it's a good thing or not. Many people in these parts are very conservative. They don't believe much in ghosts or spirits."

"Dr. Brammer brought back the proof Cathy", Josh said firmly. How can they deny the evidence?"

"It's easy for them to deny the evidence. They watch all of those conspiracy shows on television. The arrow could be a fake. They don't know for sure, they weren't there like we were."

"Thank God for that", Terrance replied.

"Then they'll believe what they want to believe", Josh said with a twinge of consternation in his voice.

"Exactly", Cathy followed. "They're going to believe what they want to believe anyway.

Josh didn't respond. Terrance pushed the button on his pain management machine. He looked tired.

"We better get going now Josh", Cathy hinted.

"Yeah, let's let Terrance get some needed rest. I just wanted to tell Terrance to call me. I'd like to come and pick him up when he is released."

"That's nice", Cathy said.

"Yeah, thanks Josh", Terrance seconded. "It means a lot to me."

"Call if you need anything Terrance", Cathy offered.

"Yeah, let us know if you need anything at all." Call me when the doctor gives you the green light to go home."

"I will Josh", he said lowly.

"Get some rest". Cathy said. She smiled at Terrance. She and Josh then made their way out of his room.

CHAPTER THIRTY-ONE

"Destiny is not a matter of chance, it is a
matter of choice. It is not a thing to be waited
for, it is a thing to be achieved."

William Jennings Bryan

The nearly full moon cast its shadow down onto the old McKenna farmstead. Once the vibrant home of Alexander McKenna, Molly McKenna and their children, it now gave off a sad and ominous vibration.

The floodlights threw off heat as well as light in the basement. Wayne Construction was putting the final touches on excavating the remains of the McKenna's.

"Sheriff, what should we do with the body remains?" Wayne asked.

Mark Preston looked down at his watch. It was eight-thirty. The Sheriff was reluctant to take action this late on a Thursday night. However, he wanted to pay the proper respects to this family.

"Merle".

"Yeah Sheriff". Deputy Vickers walked to where the Sheriff was standing.

"I know it's late, but we need to get in touch with the County Coroner. We need him or someone from his office to come collect the remains.

"I'll take a ride out to his residence Sheriff."

"Thanks Merle", the Sheriff said. "Mention to them the circumstances and that we want these bodies transferred with the same respect as anyone else. They should also examine the remains in an effort to determine cause of death. Please ask them to come as quickly as possible."

"Will do Sheriff". Merle made his way to the wooden stairs leading up to the kitchen hallway.

"Hey, Wayne?"

"Yeah, Sheriff".

"Have your men stop what they're doing at this point. Merle is going to get the coroner. They'll take custody of the remains when they arrive."

"Sure thing Sheriff", Wayne said, while rubbing the whisker stubs of his unshaven face. "Do you want us to stick around until they arrive?"

"That'd be great. We can use these flood lights down here."

"You got it." Wayne walked over to his foreman and explained the situation to him.

"Shut it down men, but leave the lights up", he barked at his crew. "Charlie, you Dale and Leroy can take one of the pickups and call it a night. Wayne and I will stick around here for awhile and shut the lights down."

The three men laid down what tools they held. They brushed the dirt from their clothes and made their way upstairs. Twenty seconds later, they heard the sound of the front door opening and closing.

"Why don't we go upstairs and grab a cup of coffee and a donut?'

"That sounds like a deal", Wayne said.

They ascended the stairs and made their way into the old living room. It was dark, so Sheriff Preston led the way with his flashlight. The lone working flashlight from the group experiment that Brian was operating sat near the north wall. The Sheriff walked over to it and turned it on. A beam of light bounced off the ceiling.

"Over here", Sheriff Preston instructed the two to join him against the west wall where the coffee and donuts were located.

"Help yourselves. I'm going to round up the Professor's equipment for him."

"Thanks Sheriff", Wayne replied. He picked up a thermos of coffee while the foreman held a Styrofoam cup. Wayne poured a cup of coffee for each of them.

Sheriff Preston walked to the center of the room where the video camera was located. It was off. To his surprise, there was some battery power left. He turned the camera on and pushed the rewind button. Once he saw the blue-green orb flash by, he stopped the camera. Hitting the play button, he watched the bizarre happenings. The light was intense, but he was able to watch it lift from the floor and fly out of the south window. The group of five was lying on the floor. As he watched the blue-green orb rush out of the window, he caught a glimpse of something odd. It was an all black object and the orb seemed to drop it outside of the window. Sheriff Preston played it back once more to verify that he did actually see something. He stopped the camera as the object fell to the ground. It appeared to be the outline of a person. Couldn't be, he thought to himself.

"Hey fella's, I'm going to step outside for a minute."

The two men nodded in his direction. They both had the larger part of a donut in their mouth.

He walked out the front door and onto the porch. Sheriff Preston pointed the beam of his flashlight below the window. Something reflected against the light. He walked over to the object. He picked it up. It was a spent bullet. It was't an ordinary bullet, this bullet was old and flattened. He wondered if the bullet had fallen out of the blue-green orb. Or, maybe the bullet fell out of the black figure? He stuck it in his front right pants pocket.

Deputy Vickers escorted the black mortuary van through the checkpoint at the main entrance and up to the old, decrepit house. He saw the Sheriff shining his flashlight on the porch floor.

Two men scurried to the back of the black station wagon. They opened the double doors and slid out a gurney.

"I don't think that you're going to need that", Merle Vickers called out to them. Just bring the bags with you."

They each grabbed a couple of long, black bags and headed toward the front porch.

"Watch your step fella's, there's a stair missing", the Deputy warned.

"You made good time Merle", Sheriff Preston told him and patted him on the shoulder.

"We made it back as soon as we could", the Deputy replied modestly.

"This way", the Sheriff directed the two men inside the house.

Wayne and his foreman were sipping coffee.

"Wayne, can you show these gentlemen what you have for them?", the Sheriff asked.

"Sure, right this way". Wayne started down the hall to the basement doorway. The others followed. It was like daylight in the basement. The floodlights were extremely bright.

"We have four bodies, or should I say what is left of four bodies", Wayne said. The two men followed Wayne to the four holes located on the east wall.

"Be very delicate in handling the bones", Sheriff Preston suggested. "They are nearly one hundred and fifty years old."

The two men from the coroner's office shot each other a puzzling glance. They both covered their hands with latex gloves. One at a time, they laid the black bags out on the ground and carefully loaded them with body parts.

"Wayne, I think you guy's can call it a night. Merle, that goes for you too."

"What about you Sheriff?" Merle asked.

"I'm going to stay out here all night. I want to make sure that nothing happens to Dr. Brammer's equipment. With the day we've had out here, I don't want to leave anything to chance."

"Do you mind if I hang out here with you Sheriff?"

"You don't have to Merle, but if you want to it would be much appreciated. Call your wife and let her know what is going on if you decide to stay."

"I'll call her now", the Deputy responded.

The men in the basement heard the sound of Wayne starting his pick-up truck. It was going to be a long night, Sheriff Preston thought to himself. He might need to send Merle on a food run.

CHAPTER THIRTY-TWO

*"Most of our failures in understanding one
another have less to do with what is heard than
with what is intended and what is inferred."*

George A. Miller

Janet Krigle often worked late into the night at the Reporter. It was eight-thirty. The radio that sat atop her filing cabinet softly played Christmas music. She pulled up her email account on the computer to check if Brian had sent her anything yet. There was an email message from Brian. After double clicking on the message line, a full screen with white background popped up. At the top of the email she noticed three attachments. One was a Microsoft Word document and the other two appeared to be photo attachments. The two photo attachments carried the suffix, ".jpeg" behind them.

She read the brief note that Brian included in the body of his email. He briefly described to her the background regarding the article that he submitted. First, she opened the two photographs. Although the items appeared a bit small in the pictures, she knew how to enlarge them without loosing much clarity.

"Oh my", she softly said aloud to herself. The wooden arrow appeared to be blood stained. Several black feathers protruded from one end. Bringing the other photo back up, she could make out the words "Indentured Servant Contract" at the top of the document.

Opening the Microsoft Word document, she began to read Brian's article. She was shocked and impressed at the same time. In his email message, Brian mentioned the experiment. He was also correct in that she'd seen several of the special news reports on television earlier that day.

It was a very well written article. It described in detail what happened out at the old McKenna place. Up until this time, she didn't know that Brian was actually a witness to the paranormal experiment. She was, however, somewhat surprised that Hank handed such an assignment to Brian. This just didn't sound like a "Hank" story. He was very conservative and this seemed more controversial than any article that she could remember in the recent past.

Janet picked her phone up and dialed Hank's number. The phone rang four times and then went to an answering machine. A female voice instructed:

"Hello, you have reached the Edward's residence. We are unable to answer your call at the current time. Please leave a detailed message at the tone including your name and a return phone number and we'll contact you as soon as possible."

The voice was very soft and sweet. She assumed that it belonged to Hank's wife. What a sweet woman for such a grouchy man, she thought. When hearing the beep, Janet left the following message:

"This message is for Hank Edwards. Hank this is Janet down at the Reporter. It's about a quarter until nine on Thursday night. I just wanted to let you know that I received an article via email from Brian. What a brilliant idea. I have to compliment you and Brian on this one. After touching it up a bit, I'm sending it down to the pressroom for tomorrow morning's edition. Please call me if you have any questions. I hope you're having a nice day off."

Janet finished prepping and proofreading the article. She emailed the Word Document and the two electronic photographs to the pressroom. After, she printed a hard copy of the article and pictures. Every emailed article also required an editor's signature for approval. She signed her name eloquently at the bottom.

Picking up her coat, she slid her arms into the sleeves. Walking over to the filing cabinet, she reached out her hand in order to turn off the radio. There was no way that she could anticipate Hank's reaction to the article the next morning. If she could, her mind would have little trouble picturing Hank behind the wheel of his car running over a newspaper stand.

Janet flipped the switch on her office light, turning it off. She'd take the stairs down one floor to the pressroom and drop the article off in the basket. After that, it was home to feed her cat and watch a little late night television.

The following morning found Hand Edwards in his pajamas. On a normal Friday, Hank Edwards would already be in his office at the Reporter. However, this was not a normal Friday. Hank took yesterday and today off work. It was getting close to Christmas and he wanted to spend a little quality time with his wife before the holiday. He threw his large, dark blue, fuzzy robe on and slid a foot into each of the beige slippers. Slowly, he made his way down the stairs and into the kitchen.

"Morning dear", Nancy Edwards said in a bubbly manner to her husband.

"Morning", he replied. Hank and Nancy were polar opposites. Hank was rough around the edges. He was a serious man who rarely smiled. Age was starting to gain traction on him. At sixty-three, he knew that his time was drawing short at the Reporter. Nancy was a happy go lucky person. She always kept a positive attitude. Even during those instances when Hank would grunt and moan, she would try to cheer him up. Nancy wore her dark brown hair short.

"I'm going to go out and get the paper", Hank stammered.

"Okay, honey", she said and smiled. "I'll start some breakfast for us. What would you like?"

"Some bacon, a couple of eggs, some toast and jelly would be nice." Hank had written off the niceties like "thank you" from his conversations with Nancy some time ago. He'd hardened and took for granted all of her efforts maintaining the household; the grocery shopping, doing the laundry, writing up the bills. He was born and raised in a chauvinistic environment.

Hank unlocked the bolt and opened the front door. Maybe it was his thick skin, maybe it was the slow blood circulation, but he didn't feel the full effect of the cold. Grabbing onto the metal handrail with his right hand, he descended the snow dusted porch steps one at a time. He spotted his prey a foot or two to the left of the shoveled walkway. It was oblong and wrapped in a pink plastic sleeve. "Doesn't the paper boy know that I'm the Editor of the newspaper"?", he said aloud. He made a mental note to himself to give Rich Groody a call when he returned to work on Monday. Rich was the delivery manager at the Reporter. Surely, he could have a talk with the driver and the kid who tossed the paper. It would only take him a few seconds to hop out of the truck and run it up to the porch.

Hank bent down and extended his arm to its limits. His fingertip snagged the edge of the plastic wrapper. First, sliding it closer to him, he gripped it fully in his hand. He looked up and down the block. Hank mumbled an obscenity. It irked him that there were so few newspapers lying on top of the snow in his neighbor's yards. Everyone seemed to be flocking to the internet. Technology, who needs it, he thought.

Hearing the front door close, Nancy happily announced to her husband, "I've got a fresh, hot cup of coffee here for you dear."

"I'm coming", he said in a monotone voice.

Hank pulled the wooden chair away from the kitchen table. It was his chair. At least, he sat in this very same chair each day for the last thirty years. The more one analyzed the Edwards, the easier the comparison to the "Bunker's" became. They could be Edith and Archie's doubles.

He sat down and pulled the rolled paper from its wet plastic sleeve. Hank put the plastic wrapper in a bigger bag located against the kitchen wall. The smell of bacon and eggs permeated the house. Another husband would be complimenting his wife, but not Hank. He took a small sip of java from the plain white ceramic coffee mug.

After setting the coffee cup down on the table, he flattened out the newspaper. It always made him proud to see the "Reporter" logo largely splashed across the top of the front page. He glanced over to the top right hand corner and spied the date, Friday, December 18, 2011. Hank glanced at the large picture in the middle of the page. It was rarely anything other than a war picture or a politician.

It was time for Hank to sprint to the good stuff. His writers' works normally appeared on the front page of the second section of the paper. He separated the two sections, setting the front section to his far left on the table.

Hank took a big sip from his coffee cup. He started to choke. Coffee came streaming out of his mouth and nose, and flew all over the table. Coughing into his hand several times, he wasn't able to stop the choking.

"Oh my dear", Nancy said, in an empathetic tone. "I'll get you a glass of water. Are you okay Hank?"

Hank couldn't find his voice.

"Went down the wrong pipe, huh?"

"No", he managed to get the word out between chokes.

Nancy walked over to the upper kitchen cabinet and grabbed a glass. She quickly made her way to the sink and filled it with water.

"Here you go dear", she said compassionately.

"Just set it down, can't you see I'm choking?" Hank was fighting to get the words out of his mouth. As usual, when he didn't feel good or something went wrong, he took it out on Nancy. She turned from the table to tend to the bacon and eggs.

Hank couldn't believe his eyes. He saw a photo of a bloody arrow and a second photo of a piece of paper where he expected to see a little beauty queen. The choking finally subsided. He forced his eyes back to the top of the page and the large, bold letters in the headline:

Experiment sheds light on one hundred and fifty year old McKenna mystery. By Brian Foster

Hank rose and peddled his way into the family room. He lifted the cordless phone from its cradle. Dialing in the seven-digit number from memory, he listened as the phone rang. After four rings, the automated system sent him to Janet Krigle's answering system. Hank was now getting the full range of his voice back.

He heard Janet's voice say the following: *"This is Janet Krigle, I'm currently away from my desk and unable to answer your call. Please leave your name, number and a brief message at the tone and I'll return your call as soon as possible."*

The beep sounded. "Janet, this is Hank. What in the Sam hell is going on down there?! Where is Brian's story about the Little Miss-Mini Beauty Pageant? Call me the second you get this message." Hank hung up the phone. He was livid. He tried to slow down his breathing. He figured that if he were ever going to have a heart attack that it would probably be now.

I need to call Christina, he thought. Christina Mayburn was the vice president of the newspaper and Hank's boss. Her brother, Andrew Mayburn, was the president. Not only were they the top two corporate officers, they were the top two stockholders as well. Their great-grandfather, Wellington Mayburn started the newspaper sometime around the turn of the twentieth century. He couldn't remember a time in his thirty-year career at the Reporter when he felt so ashamed. How was he going to smooth this over with Christina? Could he even smooth it over with her?

Hank reluctantly punched in the seven-digit phone number. Once again, he heard the phone ring.

"This is Christina", the well-spoken female voice answered. Having gone to private schools her entire life, Christina spoke properly and with perfect diction.

"Christina, this is Hank Edwards", he meekly replied.

"Hank, I thought that you had yesterday and today off, she asked?"

"Well, I do, but I need to talk to you regarding a work related matter."

"Sure, what's on your mind?"

Hank paused and thought for a second or two. He would need to dance around this fiasco like Baryshinikov at the Moscow Ballet.

"Christina, there was a misunderstanding between myself and two of my direct reports regarding an assignment. I instructed them to cover one event and without consulting with me first, they covered another."

"I see", she said sternly. "It sounds like there might be a communication problem in your department?"

"We normally communicate well. I don't know, but Janet Krigle, Brian Foster and I weren't on the same page.

"Really", she replied. "What happened?"

"Before leaving work Wednesday evening I strictly instructed Brian Foster to cover The Little Mini-Miss Midwest Beauty Pageant the next day at the old Divine Theatre. It's like Miss America, only the contestants are young girls."

"I'm familiar with this contest".

"Well, Brian covered another story instead. Without prior approval, he decided to cover the story out at the old McKenna place, the article he wrote is in today's paper.

"I read it", Christina said with no emotion in her voice.

"As the editor, I'm ultimately responsible for all of the articles appearing in that section of the paper. I'm not even sure if Janet Krigle knew what was going on. I want to apologize to you for this type of sensational journalism. This doesn't meet the high standards of the Reporter. I accept full responsibility and any disciplinary actions for tarnishing its pristine reputation should fall on my shoulders."

"Hank, let me see if I understand you correctly. Even though Brian made the decision to cover the McKenna story, you are accepting full responsibility?"

"Yes". Hank fully expected one of two things. That she would fire him on the spot or ask for his resignation.

"I remember some years ago a certain reporter who worked for our newspaper that had a fire in his stomach. There didn't seem to be a story out there that he wasn't willing to cover. I saw spunk and spark in that reporter. Do you remember that reporter?"

"I'm not sure, but I think that you may be referring to me?"

"I am referring to you. Hank Edward's was not afraid to tackle the tough stories. He relished them. I think that version of Hank Edward's is still around. It's just been dormant for a long time.

"Do you agree with me?"

"Yes", he said. "I've become a weaker version of my younger self."

"No, you're still that same version of Hank Edward's, and you'll always be that version of Hank Edward's. In my opinion, you just need to do some relaxing in order to get back in touch with yourself."

"Would you like for me to resign Christina, Hank asked.

"Absolutely not", she responded in a prompt voice. "The McKenna story has given this newspaper a breath of life. We're receiving more telephone calls regarding this article than any other article in recent memory. Ninety-five percent of it is positive. People are thanking us for keeping them informed on the developments that took place out there yesterday. In addition, our web site has lit up like a Christmas Tree with questions, comments and thoughts regarding the paranormal experiment."

"Wow", Hank interjected.

"Wow is right", she continued. "You and your people are doing a great job for this newspaper and its readers. I'd like to meet with you and your staff Monday afternoon if you are all available. It'll give us an opportunity to throw some things out there on the table that have been bottled up for who knows how long. It will allow us all the chance to get back onto the same page. Does that sound agreeable?"

"Very much so", Hank said with relief in his voice. I'll let Janet and Brian know."

"Great", she said affirmatively. If Monday doesn't work, we can do it another afternoon next week. It's important to me though that we make time one day next week. I don't want this matter to slip through the cracks. For now, let's tentatively say Monday at two- thirty in the afternoon in my office."

"I'll inform them", Hank replied. "Christina, thanks for being so understanding."

"Come on Hank, we go back along way. We grew up together at this newspaper. It's time that you and I help prepare the next generation here at the Reporter."

"I agree", Hank said, with more spunk in his voice than normal. "I'll see you on Monday afternoon."

"See you on Monday Hank. Relax and have a couple of wonderful days off."

The phone clicked in Hank's ear and the dial went silent. He walked the cordless phone over to its cradle and hung it up.

"Is everything okay dear?" Nancy asked with concern.

"Everything is alright. I just forgot to tell you something."

"What's that Hank?"

"That I love you more today than the day I married you!"

"Ah Hank". She had tears rolling down her cheeks as she ran to him. They hugged as they hadn't hugged in years. They retained the embrace for several minutes.

CHAPTER THIRTY-THREE

"A person can't change all at once."

Stephen King, The Stand

Donald Brammer crawled out of bed as gently and quietly as possible. He needed to use the bathroom, but didn't want to wake his wife. Slithering out from under the sheets, he rose while holding the mattress down with his right hand. It was eight-thirty five in the morning. At least, that's what was on the face of the alarm clock.

"I'm not asleep", Patty slyly said, as if interrupting a cat burglar.

"I didn't want to wake you babe", Donald said, as he continued on to the bathroom.

Patty picked up the remote from the nightstand next to her and turned on the television. She punched in the number's two, one, and seven. There was a live broadcast in progress just outside of the old McKenna farmhouse. Sheriff Preston stood behind a bank of microphones woven together. She turned up the volume.

"I know a lot of you in the community have been following this story", he said. He briefly paused. "Some of the reports have sounded strange and far fetched. This morning, I'd like to add a few factual details." Sheriff Preston stepped back.

There were several reporters standing just out of camera range. Topeka police officers were doing their best to control the crowd. Many citizens came out to the property wanting to get a first hand look at the bizarre scene.

Sheriff Preston stepped up to the bank of microphones once again. "First, I'd like to reassure everyone in the community that all five persons reported missing have been found. They're safe and we've secured the site for further investigation." Those on the scene could hear him clearly, as the microphones blared away through loud speakers.

"As you probably know by now, a group of students and their Psychology Professor were here yesterday conducting an experiment. An experiment designed to shed new light on the one hundred and fifty year old McKenna mystery. I can tell you today, they were successful."

All eyes in the crowd trained on the Sheriff. It was cold out, but quiet. Deputy Vickers watched from the front porch as his protégée continued giving his statement.

"I'm not going to go into all of the details with you at this time. There's still an ongoing investigation. What I can tell you is an excavation in the basement of the house last night uncovered the graves of all four members of the McKenna family." A rippled buzz made its way through the crowd as people gasped to one another.

"The discovery was made possible through the efforts of Professor Donald Brammer and four of his students. I don't think their original plan was to actually solve the mystery. However, they were able to glean information lost for over a century. I'll end my statement here and take a few of your questions."

A male reporter out of camera range shouted into his microphone, "Sheriff, do you anticipate finding any additional bodies?"

"No, we don't at this time."

Donald Brammer walked back to bed. His eyes trained on the television and Sheriff Preston.

"The Sheriff gave you and your student's credit for helping solve the mystery", Patty said this as if he were an astronaut returning from a heroic mission.

"I'm just glad that everyone made it back safe", Donald said modestly.

Patty noticed a look of concern sweep across her husband's face.

"Patty, he said, "Do you realize over half of a million soldiers died during the Civil War?" He continued, "That figure doesn't even include civilians."

He brushed his brown mustache with the thumb and index finger of his right hand, as he often did. "The McKennas, and families like theirs faced unimaginable hardships. In some extreme cases, the war pit neighbor against neighbor. On even rarer occasions, it divided families. The students and I witnessed this for ourselves, first hand."

Donald was going to tell his wife the story about the Underground Railroad but saw a small tear bubbling up in Patty's left eye.

I think I'll call the hospital now and check on Terrance. Do you mind turning the volume down a bit sweetie?"

"Sure", Patty said. She hit the mute button on the remote. Turning on her right side, she watched her husband pick up the grey, cordless phone from its holder.

After pushing several buttons on the handset, Donald heard the phone ring.

"This is Nurse Hughes, may I help you?"

"Hello Nurse Hughes, my name is Professor Donald Brammer and I'm calling to get check on the condition of one of my students, Terrance Bell."

"Dr. Brammer, I can tell you that Terrance had a real good night and is currently resting comfortably."

"Wonderful", Donald replied.

"Dr. Livingston should be making rounds later this morning."

At first, the name Livingston didn't register in his brain. Then it hit him like a ton of bricks. He suddenly felt ill. His mind recalled that fateful day at the McKenna place. He saw Major Wilkerson speaking to Alexander and Molly McKenna. The words haunted him. "My name is Major Aaron Wilkerson and this is Corporal Jeremiah Livingston", the major said.

It couldn't be him. His heart felt like it jumped in his throat. This must be the feeling that criminal defendants have just before the jury foreman announces the verdict, Donald thought.

"Dr. Brammer, are you still there?"

"Yes nurse", he said with a crackle in his voice. His mind was spinning out of control. "What time does Dr. Livingston normally make his rounds?"

"You mean *her* rounds", the nurse clarified. Her name is Dr. Mary Linda Livingston and she makes her rounds at about ten o'clock."

Donald swallowed hard. His heart began to settle back into his chest. He felt the numb feeling in his body start to subside. He shut the movie down that was playing in his mind. There would be no need to race to the hospital in an effort to defend Terrance from another deviant time traveler. Dr. Livingston was a she!

"That's what I needed to know", he said to the nurse, with a little more strength in his voice. His breathing was now less rapid and more normal.

"You've been most helpful nurse."

"Why thank you Dr. Brammer. I hope you have a wonderful weekend."

"Thank you nurse and you do the same."

Both parties hung up their respective telephones.

"Donald, you look like you just saw a ghost", Patty exclaimed.

"I've been seeing all kinds of things lately", he said, in a lost way.

"It's okay honey". I think yesterday was too much for all of us. Why don't you come back to bed and we can snuggle for a little while longer?"

"Now that sounds like a plan!"

Donald slid back under the bed covers. He fluffed his pillow and turned it over. The cool side of the pillow always seemed to calm him down. Patty shifted onto her left side, facing away from him. Donald wrapped his right arm around Patty and pressed his body against hers. He pulled her tight to him.

"Donald?", Patty asked.

"Yes", he answered, closing his eyes.

"Have you ever considered a profession that's a little less dangerous?"

"Less dangerous?", he quizzically replied. "Did you have something specific in mind?"

"I don't know", she answered, "Maybe an international spy?"

Donald let out a huge laugh. He chuckled several more times. Patty was laughing with him.

"You think you're pretty funny, don't you?", he asked, in a rhetorical way.

Donald Brammer squeezed his wife a little tighter. To him, this was as close to heaven as he could get. Besides, this was their favorite time of the year!